PRAISE FOR KARA THOMAS

Out of the Ashes

"This story simply engulfed me. I didn't trust a single seedy character that Samantha Newsom came in contact with while on her quest to unearth, after twenty-two years, who was responsible for murdering her entire family and setting their Catskills farmhouse aflame. *Out of the Ashes* is gritty, raw, and chock-full of tension as suffocating as the tiny town of Carney itself."

—Stacy Willingham, *New York Times* bestselling author of *A Flicker in the Dark*

"A masterful, smart, slow-burning suspense. *Out of the Ashes* drew me in with its sinister secrets and wouldn't let me go until the very last page."

—Elle Cosimano, *USA Today* bestselling author of *Finlay Donovan Is Killing It*

"Bold, unpredictable, and savagely beautiful, *Out of the Ashes* is that rare read that combines breakneck twists and turns with deeply woven themes of family, memory, and justice. You'll read this with your heart in your throat, desperate to know what happened that night—but afraid at how ugly the truth might be. A searing, shocking powerhouse of a debut."

—Laurie Elizabeth Flynn, bestselling author of *The Girls Are All So Nice Here*

That Weekend

"Kara Thomas is ruthless. When you descend into *That Weekend*, prepare for darkness ahead, breakneck turns, and shivery secrets. I am still reeling."

—Kit Frick, author of *I Killed Zoe Spanos*

"Deliciously twisted. Clear your schedule, because *That Weekend* is going to keep you up all night."

—Karen M. McManus, #1 *New York Times* bestselling author of *One of Us Is Lying*

"A deliciously unsettling and grimly beautiful examination of the dark and twisted potential lurking within us all. *That Weekend* is a bold and expertly plotted page-turner from beginning to end, and it firmly cements Kara Thomas as a master of the craft—no one writes a thriller like her."

—Courtney Summers, *New York Times* bestselling author of *Sadie*

"Kara Thomas deftly weaves a web of secrets, tangling you in a mystery so shocking you'll never guess the ending. My jaw actually dropped."

—Erin Craig, *New York Times* bestselling author of *House of Salt and Sorrows*

"A riveting, unputdownable thriller that made my palms sweat and my heart pound. I devoured this book in a single sleepless night; *That Weekend* is a brutal examination of what it means to survive."

—Victoria Lee, author of *A Lesson in Vengeance* and *The Fever King*

"A mesmerizing, creepy, excellent thrill ride of a book."

—Kathleen Glasgow, *New York Times* bestselling author of *Girl in Pieces*

"Thrilling, captivating, unpredictable (still reeling over those twists!) and will consume your life until you finish! And then it will haunt you afterward."

—Laurie Elizabeth Flynn, author of *The Girls Are All So Nice Here*

The Cheerleaders

"Sharp, brilliantly plotted, and totally engrossing."

—Karen M. McManus, *New York Times* bestselling author of *One of Us Is Lying*

"A crafty, dark, and disturbing story."

—Kathleen Glasgow, *New York Times* bestselling author of *Girl in Pieces*

"A little bit *Riverdale* and a little bit *Veronica Mars*."

—Riley Sager, bestselling author of *Final Girls*

Little Monsters

"A disturbing portrait of how bad news and gossip can curdle when mixed together."

—Oprah.com

"An eerie and masterly psychological thriller . . . [that] culminates in a shocking and disturbing ending. Thomas expertly captures the pointed nuances and the fickle, manipulative bonds of adolescent girls' friendships."

—*SLJ*

"Taut and suspenseful . . . this gritty page-turner will easily hook a broad range of readers."

—*Booklist*

"An intense psychological thriller that all but ensures the lights will be left on between dusk and dawn."

—*Publishers Weekly*

"Gritty and realistic . . . this mystery will leave readers in awe."

—*VOYA*

"A twisted story of obsession and manipulation, *Little Monsters* captivated me right up to its surprising conclusion—and left me wondering how well I really know my friends."

—Chelsea Sedoti, author of *The Hundred Lies of Lizzie Lovett*

"A brilliant, well-written masterpiece, full of unreliable narrators, suspense, and plot twists that will leave you at the edge of your seat."

—Inah P., *The Bibliophile Confessions*

"A twisted and evocative tale of teenage friendships, obsession, and family dynamics all wrapped up in a mystery that is as compelling as it is dark."

—Liz, *Liz Loves Books*

"The ending left me staring slack-jawed."

—Leah Lorenzo, *Bumblebee Books*

"*Little Monsters* was absolutely amazing. It pulled me in, and now that I am done with it, I am going to have such a major book hangover . . . Every time I thought I was close to having [the mystery] figured out, Kara Thomas would throw something at us and it would change EVERYTHING!"

—Stephanie Torina, *Reading is Better With Cupcakes*

The Darkest Corners

"Gripping from start to finish, *The Darkest Corners* took me into an underbelly I didn't know existed, with twists that left me shocked and racing forward to get to the end."

—Victoria Aveyard, #1 *New York Times* bestselling author of *Red Queen*

"A tight, twisted thriller, full of deft reversals and disturbing revelations—deeply, compulsively satisfying!"

—Brenna Yovanoff, *New York Times* bestselling author of *The Replacement*

"As dark as Gillian Flynn and as compulsive as *Serial* . . . Kara Thomas's mystery debut is intricate, chilling, and deeply compelling. Unforgettable!"

—Laura Salters, author of *Run Away*

"You'll be up all night tearing through the pages, gasping through the twists and turns."

—Bustle.com

"[It] will have you questioning the lies young girls tell, and the ripple effects they can have."

—EW.com

"Thomas carefully crafts the suspense, leaving present-tense narrator Tessa—and readers—to doubt even those she loves the most . . . An unsettling story of loss, lies, and violence lurking in the shadows of a small town."

—*Kirkus Reviews*, starred review

"On the heels of *Making a Murderer* and *The Jinx* comes a psychological thriller strongly rooted in the true-crime tradition . . . Expertly plotted with plenty of twists and turns—never mind a truly shocking conclusion—this gritty thriller is sure to find a wide audience among teens and adults alike. Equally concerned with a quest for the truth and the powerful motivation of guilt, this compelling novel won't linger on the shelf."

—*Booklist*, starred review

"Thomas keeps it real with a jaded heroine from the have-nots societal segment who holds on to her humanity, and a frank illustration of failure in the justice system. Hand this one to older teens who love dark mysteries or fans of Netflix's *Making a Murderer*."

—Shelf Awareness, starred review

"Clearly drawn . . . [and] alive until the twisty end."

—*Bulletin*

"Strong character development and thrilling reveals . . . this novel is a sure bet."

—*SLJ*

OUT
OF THE
ASHES

OTHER TITLES BY KARA THOMAS

That Weekend
The Cheerleaders
Little Monsters
The Darkest Corners

OUT OF THE ASHES

A NOVEL

KARA THOMAS

THOMAS & MERCER

Published by Thomas & Mercer, Seattle

www.apub.com

ISBN-13: 9781662509537 (paperback)
ISBN-13: 9781662509544 (digital)

Cover design by Caroline Teagle Johnson
Cover images: © DEEPOL by plainpicture/Mischa Keijser / plainpicture; © Blue Collectors / Stocksy; © Beth Rooney / Getty Images

Printed in the United States of America

For my father—sorry, there are no dragons in this one either.

Chapter One

The alert came in while I was camped in the break room, running the clock down on the remainder of my shift. Half a dozen iPhones going berserk, warning of severe thunderstorms, possible flash flooding. Nurses sighing over Tupperware containers of leftover pasta salad, everyone anticipating the panicked calls from the ER, begging to send them floaters. Bad driving conditions meant an influx of bodies, peeled off the pavement, needing to be stitched back together.

I slipped out of the room before anyone could remember that I was off in half an hour. A coveted 7:00–11:00 p.m. shift before three nights off was a perfectly good reason for my coworkers to turn on me in normal conditions, but tonight was going to be a long one.

Rain slapped against the hospital windows as I retrieved my vitals cart from the hall. I thought of my car, parked in a garage six blocks from the hospital, and the long journey ahead of me tonight. Too late to be searching for an out now.

I stopped outside 102A, a woman in her late sixties I'd grown particularly fond of in the days she'd spent in the ICU recovering from a bowel bleed. On this floor, it's generally unwise to get attached to patients, but Mrs. Berne made even the most arrogant attending doctors shit their pants, and I admired her.

"Knock, knock," I said, tugging my cart into the room.

Mrs. Berne muted her television. "What was all that terrible noise?"

"An overreaction to the weather." I wrapped the blood pressure cuff around Mrs. Berne's arm, careful not to disturb the network of IVs in her hands. "How are you feeling?"

"Tired. You people and these machines—how am I supposed to sleep?"

While the blood pressure machine hissed and clicked, I slipped the pulse reader over Mrs. Berne's finger. "Hate to be the one to break it to you, but the doctor ordered an abdominal scan."

"Tonight? Why?"

You're very sick, I stopped myself from saying. Most people who wind up in the ICU do not understand this simple fact, and reminding them only pisses them off. "Your white blood count is still pretty high. He wants to make sure the infection isn't coming from a perforated bowel."

Mrs. Berne's eyelids closed. I took her hand in mine, her skin rice-paper thin and mottled with abused veins. "Hey. This is just a complication. It won't be what does you in."

Mrs. Berne eased a bit under my touch. "Oh yeah? What will, then?"

I hung up the blood pressure cuff. "My money is on that daughter of yours."

"Which one?" Mrs. Berne shifted in her bed, wincing.

"The blonde. Always yelling at us?"

"Oh, that one's been a bitch from the second she was born."

I smiled behind the glow of my monitor and finished logging her vitals. I wished Mrs. Berne luck with her abdominal scan and made my way to the door but paused in the doorway, drawing her attention from the television.

"What is it?" she asked.

"Just letting you know I won't see you again for a bit." I palmed the doorframe, my opposite hand on my vitals cart. "I'm off at eleven, and then the next few nights."

"Any fun plans?"

"Yeah." I flipped the room light off for Mrs. Berne. A rare private room on this floor, thanks to the highly contagious intestinal parasite she'd been admitted with. "Sleeping."

It couldn't have been further from the truth, but the most effective lies usually are. I picked that one up from patients. Tell me you got that black eye when your husband elbowed you while reaching for the remote? Obviously I'll think he punched you out. Now, if you say you got kicked in the face by a horse—that's so wild I just might believe it.

Mrs. Berne's response was a bark of a laugh. I carried it with me on the elevator ride down to the hospital entrance, out the doors, and toward the garage under an increasingly threatening sky.

My scrubs were damp by the time I reached my 2003 Accord. Having a car in Queens was pointless, but I'd had the thing since college and felt obligated to keep her around, like a needy old friend who wants to meet up twice a year for drinks.

I turned on the air in the Accord, my fingertips pulsing with the urge to pop my glove box and check that the Ziploc bag was still there.

It obviously wasn't difficult to get my hands on a syringe. A sufficient dose of morphine was a different story—one that would hopefully not end with a twelve- to fourteen-month prison sentence.

I expelled the sigh trapped in my cheeks and clipped my phone to the dash mount, more habit than anything. No need for GPS for this trip.

The clouds formed a giant bruise over the horizon by the time I reached the George Washington Bridge. Lightning lit the sky like a camera flash, preceded by a fresh assault of rain that blotted out my view of the road ahead.

The lanes quickly jammed up ahead of the merge for the bridge. I kept right, red and blue lights in my periphery drawing my attention.

My heart sank to my bowels. An NYPD cruiser swerved around me and pulled up to a car hugging the side of the bridge. A jumper, maybe, or an accident already.

My fingers went slick around the steering wheel. I'd been skittish around law enforcement since I was a preteen, when my uncle Scott nailed a sign to the edge of our property spray-painted with the words COME BACK WITH A WARRANT. I'd grown adept at avoiding the cops that occasionally came up to the ICU with questions. *Sorry, vomit on my hands. Someone else at the nurses' station will help you.*

I kept my eyes trained on the taillights ahead of me until I passed the cruiser. No need to behave like a criminal. I hadn't killed anyone. Not yet.

I left the storm in my wake somewhere on I-84. I'd forgotten how lonely this stretch of interstate could be. I'd only made the trip back to Carney, New York, a handful of times since I left for college twelve years ago. The most recent had been three months ago, after my mother's foster brother Gil was diagnosed with stage 4 lung cancer.

Carney is in western Sullivan County, nestled between the casino at Monticello and the Pennsylvania border. The only marker one has entered the town of Carney is a billboard for Ealy Farms, a family-owned business that had kept the local economy on life support until the Great Recession and the ensuing rise in new hospital systems and health-care-adjacent jobs. Beside the billboard advertising "U-Pick" berries at Ealy's was one that simply claimed JESUS IS THE ANSWER.

To what, exactly, I was unsure. Rising opioid deaths, unemployment, white rage. Take your pick.

Thanks to the mess getting out of the city, the two-hour drive took three and change. Gil lived right off County Route 42. Keep heading north and I'd eventually pass the fifteen-acre plot of land where my family's farmhouse used to stand before the evening of September 8, 2001.

I killed my lights on the approach to Gil's, even though his nearest neighbor was a quarter mile down 42, the house hidden by a cover of trees and night. The Accord bumped and ground to a stop on the uneven terrain of Gil's driveway. Part of me longed to hit the gas and continue on the semicircle that fed back out onto 42, but a light flicked on in Gil's living room. A face, round and ghastly, appeared in the window, letting me know that I had been seen.

Gil waddled into the kitchen at the same time I stepped through the front door. Years ago, he had been the type of good-looking that had led to at least two bar brawls between women that I knew of. Now his face was twice its usual size, from the cocktail of Decadron and pain medication. Since he'd stopped treatment, white hair had started to sprout from his scalp like toothbrush bristles.

I looked from the joint between his lips to the oxygen tank he dragged behind him. "Could have let me know your plan was to blow yourself up."

Gil's face softened. He plodded over, collapsed into the chair opposite me. Stubbed out his joint in the ashtray on the table. "It wasn't fair of me to ask you."

"No, it wasn't."

After a beat, I reached for his hand, stroked the leathery skin sagging over his gnarled joints. Gil's gaze dropped to the table. "You could talk me through it. So you don't have to be the one."

I felt myself thaw a bit. Gil didn't need to explain why he couldn't just buy a Ruger and do it himself. He hadn't touched a gun since he'd left Afghanistan in 2002. Told me he couldn't bear to, not because of things he'd seen over there but what had happened to my parents and Uncle Scott here in Carney.

A slick of sweat came to my palms. I wanted to think of Gil's brains splattered against a wall about as much as I wanted to remember how the local paper had described the way my father's remains had been found. A skeleton in the ashes, half his head blasted away. It was not until ten days later that they found his jaw near the creek at the edge of our property, animal teeth marks in the bone.

"Sam," Gil began.

I tamped the grisly images down, squeezed Gil's hand, warning him not to say more. Gil had been overly sentimental during my last few check-ins, and I didn't want his last words to be a reminder of all the ways we'd failed each other over the past twenty years. Perfunctory phone calls on holidays, polite deferments of offers to visit each other—Gil did not like the city, and I could not get the time off work to come up here.

When I finally spoke, my voice clogged in my throat. "How about you lay down?"

I looped an arm through Gil's and walked him into the living room. "In here," he wheezed. "Bedroom's a mess."

I did not point out that the whole house was a mess, and soon to be my problem, as I guided Gil to the couch. The thing was older than I was, a pilling flannel bedsheet tucked over the cushions. He lay on his back, his knees bent to the side like bird wings.

"Put the TV on," Gil said, while I draped an afghan over him.

At this time of night, it's all the same. Jingles for cardboard-tasting pizza, ads for medications with so many side effects I think I'd rather just die.

As I replaced the remote, a framed photo on the end table drew my attention. Mom and Uncle Scott, seated at a picnic table. My mother wore a paisley dress that rode up her thighs while sitting, showing off an inch-long scab on her knee—I remembered it as a faded white scar.

"I thought you might like to take it home."

Gil's voice was small as I reached for the frame. Uncle Scott was seated next to my mother, his mouth fruit-punch stained around a smile, tongue poking through where his front teeth were coming in.

His strawberry-blond hair fell to his collarbone. I used to rib him about the old photos, the way he looked like a Hanson brother.

"I've never seen this one," I said, swallowing to clear my throat.

"That's the day it happened," Gil wheezed. "His eye."

My uncle Scott was seven when he lost his right eye in a playground accident. A freak thing, a slip from the monkey bars and onto a stick protruding from the ground.

Gil's fingers found the corner of the frame. I loosened my grip, let him have a final look.

"I was supposed to be watching him," Gil said. "He wanted to go to the playground, but everyone else was still eating lunch, so I took him. And instead of watching him, I was talking to a cute girl."

I was quiet, absorbing the impact of Gil's confession. My uncle had worn a patch over his dead eye until middle school, when my grandfather died. Grandma Lynn had used the money from his life insurance to pay for Scott's new glass eye, but he had already fallen in with the only kids who would accept him, the Future Drug Dealers of Carney. Most people agreed that Scott's life had been permanently derailed by the accident on the playground.

I watched Gil now, the wetness in his eyes, the way his thumb moved over Scott's face in the photo. It made me sad to think of him carrying this secret all these years. Gil had come to my grandparents as a foster child at eight and never left; despite the lack of blood relation, I'd considered him as much my uncle as Scott.

"It wasn't your fault he lost his eye," I said, even though I had no idea, really.

The answer seemed enough for Gil. He handed the photo back to me and closed his eyes. Wherever his mind had landed, he seemed at peace, until a juicy cough erupted from him. When he regained his breath: "Better get on with it."

Gil eyed the items as I fished them out of the Ziploc bag and lined them up neatly on the coffee table. "Couldn't have just smothered me with a pillow?"

"I thought that might get weird if you changed your mind halfway through."

I stuck the needle into the vial of morphine and pulled the plunger. Gil, unblinking, watched the syringe fill, his breathing filling the silence.

"I'll wait until you're ready," I said.

"I am."

I ran a finger over his veins, found a serviceable one, and gave it a tap with two fingers. I slid the needle in and pushed down on the plunger.

"Whoa," Gil said, almost immediately. "Where's this shit been all my life?"

The first rush is always like that—euphoric. Then: "Sam. I feel funny."

"I know. It'll pass."

"I don't like it." Gil sounded like a frightened child. I threaded my fingers through his.

"It's okay. I'm here with you."

Gil arched his back. "Marnie."

My fingers went still. "Marnie's dead, Gil."

"Oh." A terrible moan parted Gil's lips, and his eyes snapped open, like someone who realized they'd left the house with the stove on. "Marnie?"

"I'm not Marnie," I said. "It's Samantha. Her daughter."

His grip on my fingers tightened, like he didn't believe me. "I'm so sorry, Marnie."

Gil's eyes oscillated before settling on me, bone-deep sadness taking over his face. My stomach did an accordion fold.

"Gil." My voice warbled with the plea: *Don't go. Not now.* "What are you sorry for?"

A final exhale before his fingers twitched, then went limp. I rose from the couch, draping the blanket over Gil's body, letting one foot stick out to catch the breeze. The only way I could ever fall asleep.

It was nearing five by the time I reached the GW. Half past, and I was outside my apartment building in Long Island City. An eerie quiet blanketed my street. Even the homeless man who hung outside the foyer and made slurping noises at me wasn't up for the day yet. Last night's storm had given way to thick, lazy drops of summer rain splattering the overhang as I punched in the front door code.

The silence in the hallway unsettled me. I found myself yearning for the woman across the hall to wake and begin screaming at her husband for being a useless piece of shit, just like she had every morning for the six years I'd lived here. She was more reliable than the hot water in the building, and sometimes she went at it for so long I had to bang on her door and tell her I was trying to sleep. I didn't even know her name, but she was my only source of human interaction in the building since my ex-husband moved out two years ago.

Sometimes I thought about getting a dog—there was no shortage of snaggle-toothed geriatrics on the shelter's website—but it hardly seemed fair, considering my work schedule. I hadn't slept an entire night since my family was murdered, which was why I'd found health care so appealing to begin with.

My scrubs smelled of Gil's final joint. I stripped down to my underwear and nestled under my comforter, the rain plinking on the AC unit outside my window.

I'm so sorry, Marnie.

Mining Gil's final words for meaning was a pointless exercise. I'd witnessed enough people leave this world to know that regret is the last thing most will feel.

I'm so sorry.

My last real conversation with my mother before she was murdered had been a screaming match. She hadn't wanted to drag my twenty-two-month-old sister out at nap time to give me a ride to Caroline Mason's house so her mother could drive us to the movie theater to see *The Others*.

I'd gotten vicious in response. *You don't give a shit about anyone but that baby.* Despite our sniping at each other the entire ride to Caroline's, Lyndsey had fallen asleep in her car seat, pacifier dangling from her lips like a cigarette, by the time we pulled into the Masons' driveway.

I was pissed that I was late, once again, so I slammed the car door on my way out. My mother rolled down the window, shouted at me over the sounds of Lyndsey's wailing from the back seat. *What the hell is wrong with you, Samantha?*

Later, when Caroline's mother picked us up from the theater, she said my mom had called. My mother had a migraine and her hands were full with my sister; would Mrs. Mason mind letting me stay the night?

Her dinner plans disturbed by another mouth to feed, Mrs. Mason took us to the Ruby Tuesday across from the cinema. Caroline and I sipped Sprites, giddy with the thrill of pulling off a sleepover without the usual pleading and negotiations.

"I wish my mom was like yours," I'd said to Caroline while we were elbow to elbow at the salad bar. "Mine hates me."

It wasn't until the following afternoon, when a police officer sat me down and told me that they were all gone, that none of them had made it out, that he had blasted all their skulls away before the fire was set, that I realized my mother's plea had saved my sorry little life.

Chapter Two

I woke to my ringtone splintering the quiet. By the time I emerged from my cocoon of sheets, head gauzy, my phone screen had gone dark.

I rubbed my eyes until the time came into focus. A little before 4:00 p.m. Gil had been adamant no one would find him until tomorrow morning, when a nurse from Medicaid was scheduled to come to the house to change his IV port.

The missed call was from my shift supervisor. I toyed with the idea of leaving the country and changing my identity, before cursing under my breath and calling Nancy back.

"Sam? Oh, thank God, I got you."

"You sure did." I fumbled on my nightstand until my fingers found my steel Hydro Flask. I chugged stale, tinny water until my throat was clear enough to say, "I'm off tonight, Nance."

"I know, I know. But two nurses called out."

"Can't you try someone else?" I pinched the bridge of my nose, massaged the bone with my thumb and forefinger.

"I already did. No bites."

I didn't know what the other nurses were doing that they couldn't pick up an extra shift tonight. Most of them were twentysomethings, the type to unironically identify themselves as "dog moms." They seemed fueled by boozy brunches and countdowns to Disney World trips and attended spin classes straight off twelve-hour shifts.

I had no problem with any of these girls, even if I avoided becoming friendly. They were not like Nancy, like my other carefully vetted friends. They were the type to ask too many questions, and working in a hospital, personal information is currency. The younger nurses traded it, banked it, whittled it into weapons. I was not going to let my guard down and get shanked in the break room.

I sighed. "Goddamn it, Nance."

"Thank you," she said.

I brushed my teeth, hunted down a pair of clean scrubs, and was waiting for the subway by 5:30. By 5:53, I was stepping through the doors of Long Island City Hospital, crushing the thought that the last time I'd made this journey, I had stolen morphine in my backpack.

The woman next to me in the elevator wept openly the whole ride up to the ICU. I screwed around on my phone to avoid looking her way; I could feel her staring, waiting for me to make eye contact, reassure her somehow.

I used to try harder with the patients' families. I knew from experience that being the person left behind was worse. But there's no comfort in what we do here for the living. No one who visits this floor is ready to say goodbye.

At 5:57, the elevator doors opened to chaos.

A chorus of gongs—empty IV drips—went ignored as a rapid-response team raced past me. In a room adjacent to the nurse's station, a security guard was attempting to break up a fight between two family members.

The attending on call tonight, Dr. Farkas, was berating a medical intern so savagely that she'd begun to cry, choking sobs that were so loud, my elevator mate abruptly stopped weeping and gaped at them.

"Is it you who has the traumatic brain injury, or is it the patient?" Farkas demanded of the intern while I whisked away my elevator mate, who was now chattering at me in panicked Spanish, and deposited her next to my coworker Gloria, who hadn't even set down her backpack and coffee yet.

Gloria put a hand on the woman's forearm. "A quién estás buscando?" *Who are you looking for?*

By the time I returned to the nurse's station, Dr. Farkas was gone. The intern he'd reamed out was sniffling in front of a computer. Nancy looked at me and said, "Woof," before answering the phone that had been ringing off the hook for the past several minutes.

I sat in the chair adjacent to Nancy's, spinning small semicircles while I browsed tonight's charts and waited for the outgoing nurse to show up and give me the rundown on which patients were ready for their peanut butter and Seroquel sandwiches. The sounds of the unit created a maelstrom in my brain, and I could think of nothing but Gil's body on the couch.

A Mary Kay–scented hand rested on my shoulder. "Samantha."

I startled in my chair as if Nancy had screamed it in my ear. I spun to face her and snapped, "What?"

Nancy blinked at me. She was what Gil would have called a "brick shithouse" of a woman. Her magenta scrubs partly concealed the Betty Boop tattoo on her bicep. "You remember 10A? Little old lady? Reitman was the last name."

Well, fuck.

I'd been careful. I'd chosen a patient who didn't have much time. A ninety-two-year-old woman who had been intubated for several days. No family hanging around to notice that the morphine dose I'd administered was actually saline.

After a beat too long, I said, "Yeah. I was with her when she passed away."

God, I hated that phrase—just fucking say *died*—but I needed to soften Nancy, and I'd never in almost ten years heard her say a patient had "died."

"Her son is requesting a meeting to talk about her care plan." Nancy glanced down at the Post-it stuck to Mrs. Reitman's file. "They're suggesting tomorrow afternoon."

The coil of panic in my gut tightened. "Isn't it a little late for a care meeting?"

Nancy didn't look up from the chart. "They want to know we did what we could."

"She was ninety-two years old with multiple organ failure. What were we supposed to do?"

Nancy removed her reading glasses to get a full look at me. "What's going on, Samantha?"

My heart was trying to blast its way out of my chest. "I'm off the next three, Nance. Unless the son wants to drag his ass here in the middle of the night, I'm not meeting with him."

Nancy let her glasses, tethered to her by a beaded chain, drop. "All right. Now I'm not asking. What's going on with you?"

Gil calling me Marnie. His apology with his last gasping breath. I pushed the thoughts down, prepared for a whopper of a lie. Shades of the truth. Whatever I needed to do to get Nancy out of my ass.

"My uncle is dying. Stage 4 lung cancer. It should be any day now."

"Oh, Sam. I had no idea."

Nancy's reading glasses rose and fell with her bosom as her breathing became more labored. Information overload. I'd spent every holiday with her family since my divorce. I knew every detail of her daughter's eating disorder and her gay son's adoption, but as far as Nancy was concerned, I had no family. I'd only told her my parents died when I was a kid and that I was raised by an aunt I no longer spoke to.

"Don't make me meet with Mrs. Reitman's son," I said.

Nancy replaced her hand on my shoulder. "I'll find someone else. Promise me something, though?"

I willed the tremor in my hand to quiet. "What?"

"Run a leave request by HR. Take a few extra nights off to be with your uncle." Nancy turned back to her computer. "And for Christ's sake, don't you ever come in here smelling like pot again."

❧

I could not stomach the idea of the subway, so I walked home.

Thanks to my dawdling, the woman across the hall was already up for the day, informing her husband he was a useless shit-for-brains. I shut myself in my apartment, their shouting muffled by the thrum of my pulse in my ears.

On the table, my phone lit up. The Sullivan County area code turned my nerves into live wires.

I let the call go to voice mail.

"Hi, I'm looking for Samantha Newsom. This is home health services of Sullivan County—please call me back at your earliest convenience."

I'm coming, I thought as I listened to the voice mail informing me of Gil's passing. No one had asked me to, or expected me to, but I was going to Carney.

Finding an opportunity to get some sleep would be Future Sam's problem. I threw a change of clothes and my cell charger into my backpack and made the pilgrimage to the parking garage.

I'm coming, I thought, a promise to no one.

I would lie low for a few days until Mrs. Reitman's son was off the hospital's ass. Empty Gil's house and get a Realtor in. And then I could turn my back on Carney for good.

❧

A month ago, when Gil had opted to stop treatment, he had suggested that I might want to keep his house. Might be a nice place to get away from the city for a weekend, with its spare bedroom and patch of woods in the backyard. The thought had nearly made me erupt in hives.

He'd left me a key, tarnished and resistant to the fussy lock. When I got the door open, my sternum hardened at the silence.

Someone—the home nurse, maybe—had turned the TV off. I couldn't bear to go back to the living room, even though the county had moved Gil's body to the morgue hours ago. He'd been adamant that he didn't want to rot in a box underground and had prepaid for his cremation.

In the unforgiving light of the afternoon, the house looked like a Realtor's nightmare. Cabinets with the handles falling off, and entire tiles missing from the kitchen floor. It seemed like a joke that Gil had left an entire house to me. In my adult life, I had only ever lived in apartments the size of postage stamps, and I had never so much as fixed a leaky sink.

I did know how to clean, though, and Gil had left no shortage of grime and mess. A skillet was abandoned on the stove, a film of bacon fat coating the cast iron. Gil used to sprinkle rolled oats over the grease to feed them to the birds.

I cracked the window over the sink, tugged open the cabinet drawers in search of something with which to scrub the pan. After an excavation of the junk drawer, I turned up nothing of value but a baggie of neatly rolled joints.

Just a hit or two, I thought. *To sleep a bit.*

I didn't like to touch matches or lighters for obvious reasons. I used the flame from the gas stove to light the joint and wandered into the bathroom. Sat on the edge of the tub and blew smoke into the shower fan.

I'm sorry, Marnie.

I thought of Gil's skillet and the oats, the delighted way my baby sister would grab a fistful and toss them to the robins out back. Lyndsey's Cheerio-crusted fingers in my hair, pudgy baby feet stomping my ribs while she toddled to the other end of the couch to where my mother sat. Always as far as possible from us, as if it were the only way she could breathe.

Memories were a riptide. Innocent enough on the surface, but let your guard down and next thing you know, you're drowning in four feet of water.

They never found Lyndsey's remains. The chief of police said a child her size, after a fire that burned for hours, wouldn't have left behind much, if anything at all.

She was a beautiful child. Maybe if more than one picture of her had survived there would have been an outcry about the Carney Police's fuckups in the investigation. *Justice for Baby Lyndsey.* Maybe she would have made the national news, had she not been murdered on September 8, 2001.

The smoke hadn't yet cleared from our property before the first plane hit the North Tower. Why would anyone care about a murder-arson in upstate New York when the whole world was burning?

I let a door slam on the memory. I closed my eyes and searched for the sounds I knew I would not find up here in the mountains. None of my usual noises—sirens and endless construction and the ranting next door. Every day while I tried to sleep, the noises formed a totem to keep my thoughts from drifting back to the little girl lost in the ashes.

I threw an arm over my face, my blood jackhammering in my temples. I elbowed my way to sitting up, expecting to see that the sun had sunk behind the trees. The time on Gil's cable box said it was a little after two. I had been out barely an hour.

My heartbeat was uneven, giving away that some noise must have woken me. I swung myself off the couch, padded into the kitchen, my mouth thick and dry. I poured myself some water from the kitchen sink, eyes on the window overlooking the driveway.

A sleek gray car was parked at the edge of Gil's property; its driver, a tall Black guy in a suit, surveyed Gil's house as if trying to determine whether he was in the right location.

My fingers went rigid around the water glass. The man shielded his eyes against the sun and headed up Gil's driveway, disappearing from my sight. I swallowed a burst of panic at the two quick raps at the door.

I set my glass on the counter with a palsied hand and made my way to the living room. I unlatched the door and pulled it open, catching the man mid-knock.

He had warm brown eyes, cheekbones that could cut glass. He stuck his raised hand in his suit pocket. "Good afternoon."

I hooked a hand over my right shoulder, massaged the massive knot that had managed to form in an impressively short period of time. "Can I help you?"

"Is Gil Ramos home?"

"He died yesterday."

The man blinked. "Really."

He cocked his head slightly, unable to contain the question that had been brewing behind his eyes from the moment I'd opened the door. "Are you Samantha Newsom?"

I tucked my hands under the armpits of my T-shirt, feeling chilled despite the heat.

"I'm sorry, how did you know Gil?"

"I didn't. Travis Meacham. New York State Police."

Police. Swatted away the memory of Gil's limp body, ditching the needle and morphine bag in a bin of used maxi pads at a rest stop bathroom.

Travis Meacham rocked back on his heels, drawing my eyes to polished dress shoes, miraculously unmarred by the dust of Gil's driveway.

"Maybe we could talk inside?"

There was no way the state police would investigate the natural death of a terminal cancer patient. I did not offer Travis Meacham coffee.

"Your family's case recently came across my desk," he began.

"Right," I said flatly.

I'd heard the exact line before. My senior year of college, I'd gotten a call from the man who took over my family's case when the original detective retired. He drove to Binghamton to meet with me, took me to a pub off campus. They had no new leads, of course, but remained hopeful every day. In between meat loaf burps, he pleaded with me to get my cousin Rhiannon to stop posting flyers around town. A photo of my family, accompanied by DO YOU KNOW WHO KILLED ME? THE CARNEY POLICE DO! They were becoming an embarrassment.

Meacham broke my gaze and reached into his jacket. My fingers moved to my lips, the blood in them thrumming, as he removed a photo from his pocket and set it on the counter. All the air seemed to zap from the room as I slid the photo closer to me.

It was a mug shot of a man, his lips parted and his eyes wide with shock. He had barely any neck and sagging skin mottled with red. Wiry gray hair hung just above his shoulders.

Meacham's voice drew my attention away from the picture. "Do you recognize this man?"

"I don't know," I said. "I don't think so."

"His name is Leonard Boggs."

I reached back, hoping the name would ping some long-dormant memory. Nothing. "Did he kill my family?"

"He was picked up for breaking into a car a few weeks ago," Meacham said. "Cops ran his DNA through CODIS—it matched an unsolved home invasion and battery in Cayuga County back in 2004."

Cayuga County was three hours northwest of here. "What does this have to do with my family's case?"

"Leonard Boggs lived in Carney in 2001," Meacham said. "He worked with Scott at the beer distributor. He's claiming he was on your property the night of the murders."

Finally, I said, "He's full of shit, right? It's been twenty-two years and now he's ready to come forward?"

"I was skeptical as well. But when I spoke to him, he described the inside of Scott's trailer accurately. I even called up the woman Boggs was living with at the time. She says he told her he was going up there that night to buy marijuana from Scott Ginns."

I pictured the inside of Scott's trailer—a poster for the Who's *Tommy* on the wall, flannel sheets on a never-made-up bed. My mother sent me over sometimes with green beans or tomatoes from the garden. If he was alone and I was bored, Scott would let me play *Duke Nukem* with him until my mother came banging on the door.

The room was starting to whirl around me a bit. "What did he say he saw?"

"He claims he was waiting by Scott's trailer when he heard gunshots, so he ran to the woods for cover. He says he saw a man leave the house."

"Okay. Did he see the man's face?"

Meacham's hands found the back of one of Gil's kitchen chairs. "Samantha, I think you should sit."

I ignored the tremor in my knees, the sense the floor was about to cave in. "I'm fine. Did Boggs see the killer's face?"

Travis Meacham hesitated just long enough to stall my heartbeat. "He says the man was carrying a screaming kid."

Chapter Three

I found out I was going to be a big sibling the way I acquired most information as an eleven-year-old perpetually outnumbered by adults: through eavesdropping. That afternoon, after a secretive and rushed visit to the doctor, Aunt Michelle had come over to have coffee with my mother. When Mom told me to go watch TV in the middle of the day, I knew something juicy was coming. I parked myself in the hallway outside the kitchen, dragging a brush through my Barbie's hair.

My mother was slumped over the table, crying. "I can't do this, Mitch."

"You have to."

There was a pause. "I don't. Not really."

"That's evil." Mitch's response was swift, her voice like a backhand to the face.

"We're barely scraping by with one kid. What am I supposed to do?"

"Pray it's a girl," Mitch had said. "Then she can wear Samantha's old things."

Unexpected as she may have been, the baby became the center of our worlds as soon as they brought her home. My father, too old for piggyback rides, seemed to age in reverse when Lyndsey was in the room. He and Gil both stopped smoking cigarettes finally, the effects of secondhand smoke on children more clearly advertised than they had been when I was born.

And me. I was elated when I found out, even if it escaped me that the age difference meant my sister would never be the companion that I'd longed for most of my life. I was not prepared for the crayon scribbles over my math homework, falling asleep in homeroom because the baby was teething, for the way my mother had turned into a virtual stranger to me, milk and sweet potato staining her shirt when she picked me up from ballet. In the back seat, always, my sister.

My sister might have survived the fire.

"He has to be lying," I said finally. "Right? He's one of those fucked-up men who start making shit up to get attention in jail?"

"I was skeptical, of course, when I got that call." *But.*

"There's no way," I said. I waited for Meacham to tell me there was no way. But he wouldn't be here if there wasn't, would he?

"I requested the fire report from the town when I got this case. I was told that no such report existed, according to their records."

"What does that mean?" I asked.

"Apparently when the coroner determined that your parents were dead before the fire was set, Detective Holcombe didn't request a full arson report." The tenor of Meacham's voice suggested that it meant exactly what I suspected: the Carney Police had fucked up the case.

"Why the hell not?" I asked.

"He didn't think it was necessary. It was clear from charring patterns that the fire was set by the killer to cover up the homicides. Holcombe's position was that the photos from the scene and the fire marshal's notes were sufficient to prove arson, should the case go to court."

"And you disagree with Holcombe."

"When I inherited the case, I sent everything to a team of arson investigators. Every single one of them feels, very strongly, that even a fire that burned for more than five hours wouldn't be enough to completely cremate a child Lyndsey's age. Or there *were* traces of her, but no one bothered to save enough for any concrete testing."

The exact opposite of what I'd been hearing for twenty years.

Some bone fragments had been found, I'd heard, not far from Lyndsey's room. The state crime lab could not say, definitively, whether they came from a very small human or an animal. A few years ago, I emailed the lab to ask if DNA technology had come far enough to retest the fragments. Several weeks later, I got a perfunctory response stating that the evidence in question was no longer in the state's possession.

I recalled an online discussion of my family's case I'd once read. A Reddit thread full of bickering armchair sleuths about whether the handling of the crime scene was evidence of a conspiracy to protect Stephen Rhodes or simply small-town police incompetence. The comment that had gotten the most upvotes had read, simply, The cops in Carney couldn't find their own dicks with a mirror.

Meacham rubbed the back of his head, the crop of sweat above his collar. "The handling of the scene was sloppy."

Sloppy. A laugh bubbled in my throat. My aunt had witnessed one of the cops at the scene take a piss on the ashes near my parents' remains. Another had posed by my uncle's COME BACK WITH A WARRANT sign, flashing two thumbs up and a grin.

"So no fire report, no bone fragments, and now a man who says he saw my sister leave alive." My voice strained on the last word, thinking of the tiny headstone Aunt Mitch had picked out for Lyndsey, the simple engraving of three interlinked hearts below her name.

"There are a number of issues with Boggs's account." Meacham's voice was equivocal, as if I were a child and he'd already overpromised me something. "Certain things don't make sense."

I asked the question I'd been circling, the one thing I could not even begin to work out. "Why would someone kill everyone else and save Lyndsey?"

Meacham exhaled, his shoulders slumping in a way that suggested the question had been taxing him. "I would think the killer couldn't bring himself to hurt a child who couldn't identify him."

"So then what the hell did he do with her?"

"The logical thing to do would be to leave her somewhere safe. A gas station, a hospital maybe," Meacham said. "But a child that young, abandoned without explanation—she would have been identified quickly."

I thought of the weeks following the fire, tucked into the corner of Michelle's couch, watching the evening news through swollen eyes, waiting for my family to have their turn. It never came.

"9/11 was that week," I said. "No one would have been paying attention. Maybe he gave her to someone—a family who promised to take care of her."

"The killer would have to be spectacularly lucky to pull that off," Meacham said.

"Maybe not lucky. Maybe they just knew how to keep someone quiet."

Neither of us said it, the silence ballooning between us. I imagined that Travis Meacham was thinking along similar lines. To hide Lyndsey somewhere no one would ever find her, to keep her caretakers silent for twenty-two years? Only one type of person could pull off such a thing.

A cop.

"I want to talk to Boggs," I said.

Meacham didn't look surprised. "Are you sure?"

"That's why you're here, right? You can't get him to talk, but maybe I can if I play the grieving-sister card."

"I mean, well . . ." Meacham's hands moved guiltily to his pockets. "It does help, in situations like this, if you have a surviving family member who is available and willing."

"Tomorrow," I said. "It has to be tomorrow."

Meacham did not ask why. Maybe he understood that I wasn't willing to wait any longer. Not after twenty-two years of knowing exactly who killed my family and not being able to do a goddamn thing about it.

A little after 11:00 p.m., I was curled on my side on Gil's couch, its skeleton digging into my ribs. A few months ago, Gil had bought his first new mattress in two decades, right before his terminal diagnosis. Queen, memory-foam top. It was practically new, but sleeping in his bed felt ghastly to me. I'd parked myself on the couch with an afghan, the pattern similar to the ones Grandma Lynn was always knitting, boxing up to send to the soldiers stationed overseas.

The blanket was too itchy on my bare legs, the room too cool without it. No matter. Sleep wouldn't come anyway. My brain was lit up, turning the idea over in my head, polishing it like a river stone. Lyndsey wasn't in the house.

If she was alive, I had to look for her. But how? Time had had too great of a head start. After the murders, one of the fire marshals had said searching for my sister's remains was akin to looking for a needle in a haystack. But at least a haystack was a place to start.

Looking for her now would be like trying to find a single grain of sand in the ocean floor.

She could not possibly be alive.

Because why would he let her live?

I grabbed my phone from the coffee table beside me and googled *Officer Stephen Rhodes*. All I could produce was a photo from many years ago, a headshot archived from the Carney Police Department's website.

I put Rhodes at about forty in the picture, not much older than he'd been in 2001, when he had pulled my uncle over for a drug bust and beaten in his skull.

Rhodes's head was shaved smooth, the hike of shoulders perhaps an attempt to appear taller. I'd never seen the man in person, but everyone talked of his short stature, how my uncle Scott was twice his height.

The look in his eyes could only be described as enthusiastic psychosis. His mouth formed a smirk that I've always believed to be the one of a man who knew he had gotten away with murder.

Fucking cops, I thought, my anger forming a heat-seeking missile. *The fucking cops killed my family.*

My temper comes from my mother's side. The Ginns are quick to forget themselves in anger, ready to go for the lowest blows. Ask anyone in Carney why Marnie Ginns and her brother Scott were murdered, along with my father and sister, and many will say it was Scott Ginns's temper, and the fact that he had fucked with the wrong cop.

In August of 2001, Stephen Rhodes pulled my uncle over for a broken taillight and found a dime bag of pot in his glove box. There were no witnesses to the encounter, which left Scott concussed, with a broken collarbone and several cracked ribs.

My family talked of suing the department. A month later, they were all dead.

Sleep came in short bursts, punctuated by dreams that stretched for what felt like hours. I could feel the heat of her giggle by my neck, her way of pleading with me: *Again.* I saw myself rolling her in her favorite Mickey Mouse blanket like a burrito, Mom watching from the kitchen sink, making sure I wasn't being too rough.

I woke, sweating, trapped in the jaws of panic. The time on the cable box read 6:25 a.m. I decided to cut my losses and peeled myself off the couch.

Meacham told me to meet him at the Cayuga County jail at 10:00 a.m. He had offered no preamble about what to expect upon our arrival, no instructions on how to dress for a meeting with a violent felon. The nicest thing I'd packed, a white V-neck tee from Stitch Fix that had cost at least three times what it was worth, offered a peek at my bra if I bent over too far.

I stood by the bathroom vanity and buttoned Gil's flannel over the T-shirt, studied my face through the grime on the mirror as I brushed my teeth.

An old boyfriend had described me as the "girl next door." I'd taken this to mean that I was not hot but just attractive enough for men to feel entitled to my attention. I was used to being slipped phone numbers from the sons and grandsons of patients and once, in a particularly shameful display, the husband of a woman on a ventilator.

Still, I was not pretty enough to make other women feel threatened, and I was guilty of using this to my advantage to net myself goodwill with people I needed something from. I'd fucked up a dose once, and the attending doctor had told me he believed me over the medical intern because I had a kind face. But I was unsure how to deal with a man like Leonard Boggs. And the face in the mirror now was anything but kind.

I raked my fingers through hair, matted from the braid and the rough flannel of Gil's pillowcase, and headed outside. The sky was gray, stippled with gold clouds that hung low over the Catskills. I stopped to top off my gas tank and set my phone navigation for Cayuga, steeling myself for eighty miles of I-81.

I arrived at the Cayuga jail ten minutes early. I found a spot and parked within view of Travis Meacham standing in the row adjacent to mine, smoking a cigarette.

I locked my car, Meacham looking up guiltily at the bleep of my key fob. He dropped the cigarette, crushed it under his shoe. People tended to get sheepish around me about this sort of thing, as if being a nurse meant I was automatically judgmental.

"Nasty habit," he said.

"We all have them." I shrugged. Truthfully, I hated smoking, always associated the smell with Aunt Mitch's house. "I thought you said ten."

"If you're not at least fifteen minutes early, you're late."

"You military?" I asked. Gil was always using the phrase, despite the fact he could not arrive on time if his life depended on it.

Meacham glanced at me with surprise. "No. My father was."

"That why you became a cop?"

"I'm not a cop," Meacham said.

"You said you were with the state police." I kneaded my thumb knuckle. The skin there was cracked, raw, from the constant washing at work. "What are you, then?"

"Technically, I'm an attorney. I was a prosecutor for fifteen years." Meacham held the front door open for me. "My official title is special investigator, if that's your next question."

I watched Meacham flash his badge at the security desk, getting us out of the line for peasants and onto one marked LAW ENFORCEMENT. It wasn't until he tossed his keys and wallet into the security bin that I noticed the lack of a gun at his hip.

"License," the guard said to me. "And sign in."

I passed my ID to her. While she propped my license up on her computer monitor, I signed myself in with a shaky hand. The guard tapped away at her keyboard, the clacking of her acrylic nails like a chain saw in my skull.

"Background check," Meacham explained to me, one elbow propped on the counter. With his other hand, he smoothed down his steel-gray tie. "You don't have any warrants out for your arrest, right?"

"Ha-ha," I said as the guard passed my ID back to me with an exaggerated yawn. She covered her mouth with a neatly manicured hand. "Excuse me."

I slid my license back into my wallet and followed Meacham through a metal detector. The uniformed guard who met us on the other side acknowledged us with a nod and led us down a crappily lit hallway.

There was bullshit between Meacham and the guard about the Bills before he deposited us in a room the size of a walk-in freezer. "I'll be right outside if you need me."

Meacham thanked him and closed the door. At the table was a behemoth of a man, handcuffed hands knotted together on his lap. Meacham nodded at the chairs on the opposite side of the table. I sat, but Meacham remained standing.

Opposite me, Leonard Boggs wheezed, as if overtaxed from the trip from his cell. He hadn't changed much from the driver's license photo

Meacham had shown me. Older, fatter, but still the same droopy basset hound face.

"Hello, Leonard," Meacham said brightly.

"You again," Boggs muttered, his eyes darting away from Meacham. They landed on me. Something clicked into place in Leonard Boggs's expression. His enormous figure straightened.

"Who's she?" Boggs's eyes, watery and ratlike, flicked back to Meacham. "The DA?"

"This is Samantha Newsom," Meacham said. "Scott Ginns's niece."

Boggs licked his lips, a nervous tic I saw in my patients. Usually when I asked when was the last time they took drugs. Sure, just a little bit of Xanax three months ago.

"I thought I told you don't come back without the DA," Boggs said.

Meacham took Boggs in, folded his arms across his chest. "Leonard—"

"Lenny," Boggs said. "My nan was the only one who called me Leonard."

The bitterness in Boggs's voice suggested Nan, whoever she was, was certainly the root of his issues with women. I thought of the woman Boggs had beaten during the robbery. Seventy-eight years old.

"Lenny. All right." Meacham eased into the chair finally, dragging himself closer to the table. "Samantha drove all the way from New York City to speak with you, Lenny. I think you ought to hear her out."

From my seat beside Meacham, I stared at Boggs, who could not meet my eye.

"How old are you?" I asked.

Leonard Boggs lifted his chin, the loose skin there wobbling when he opened his mouth. "Sixty-four in February."

I turned to Meacham. "What's he looking at for the assault?"

Meacham leaned back in his seat. "Minimum five, but since it occurred during a break-in, Christina will go for the max. Twenty-five."

"What about the robbery itself?"

"Minimum three and a half years, max fifteen."

"The fuck is going on?" Boggs looked at Meacham, who simply shrugged.

"You're looking at up to forty years in prison," I said. "Even if the DA drops the burglary, that's twenty-five for the battery."

I made a big show of peeking under the table, even though I'd caught a glimpse of Boggs's swollen ankles below his jumpsuit when I walked in. "You on medication for the hypertension?"

"Lasix," he muttered.

"That clubbing around your fingers," I said. "Lifelong drinker, right?"

He was also probably about a hundred pounds overweight, but I felt it was impolite to point this out. Meacham and Boggs were both staring at me now.

"You're not living another twenty-five years," I said to Leonard Boggs. "You're never going to see the outside of a prison again."

Boggs said nothing. Beside me, Meacham's body made a hissing sound, like air escaping a valve.

"You can wait for your deal to tell me what you saw the night my family was killed," I said. "Or you can stop wasting everyone's fucking time and enjoy playing Uno for the next eight to ten years."

For a long moment, no one spoke. Then, slowly, Leonard Boggs rested his hands on the table. "I was supposed to pick up my weed at Scott's trailer. Only when I got there, he wasn't around. I waited maybe fifteen, twenty minutes. Didn't have a cell phone to call him."

"Why didn't you go see if he was at the house?" Meacham asked.

"There was a vehicle I didn't recognize. Somethin' told me to stay away."

"Can you describe the vehicle?" Meacham was studying Boggs, one corner of his mouth bent with disgust. I didn't like how he'd said the word *vehicle*. He'd used a tone most people reserve for terms like *UFO* or *bigfoot*.

Something in Boggs's expression shifted. Darty eyes like a cornered animal. He was a man concerned only with his own survival, one who had sensed the odds shifting in his favor. "Sure. Once I have a deal."

"That's not up to me," Meacham said. "They've got your fingerprints and DNA, man. You have to give us information that proves to be substantial before she'll even talk about a deal."

"You want something substantial, huh?"

Meacham's hands moved to his hips, his jacket pushed back, as Boggs shifted in his seat until his eyes found me again. "While I was waiting by the trailer, I saw someone leave the house."

"Who, Lenny?" Meacham leaned in, just close enough, I thought, that my heart sank. He'd tipped his hand.

I could think of nothing but the crying from the nursery beside my room in those early months. Me, racing to get to her first. Rocking her in that glider chair, tiny baby fingers winding themselves in my hair. My mom, exhausted by pregnancy and the most basic preparatory tasks, had let me pick out her name. *Lyndsey*, the indulgent spelling a tribute to Grandma Lynn.

Leonard Boggs's voice drew me back. "He had her wrapped in a Mickey Mouse blanket. She was crying."

The air seemed to have been jettisoned from the room. I clawed at the collar of Gil's flannel.

Beside me, Meacham tucked his hands into his armpits. For the first time, I saw a flicker of emotion in his face.

"I think you've wasted enough of our time, Lenny," Meacham said, his voice thick, betraying his thoughts. *How dare he.* How dare this piece of shit string me along, make me think my baby sister had escaped that house.

"Then get the fuck out." Boggs fluttered his hands toward Meacham. "Goodbye, now."

The guard raised his eyebrows at Meacham. He opened the door, shrugging, as Meacham gathered his things.

"Don't come back until you got my deal," Boggs called after us. "Except you, sweetheart. Come back anytime."

Outside the jail. Meacham was on his phone, pacing the length of a planter box of impatiens. Despite the assault of sunlight on the back of Gil's flannel, I was kneading the cold out of my fingers.

Meacham ended his call, slipped his phone in the pocket of his jacket, now draped over his forearm. I was aware of him moving toward me, his mouth opening, but his words dissolved before they could reach my ears. I shielded my eyes against the sun, said, "What?"

"Long drive," he said. "I could go for a coffee."

"No. Alcohol, please."

"I know a place on the way back to Carney. Follow me."

Meacham texted me a pin, should we get separated on the drive.

The Neversink Lodge was a hotel on the eponymous river, about twenty minutes north of Monticello. I waited behind Meacham as he effortlessly squeezed into a metered spot outside the fusty redbrick building.

I looped around, parked behind the building. Meacham was waiting for me out front.

The only employee inside was an older woman, box-blonde and cigarette-skinny, behind the bar. She blinked at us, her clumpy mascara flaking under her lower lash line. "Sit anywhere."

Meacham draped his suit jacket over the back of a chair at a high-top by the bar and excused himself to use the restroom.

I sat, resting my palms on the tabletop, and stared at my hands until I no longer felt they were part of my body. Being a nurse required a high degree of detachment. I'd seen babies shaken into comas and emaciated toddlers who had been starved as punishment. There was no point in trying to understand why people hurt children.

But to save my sister from the burning house, only to—I could not complete the thought. I could not think of a single reason why someone would take Lyndsey and not return her safely to us.

While I sat alone, on the verge of unraveling entirely, I was aware of the bartender hovering, watching me with a look that was either motherly concern or morbid curiosity. She pounced the moment Meacham returned. "What can I get you folks?"

"Just a seltzer, please." Meacham settled into his chair and nodded to me, jolting me back to the Neversink Lodge. His eyebrows lifted when I asked for a whiskey neat.

When the bartender disappeared, I said, "You brought me to a bar and didn't expect me to order booze?"

"I pegged you as a martini type, that's all."

Whiskey had been my father's drink of choice. I didn't care too much for it, but I'd never really developed my own taste in booze. I thought of my father, in his armchair after work, a glass of Wild Turkey balanced on one knee, my baby sister on the other.

"My mom's work friends threw her a baby shower," I said, when I found my voice. "They gave Lyndsey the Mickey Mouse blanket."

I saw her now, dragging that blanket around, tiny feet getting caught in it. Gil had playfully called her Linus; she was so reluctant to part with it that the seam had already begun to fray from her tiny fingers gripping the corner, from being washed so often.

Meacham's lips parted, but he said nothing.

"How could Boggs know about the blanket unless he'd seen it?" I asked.

"Eyewitnesses can get things wrong twenty minutes later. It's been twenty years. He's had a lot of time to conflate the night of the eighth with another time he'd been at your place."

The bartender returned, set down Meacham's glass of seltzer and a flimsy pour of whiskey for me. I took a greedy gulp to give myself something to do with my hands. I was embarrassed at how the visit with Boggs had shattered my nerves.

"Boggs said he heard the gunshots and saw the man leave the house between eight and nine," I said.

The grandfather clock in our hallway had given the strongest clue to my parents' time of death: the metal hands, sticking out of the ashes. The arson investigator used their position to determine that the fire had likely destroyed the clock's inner workings around one thirty in the morning.

I looked up at Meacham, the whiskey warming the inside of my chest. "That means Rhodes doesn't have an alibi for the time they were shot."

"He still couldn't have set the fire if he was in bed when his wife claims," Meacham said.

"Maybe he killed them around the time Boggs says he saw him and he had someone else go back to set the fire and get rid of the evidence."

"It's risky," Meacham said. "Involving someone else, returning to the scene. More likely we're dealing with one killer."

For years, that melted clock had kept any real heat off Stephen Rhodes. In a statement he voluntarily submitted to investigators, Rhodes said he had gotten knocked out of a poker game around 8:00 p.m., driven a colleague home, and retired to his own place approximately thirty minutes later. Rhodes's wife insisted he was in bed, asleep, when she got home from work shortly after 11:00 p.m. According to the arson investigator, Rhodes could not have been the person who set the fire sometime after midnight.

"What if they were wrong, about the clock?" I asked, feeling increasingly pathetic.

"The clock was close by the fire's point of origin. I had an expert in a lab out of state perform a test with a similar model clock—their theory that the fire started shortly before the clock stopped working is sound."

I picked up my drink, sucked at my teeth petulantly.

"Sam, science doesn't lie," Meacham said. "Only people."

I set down my glass. "You think Boggs is lying? Or Rhodes's wife is?"

"Ex-wife," Meacham said. "And I think all that matters right now is getting a description of the vehicle Boggs saw."

"And what are the chances of that?" I thought of the phone call Meacham had made outside the jail. "Is the DA or whoever going to consider pleading him down?"

"I'll be real; she doesn't want to do this guy any favors. Boggs is a career criminal, and his assault victim was a seventy-eight-year-old widow. He knocked her down, caused a brain bleed. She's lucky she survived."

What about me? I thought sullenly. *Doesn't my tragedy matter too?*

Meacham said nothing as I knocked back the rest of my drink. The bartender returned, wordlessly depositing a bill in front of Meacham. He slipped a twenty inside the check holder before I could object.

We watched each other for a bit, neither of us speaking, as if we'd reached the end of a first date that had run its course. "Boggs isn't going to talk without a deal, is he?"

"There are other ways to apply pressure to him. Don't lose hope yet."

"Hope," I said. "That's what you think I feel?"

Meacham eyed me as I slid out of my chair.

"Thanks for the drink," I said.

"Safe drive home, Sam." He smiled, his face kind. He really had a lovely face. A shame, I thought, that I would likely never see him again.

❧

The sky was on fire by the time I reached the exit for Gil's house. Onto 42, single lane, and I was trapped behind a delivery truck moving approximately three miles an hour.

The driver eased around the bends in the road as if the truck were loaded with live grenades. I backed off the gas, exhaling annoyance. No way to pass him. I rolled my shoulder until it popped, eyes on the road beyond in time to see a doe springing from the wooded area. The deer hopped over the median, and the truck driver slammed to a halt.

"Fuck." I crushed my brake pedal. A screech of tires on the pavement, the gentle bump of my fender meeting the bumper of the truck.

"Son of a bitch." I banged a fist on the top of the steering wheel. "Son. Of. A. *Bitch*."

The man behind the wheel of the truck was already hopping down from the driver's side. Denim shirt, mesh trucker hat on backward, golden-brown hair peeking out the bottom. When his face angled toward me, I noticed the small scar over his cupid's bow, from a cleft lip surgery he'd had as a kid.

I cursed again, because I had rear-ended Taylor Edwards.

Taylor had been a year ahead of me in school. Nice kid, unlike his half brother, Bo, who had fingered me in the bed of his truck and never spoken to me again.

I unbuckled myself. Taylor was bent over, hands on his knees, inspecting the truck's bumper. Also muttering "Son of a bitch" under his breath.

"I'm so sorry," I said from behind my fingers.

"Yeah, well, why were you riding my ass?" Taylor straightened, eyes locking on me. "Sam, holy shit!"

"Yep. Me."

Taylor's face softened. Smooth, clear skin, a smattering of summer freckles. It appeared he hadn't aged himself with drugs or booze, which Facebook told me that many of our classmates had done.

I craned my neck to get away from his stare. "Is there any damage?"

"Just a little scratch." Taylor was still studying me, as if I were a ghost. I bent to examine my bumper. I licked the pad of my thumb and wiped away a white smudge where the Accord had met the back of Taylor's truck.

When I stood, preparing for an awkward parting handshake, Taylor had his cell phone out.

"Wait, who are you calling?" I asked.

"I'm supposed to call my boss if I get into an accident."

"Accident? There's no damage."

"I'm sorry. It's company policy."

"What company?" I said, immediately feeling stupid for asking. Taylor wore the telltale shade of hunter green. Ealy Farms.

I wasn't surprised he'd gone into the family's business. Taylor's mother had been an Ealy, although she was as much interested in farming as she was in parenting, to hear my parents speak of Wendy Ealy-Edwards.

"Sorry," Taylor said again, lifting his phone to his ear.

He looked like he really was sorry. I slapped a mosquito off my thigh, leaving a smear of blood and guts below the hem of my shorts. I walked to the side of my car slowly, ears trained to catch what Taylor was saying into his phone. It sounded like his boss was tearing him a new asshole.

"I *did* call you right away—literally just happened." Taylor caught my eye and mouthed *Sorry* around a grimace. I shrugged. Unsure of what to do with myself, and dreading the thought of small talk with a classmate I hadn't seen in fifteen years, I returned to my car and blasted the AC.

Taylor rapped on my window. "She says don't go anywhere until she gets here," he said, upon my lowering it. "You didn't tell her you're in town?"

"What are you talking about?"

"Rhiannon." Taylor frowned.

My stomach went wormy. I had barely spoken to my cousin since I graduated college and took a job in the city. I knew that she'd stayed in Carney, working for the Ealys, and that she'd had a daughter with Clinton Ealy Jr., heir to the farm.

As I was considering whether some light jail time for leaving the scene of an accident would really be that bad, a Tahoe peeled onto the shoulder. The driver's face was hidden behind a pair of aviators, despite the fact that the sun was buried below the horizon. I killed my engine and stepped out at the same time the Tahoe driver's door opened. A pair of long, tanned legs in denim cutoffs unfolded themselves.

Rhiannon Newsom stepped out. She said, simply, "Samantha."

"How are you?" I asked.

"Not happy to be dragged out here at bedtime because my bum-ass cousin can't drive." She lifted her sunglasses, the skin on her forehead shiny. Hair the color of cherry cola fell to the collar of her Rolling Stones T-shirt.

"It's really fine," Taylor was telling Rhi. "No damage."

"Be quiet, Tay."

Taylor clamped his mouth shut as Rhiannon inspected the bumper of the truck and snapped a photo with her phone. After considering the truck for a painfully long moment, she slipped her phone in her back pocket and told Taylor, "Go."

Taylor put his hat back on. "Maybe see you around, Sam?"

"Maybe," I said. "Sorry again."

When he was gone, leaving a dust cloud in his wake, Rhi turned to me. "How long've you been in town?"

"Since last night."

"You could've called us."

"It wasn't a planned trip. Gil died. Lung cancer."

Whatever was making her lip curl up at me would not be settled the way it used to be: me, pinned down on the living room floor, trying to sink my teeth into Rhi's wrist while she had a fistful of my hair. A fight born out of boredom, us growing sick of each other in those long summer days at the farmhouse.

"Are you gonna tell Mitch I'm here?" I asked.

Rhi shrugged. "You'd rather someone else tell her?"

With a nod goodbye, she retreated to her Tahoe. I watched her leave in a cloud of dust, my scalp throbbing with the memory of the tussle that had ended with my father separating us until my aunt Mitch came to pick up Rhiannon after work.

My father had shouted at me, and it had stung a thousand times worse than whatever slight from Rhi had prompted the argument to begin with. Dad rarely screamed, so I'd cried, and he'd folded me to his body and explained.

He wasn't that much older than I was when his mother left, when his father began to drink himself to death and he realized that he would have to look out for Mitch because no one else would. Michelle Newsom was neither a beauty nor a woman of natural charms; when she wound up pregnant by way of a married meat truck delivery driver, there was never a question about whether the man might be involved in Rhi's upbringing.

That day, after that awful fight with my cousin, my father needed me to know that in many ways, being a Newsom meant being alone in the world.

"I know Rhi can be difficult," he'd said. "But you're lucky to have each other."

I gripped my hair at the root, checked my urge to scream into the void. I wondered what my father would say if he could see us now. If, in his opinion, he would still consider us lucky.

Back at Gil's, my mood permanently dented by the visit to the jail and the clusterfuck with my cousin, I tried to recall the last time I had heard from Rhiannon, and if the transaction had been as unpleasant as the one this evening. There had been the perfunctory text about two years ago, informing me of Kaylee's birth, accompanied by a photo of a swaddled infant, pudgy face turned away from the camera. I had congratulated Rhi and the conversation had ended. It was not expected of me to visit the baby; in the years prior, our discomfort around children was one of the few things Rhiannon and I had been able to bond over.

A couple of months ago, a friend gave birth to twins who were staying in my hospital's NICU. I had stopped by when I knew she would be feeding in order to avoid the awkward excuses about why I should not hold the infants. *Nasty cold going around on my unit, better to be safe.* The last new baby I'd touched had been my sister. She'd been so small, fit in the crook of my arm so perfectly, that it seemed impossible I'd spent the previous few months terrified to hold her.

I thought, again, of Detective Karl Holcombe's insistence that Lyndsey's body had been incinerated. I needed to know where it came from, his confidence that my sister had died that night.

It took me approximately thirty seconds to track down Detective Karl Holcombe. He had an uncommon name, and according to the *Tri-County Independent*, he had opened a fishing supply shop in Lake Ariel, Pennsylvania, after retiring in 2011.

I scrolled through the article on my phone, a fluff piece about last summer's barbecue bash at the lake. In one of the photos, a man stood under a red tent, posing next to a steel pot. His face was obscured by polarized sunglasses and a wide-brimmed fishing hat. He brandished a soup ladle, displaying a white scar on his forearm that had probably housed a cancerous mole, judging from the sun-worn quality of his skin.

> Karl Holcombe, owner of KJ's Bait & Tackle, doles out his famous chili con carne.

KJ's Bait & Tackle closed at 6:00 p.m. If I left now, I could make it there by a quarter to.

Clouds hung low and gray over the Pocono Mountains. A fine mist sprayed my windshield. I stopped at the nearest Turkey Hill and filled my car. I bought a stale croissant from the convenience store and fed myself rabbit-size bites the entire drive to Lake Ariel, my fingers stinking of gasoline.

This part of Pennsylvania and upstate New York were a near genetic match. Raised A-frame houses, a few displaying oversized Trump 2024 flags. Family-owned burger and shake joints, the facades peppered with Help Wanted signs.

KJ's Bait & Tackle had a similar sign in the window. I parked; inside, I waited over a sweating cooler of ice creams for six minutes before a woman wandered out. Her wiry gray ponytail was held back in a scrunchie.

"Hi," I said.

The woman eyed me. "Hello. Help you?"

"Is Karl here?" I asked.

"No."

"Do you know when he'll be back?"

"He's out through the month. Had a knee replacement few weeks ago."

"Is there a number I can reach him at?"

"Can I ask why you need to speak with my husband so urgently?"

"My name is Samantha Newsom."

Holcombe's wife stared at me without a trace of recognition. "And how do you know Karl?"

"He was the lead detective on my family's murder case."

This little tidbit about my family usually prompted a reaction from people, but the woman remained unmoved. "Karl's retired, and he doesn't like to talk about any of that."

"I drove all the way from Carney. All I want is fifteen minutes with him."

"All right." The woman seemed exhausted by me. "Hold on. Wait right there."

She shuffled into the back room. I eyed the television visible through the doorway, tuned to a news segment.

She poked her head through the doorframe, phone pressed to her chest. "What did you say your name was again?"

"Samantha Newsom."

The woman muttered into the phone. A long pause before she held the phone to her chest and found my gaze. "He says go on up to the house."

"The house" was on Lakeview Road, a short drive from the tackle shop. Holcombe's wife declined to provide a house number—only an assurance I would not be able to miss it due to the flag at the end of their driveway.

I followed my GPS to Lakeview Road, continued straight for a mile as Holcombe's wife had instructed me, until a Thin Blue Line flag the size of a barn door came into view.

I ate my discomfort as I pulled into the driveway. My line of work meant I'd had to deal with a fair number of cops over the years. Very rarely did I encounter ones on a power trip who fit my image of cops like Stephen Rhodes. Most were like Karl Holcombe, resolute in their belief that policing made the world a safer and better place. Try to suggest to them that maybe, sometimes, law enforcement makes people's lives much worse and you'll be met with an impassioned speech about duty, and sacrifice, and a few bad apples.

It's cops like these who worried me more than the Stephen Rhodeses of the world.

After several hundred feet, a log cabin, impressively built, came into view. I parked alongside an aging Suburban, a sticker in the shape of a lure on the back window accompanied by the words Bite Me.

I passed a wheelbarrow filled with rusted rainwater, mosquito larvae dappling the surface, and a stack of firewood covered by a tarp. The snap of twigs beneath my feet startled a doe that had been munching on the leaves of a tomato plant poking through the deer netting arranged around the planter. The doe bolted, disappearing behind the log cabin and the woods beyond.

On the porch, Karl Holcombe was wedged in an Adirondack chair. A salmon-colored Life is Good shirt stretched across his chest, his candy-floss white-blonde hair tucked behind his ears. On my approach, he wordlessly reached for the two cans of Coors Light at his feet.

He cracked one open. Took me in, said, "I always wondered if someday you'd track me down to shout at me."

"Do you think you deserve to be shouted at?" I asked.

Karl Holcombe smiled and offered the other Coors to me. When I declined, he shrugged. After a long swig, he looked at me and said, "You don't remember, do you? That morning?"

I reached back, to the morning of September 9, eating bacon and eggs at Caroline's kitchen table. Mrs. Mason's face when she'd answered the phone, the way her eyes widened with horror before locking onto me at the table, as if I'd been dropped there from the sky. *No, no, she's here.*

No one could tell Mrs. Mason with any confidence what to do with me, so she'd driven me up to Sunflower Hill Road. Mitch was waiting for us at the bottom of our driveway, which was blocked off with police cruisers. I'd screamed, made a break for it when my aunt said the house was burned, there was nothing left. It took two grown men to wrestle me into the back of a police car.

I sat there alone, in my piss-soaked pajama pants, for what felt like an absurdly long time before the back door opened. I recalled the pity on Karl Holcombe's face as he held up a finger, ducked back out of the car. The pop of the trunk, and then he returned holding a Capri Sun, beefy fingers struggling to pierce the pouch with a straw.

"I keep these on hand for my little guy," he'd said.

This gesture, the familiar taste of the juice on my tongue, had calmed me down for long enough to answer Holcombe's questions. It was the last time I ever saw him. When the police determined my family had been murdered, they sent the department's sole female employee, some newly christened detective, to speak with me at Michelle's house. The only detail I could recall from the interview was that I had been so distraught that the detective could barely look me in the eye.

For whatever reason, Karl Holcombe's expression suggested that it was important that I remembered that moment in his car.

"It was you," I said. "You brought me the juice."

Holcombe smiled, and I wondered if the memory was meant to disarm me. A reminder that he was on my side, despite the rumors he'd seeded about my family and why they were killed.

"How old is your son now?" I asked him, settling into the Adirondack chair adjacent to his.

"Would have been twenty-six last week."

"I'm so sorry."

"He overdosed seven years ago." Holcombe sipped his Coors. "Not all people are born strong."

I said nothing. It was not my place to challenge how Holcombe qualified his grief, how he explained the loss of his son.

"I remember like it's yesterday." Holcombe shifted in his seat, drawing my attention to the scabbed-over incision on his knee. "I remember you sitting there, answering my questions. I could tell you were different from most. That you would be okay."

Well, here I am, I thought. *Am I okay?*

"I suppose there's a lot you'd like to ask me," Holcombe said.

"I really don't know where to begin," I said. "I guess I want to know if you ever really considered Stephen Rhodes a suspect."

Holcombe shifted in his chair at Rhodes's name. "Officer Rhodes was a terrible cop and a son of a bitch. There was no shortage of bad blood between him and your family, but he did not kill them."

"Because he was home in bed around the time the fire started, I know." I thought of Meacham's parting words after he stopped by Gil's yesterday; he'd asked me not to tell anyone about Leonard Boggs. News traveled fast in Carney, and Meacham was afraid of tipping the killer off to a potential new witness.

"But there was no way to determine exactly what time my parents were killed, right?" I leaned in my chair, elbow on the armrest. "Which means it's possible they were killed earlier and someone else went back and set the place on fire."

"Anything is possible when you don't know anything." Holcombe perched his beer can on his good knee. "But the state of the bodies in the house—there were clues to tell us how it went down. Obviously, details that wouldn't have been shared with a surviving family member your age."

I was suddenly too aware of the gnats droning by my ear. "I'm a big girl now. I can handle it."

"Your father's hand was shattered, as if he'd tried to grab the barrel of the gun. Your mother had been shot from behind. The chaos of it all—the killer was unsophisticated. He probably hadn't planned to go to that house and kill everyone inside. I think he wanted something, and when he didn't get it, things went south very quickly."

"You sound convinced it was only one killer," I said.

Holcombe shrugged. "The shells we found suggested they'd all been shot with the same gun. The system never turned up a ballistics match, which you'd expect of an unlicensed firearm that belonged to someone in the drug trade."

"Why are you so convinced they were killed over drugs?" I asked. "They left Scott's plants."

Holcombe said nothing for a long beat. "I don't know if anyone has ever told you this, but on the morning of the murders, your mother took out a large sum of money. Eighteen hundred dollars, spread across different ATMs throughout the day."

I had never heard this before. Who even would have told me? Meacham should have told me. My hands started to sweat.

"I don't understand," I said. "If she got the money for Scott, why would the dealer kill them anyway?"

"Maybe it wasn't enough. Maybe it was to make a point. There's no way to say with these people. They're not like you and me. It's not about the money but the message it sends if you let someone get away with ripping you off."

Holcombe fiddled with the can of Coors on his knee. "That fire—I always thought it wasn't just a way to destroy evidence. It was overkill. Whoever set it wanted to send a message: this is what happens if you screw with us."

"So, who was the 'us'? You must have had an idea."

"There were names thrown around, sure, and I had a few people in particular I thought warranted a closer look."

"You're retired," I said. "You can't give me one name?"

"Personally, I always thought it was Ed Robinette."

"Who is Ed Robinette?"

"A degenerate and a dope dealer, among other things."

"Heroin," I said. I felt as if Karl Holcombe's porch had bottomed out, the wreckage swallowing me whole.

In the fifth grade, we'd had a sheriff's deputy visit our class to give a D.A.R.E. presentation. At the end, a boy's hand shot up and he asked, "What's heroin?" The officer mumbled something about it being a narcotic and asked if there were any other questions.

When I got home from school, I knocked on Scott's trailer door and asked him if he knew anyone that did heroin. He grabbed me by the shoulder, gave me a shake that rattled my brains, his face inches from mine. "What the *hell*, Samantha? Why would you ask me that?"

I'd sputtered something about a kid at school mentioning heroin, and Scott went red in the face. "I don't do any of that shit. And you better never do it either."

It was the first time in my life that my uncle had spoken to me like I was a child. Scott was only twenty-five when he was killed, practically a kid himself.

"My uncle didn't do heroin," I said.

"I thought the same of Andrew. He was a good kid, had good friends growing up, even if I did catch them doing some things they shouldn't've. Then he started college up in Albany." Holcombe's voice went tense. He took a long sip of Coors. "My ex-wife saw it, but I didn't want to believe it. Not until I got a call in the middle of the night that he'd been arrested trying to break into a pharmacy. We sent him to rehab. He got out, enrolled in community college, found a job.

Two days later, my wife came home and found him in his bed, needle in his arm."

Holcombe cleared his throat. I felt sorry for him. Truly, I did. "My uncle didn't do hard drugs."

"We had a number of people telling us that Scott started hanging around Crazy Ed after his arrest."

"You mean after his assault."

My uncle had to sleep sitting up for a month after Stephen Rhodes beat the shit out of him. I'd seen people develop a $1,000-a-week pill habit over less.

"Ed swore Scott was just a smoking buddy, that he never sold him pills." Holcombe sipped his beer, his eyes never leaving mine. "But Ed Robinette is the type of man that couldn't tell the truth if his life depended on it."

"There was nothing else to link Ed to the murders?"

"He had an alibi for the night of the eighth, albeit a flimsy one. He had no vehicle, no means of getting to the house." Holcombe shrugged.

"Then why do you still think it was him?"

"Because when I think of the type of individual who would let a baby girl burn to death in her crib, I think of Ed Robinette."

"Unless Lyndsey wasn't in the house."

At this, Karl Holcombe shifted in his seat, as if I'd finally said something to surprise him. "Someone telling you otherwise?"

"I mean, you never found her."

"There was nothing to find."

"An investigator with the state has been looking at the case," I said. "He talked to an expert who said it's unlikely there would have been nothing left of her."

"And I can get you someone on the phone that'll say the opposite." Holcombe set his beer can on the deck, by his feet. "I was there. All that was left of your sister's crib was the little metal wheels. One of my men broke down sobbing when he saw it."

Holcombe cleared his throat. "I'm sure your statie friend means well, but there's not a shred of evidence to suggest the child left the house that night."

Except an eyewitness, I thought. *One you might have found yourself, if you'd looked a little harder.*

"All I want to know is if you ever considered the possibility she was taken," I asked.

"Taken by who?"

"She couldn't identify them. Maybe at the last minute, the killer heard a baby crying. He couldn't bring himself to leave her, so he brought her somewhere safe."

"Safe," Holcombe said. "Why on earth would he do that and risk being seen?"

Because she was a child. Because for every creep who would take a child from her bed and cut her into pieces, for every fucked-up person who would walk into a school and shoot a bunch of first-graders, there are millions of people who do not hurt children.

Motion, off to the side of the deck. The deer had returned, taking slow, cautious steps toward that tomato plant again. Karl Holcombe was the one to break the silence finally, scaring the creature back into the woods.

"If someone took that baby, you'd better pray it wasn't Ed Robinette."

Chapter Four

Back at Gil's, I plugged my phone in and googled *Ed Robinette*. There was no mention of him in any of the threads dissecting my family's case. But there was a registered sex offender named Edward Paul Robinette living in Spring Meadow, a mere twenty minutes from Carney.

> DATE OF OFFENSE: 7/30/1998
>
> OFFENSE DESCRIPTION: Bribery to commit a sexual act
>
> AGE OF VICTIM: 5 Y/O F

Five-year-old female. A slick of sweat came to my hands as I scrolled to Robinette's photo.

My first thought was that Edward Robinette looked like a pedophile. His eyes bulged, bearing the look some of my patients got right before they started ranting about the 5G-emitting device I had implanted in their brains.

There was no other information about Robinette's crime, but I had already seen enough. I thought of my sister, rolled up in her blanket, screaming for my parents, too dead to save her.

I closed my eyes, and I tried to summon a memory, any memory. A creepy man at the grocery store whose gaze lingered on Lyndsey too long. Scott, expression hazy from what I thought were prescription painkillers for his broken collarbone.

Heroin dealers, pedophiles, men who attacked little old ladies alone in their bedrooms. These were the types of people my uncle had invited into our lives.

At some point, my body gave in to the pull of exhaustion. Light filtered through the bay window as I disentangled my legs from the afghan, caught the time on the cable box. A little after eight in the morning; I'd netted enough sleep to get me through the day. Already the shimmering heat outside battled with the rheumatic AC unit in the window.

I was afraid to move, to open my eyes and accidentally begin to exist. I was fifteen again, waking in my bed in my aunt's house, the prospect of a whole summer day to fill feeling like staring down the barrel of a gun. I thought of the *before*, helping my mother in the garden, green beans pouched in the hem of my shirt. In the evenings, Grandma Lynn teaching me to sew, before she became too sick to thread a needle. Gil chasing the dog and me through the spray of the sprinkler out back, Scott watching from his lounge chair, smiling but too stoned to partake.

My aunt's house, I learned very quickly, was a place without any joy. On the days she was at work, Rhi and I divvied up our chores before rotting in front of MTV together, provided we woke up in the morning able to stand the sight of each other. When my aunt was home, we retreated to our respective friends' houses, afraid an errant remark or shoes left in the hall might provoke Mitch into war.

You're at Gil's, I reminded myself. *You're safe.* Surrounded by mess, perhaps, but in no shortage of ways to fill my time.

The humidity was oppressive, despite the early hour. One of those summer mornings where I couldn't fully remove the damp from my body before getting dressed, and the resulting effect made my Gap jeans feel like a prison. I'd packed thoughtlessly, in a rush; if I wanted to avoid heatstroke, I would need to hit up a Walmart and adopt the local uniform of terry shorts and a spaghetti-strap tank with a built-in bra.

There was a Walmart Supercenter outside Carney. Tourists clogged 42, desperate to fit in another getaway before the Labor Day crowds hit. I filled my cart with trash bags, industrial-strength cleaners, a sleeve of Diet Coke, and a five-dollar pair of shorts.

After a stop for a decent face wash, I made a detour to the children's aisle for a stuffed Fisher-Price puppy.

At the register in front of me, a woman loaded her items onto the belt while her preteen daughter lingered by the cart, body bobbing to a silent tune. When the cashier spoke, the girl turned to answer her question with a polite yes, her smile placid.

I was startled to see that she was not a preteen at all. The girl was at least twenty, and in the seat of the cart was a naked baby doll.

The girl's mother stuffed her wallet back in her purse, one hand on her daughter's back, guiding her to the exit. The cashier waved goodbye to the girl, who returned the gesture shyly.

My heart tugged as I set the Fisher-Price puppy on the belt. I could not shake the image, that woman, the protectiveness on her mother's face when she had caught me staring at her adult daughter with the mind of a child. It couldn't be easy, but at least the two of them would never outgrow each other.

What the hell is wrong with you, Samantha?

My mother and I hadn't always lived at each other's throats. Before Grandma Lynn died, before the surprise pregnancy with my sister, I remember having all my mom's attention. Curled into her body while I was home sick, her fingers in my hair, watching daytime soaps together on my parents' bed.

I got off at the exit for South Carney instead of the exit for Gil's. There was no formal distinction between the parts of town, but everyone called the houses tucked in the mountains North Carney. South

Carney was composed of Main Street and the row houses surrounding it. The types of homes where wire fences corralled various pieces of furniture, stained from the tannins of leaves of winters past. Dogs with drooping bellies.

As I turned onto my aunt's street, I thought of Penny, the black Lab puppy my father had brought home after finding her abandoned on the farm. The dog was skittish, prone to running away for a day or two after a bad thunderstorm. We always found her somewhere on the property, cowering under a bush.

After the fire, I waited for her to find her way to me, filthy and trembling. I cried myself to sleep every night for weeks until my aunt entered my room, wordlessly and like a specter. She yanked me from my bed and split my lip open with the back of her hand.

Enough about the goddamn dog.

I had not seen my aunt in over a decade. In that period, I'd spoken to her fewer times than I had fingers on my hand.

I killed my engine at the curb. Eyes closed, skull tilted back against the headrest, the sun warming my face. The past twenty-four hours weighed on me. That girl in the Walmart, the baby doll, the protective look in her mother's eyes. For the first time in a very long time, I felt really, really bad.

My aunt's house needed a good power washing. Her trusted station wagon had been replaced with a Camry the color of oatmeal. Gone was the spider-infested plastic playhouse in the backyard where I'd lost my virginity. The gallant gentleman who performed the honor lived two houses down. He was a year older than me and had two kids of his own by the time I left for college.

Before I could raise my fist to rap on the frame of the door, a gravelly voice called, "Who's there?"

"Samantha," I said, peering through the screen.

Despite the heat, Mitch was wearing a flannel shirt. Her thinning black hair was streaked with gray, her part wide and exposing a scaly scalp. Fingers, knobby and gnarled from a rheumatoid arthritis diagnosis in her late twenties, gripped the remote and muted the TV. She rose, slowly. Mitch had always been lumpy, completely sexless. If it weren't for a photo I'd seen in a shoebox in our house when I was younger—Mitch helping my mother prepare Thanksgiving dinner, her belly swollen with Rhi as she bent before the oven to check on the turkey—I'd refuse to believe a man had ever been inside her.

About a thousand years later, Mitch reached the door and held it open for me. "Did you call?"

"Yeah. You must not have heard it over the TV."

She didn't push back, but I knew she would check the log on the home phone later. She released the door, and I caught it before it could swing back and smack the frame. Muscle memory.

"Rhi fixed that hinge years ago." Mitch deposited herself back on the recliner. I set the Fisher-Price puppy on the coffee table and sank into the couch, the cushion sagging so much I felt its ribs.

Mitch reached for a mug of tea on the table adjacent to her recliner. Her fingers were curled into claws. When they grasped the mug handle, she winced.

"How have you been?" I asked.

"How's it look?"

I bit the inside of my cheek. "I'm sorry you're not well."

"It's just pain," Mitch said. As if it were that simple—as if people didn't destroy their lives trying to escape pain.

Every morning for fifteen years, Mitch had hauled herself out of bed before the sun was up to cook egg sandwiches and slice deli meat. I heard her engine below my bedroom window even if she'd been up the whole night before, soaking her joints in the tub across the hall. The deli was open from six to three, which meant Mitch was home to haunt me before school even let out for the day.

My mother used to say Mitch was unhappy because of her illness. I had no doubt my aunt was in pain, but I also suspected it had been so long that she had no identity outside of it.

"When was the last time you saw a doctor?" I asked.

"Couple months ago. Wants me on some experimental drug that's like chemo."

"Are you gonna do it?"

"Medicaid won't pay. And who would watch Kaylee?"

"Maybe when she's old enough for preschool," I conceded.

"I'll be dead by then," Mitch said.

I watched my aunt remove her tea bag from her mug and set it on the napkin on the end table. It was already stiff and stained brown in spots, because Mitch was not the type of woman to throw out a perfectly good used napkin.

"How long are you staying?" she asked.

"Until I can list the house, I guess." As I said it, I realized she had probably meant how long I planned on staying in her house, not in town. "Aunt Michelle."

She looked up sharply. For a moment we were both struck dumb, probably from the shock that I had acknowledged it. *Go ahead and treat me like a stranger. We still share DNA.*

"Does the name Ed Robinette mean anything to you?" I asked.

Mitch seemed to be thinking, for a long beat, as she reached for the remote beside her mug of tea and aimed it at the AC. The air gave a final rattle in the vents before the unit went quiet. "Who?"

"He's a sex offender." A chill cropped up on my arms, despite the heat. "Karl Holcombe thinks Scott owed him money for drugs, and when he couldn't get it to him, Ed killed them all."

"Karl Holcombe knew it was Rhodes, and he knew Rhodes had help. Why else would he refuse to turn the case over to the state?"

I'd heard this theory ad nauseum as a kid. That Holcombe stubbornly clung to the murder case because of what a statie investigation would uncover about the police department. But he'd retired more than ten years ago; the state had been sitting on the case ever since, and in all that time, they hadn't managed to produce anything to prove the murders were an inside job by the Carney Police.

The doubt made me feel queasy. Maybe I'd been too swayed by Karl Holcombe's pitch for Ed Robinette being the killer. Maybe, on some level, I wanted him to be right, because a pedophile would not murder an entire family and steal a twenty-month-old only to let her live a long and happy life.

My lack of a response seemed to agitate Mitch. Her voice was practically a growl as she said, "Is that why you came here? To grill me about a kiddie diddler?"

I eyed the toy on the table for Kaylee, which Mitch had not acknowledged, my chest tightening. "I shouldn't be finding out, all these years later, there were other suspects."

Mitch shook her head at me.

"What?" I asked petulantly. "Say it."

I shut my eyes, inhaled through my nose. I would not get anywhere with Mitch by being hateful, but the problem was, tenderness had never worked either. The one time I had ever tried to hug my aunt, she had physically recoiled, a startled look in her eyes as if I had attacked her. I was four.

I stood now, so swiftly the blood drained from my head. "I need to use the bathroom."

My aunt's gaze trailed me as I made my way down the hall leading to the only bathroom in the house, as well as the rooms that had been mine and Rhi's. My father's and Mitch's as kids, respectively.

Mounted to the wall outside the bathroom was Rhi's kindergarten photo, next to the only photo of my father I had for reference in the years after the fire. He was in his early twenties, I guessed, standing next to my aunt, her bangs teased like Stevie Nicks's.

My fingers ached to reach for his face. My father, not handsome in a typical sense, but the type of man you noticed, if not for his height, then his nose. The bridge was flat and crooked. On his cheek, below his right eye, was a white scar in the shape of a crescent, obtained during the locker room fight that had gotten him thrown off the middle school baseball team. My father would not talk about the incident, but my mother had let it slip that he had attacked a group of boys who called his mother a dyke.

The grandmother I'd never met was absent from the hallway photos. She had left when my father was thirteen, had packed up and moved to Alaska with another woman.

The only change to the bathroom was the addition of a nautical striped shower curtain. I lowered the toilet seat and sat on the shag cover, my legs weakening under me.

I shot a glance at the bathroom door before I stood and opened the medicine chest, my own reflection in the mirror reproachful of my behavior.

I popped open the bottle of aspirin. Aspirin pills inside only. There were no prescription bottles in someone else's name, nothing stronger than naproxen. I felt a small seed of disappointment root in my belly.

This was, perhaps, the ugliest thing about me. People like my aunt, who were so convinced of who they were, made me deeply uncomfortable. They activated my impulse to study their exterior for cracks, to expose their fraud.

As I shut the medicine cabinet, a noise in the hall. The small cry of a child. Alone and scared.

Panic, low in my belly. I bolted into the hall in time to see my aunt emerging from the bedroom that had once been mine, a child in her arms. The girl rubbed her eyes and took me in, this stranger. Blonde curls clung to her forehead.

Mitch made no motion to introduce the child to me. Kaylee squirmed against my aunt before her eyes settled on me, disinterested. Long, dark lashes. Irises the color of milk chocolate.

Mitch deposited the child in a playpen tucked behind the couch, concealed from view upon entering the house. She then lowered herself into her armchair, wordlessly, and I thought of how foolish I must have looked, bounding into the hall when I'd heard Kaylee's cries.

A heaviness mounted in my chest, at the memories so faded I wasn't sure they even belonged to me.

In the playpen, Kaylee pulled herself to standing, began to fuss. Mitch turned on an episode of *Peppa Pig*, and the two of them stared ahead at the TV, as if I were not there at all.

As a child, I sensed that my aunt simply did not like me. I must have seemed spoiled compared with her own daughter. I noticed it on her face when I was very small, how she watched with disgust while Scott and Gil chased me around the wooden playhouse my father had lovingly crafted for me.

Most of my cousin's toys came from Happy Meals. While I took ballet classes with girls like Caroline Mason, Rhiannon withered in after-school programs, already too tall for the hand-me-down clothes Grandma Lynn had sewn for me.

After the murders, I moved in with my aunt, another child to care for in between her ten-hour shifts slicing meat at the deli. A child who, at eighteen, was set to inherit more money than Michelle Newsom had ever seen in her life. The insurance payout from the farmhouse and the property sale was placed in a trust, Mitch given a meager stipend to feed and clothe me. Late bill payments, talk of Mitch going on Medicaid, Rhi picking up a second job after graduation, all while I put my college tuition on my credit card.

My junior year of college, when I phoned to inform her that I had found housing near campus for the summer, Mitch had seemed relieved. When I texted Rhiannon to let her know that I was getting married and would love for her and Mitch to come to the city and attend the city hall ceremony and dinner, it took her three days to respond and say that Mitch wasn't well enough to make the trip.

We had no expectations for each other, my surviving family and me. Any pretense of that had been gone for years. And still, Mitch's dismissal of me this morning stung, gnawed at me while I tackled Gil's kitchen.

A little after 10:00 a.m., every window in Gil's house flung open. I stunk of kitchen grease and industrial-strength cleaner. With gloved hands, I ferried a fossilized bag of sugar, taken over by a colony of ants, straight to the outside trash can.

The driveway was rapidly filling up. Black trash bags filled with detritus, and white ones of kitchen junk, passable enough for Goodwill. Sweat adhered my T-shirt to my back, and my nose ached from the amount of bleach I'd inhaled.

Back inside. I steeled myself for entry into Gil's shower, which I wagered had not been cleaned since a Bush was president. I left my flip-flops on. The water stalled out at tepid; I couldn't pry away the cracked bar of Irish Spring soap adhered to the ledge of the tub, so I rinsed and got out, feeling dirtier than I had when I'd stepped in.

As I dressed, my phone lit up on Gil's coffee table. I had not saved his number, but I recognized it as Travis Meacham's.

"Hi," I said.

"Morning. Are you free for coffee and a chat?" Meacham's voice was aggressively chipper. I imagined him as one of those people who naturally awoke before the sun, ready to hit the treadmill and cook an egg white.

I bent and tied my sneakers, cell wedged between my ear and shoulder. "That depends on the topic of the chat, I guess."

Meacham chuckled. "I'm headed to the office in Port Jervis. That's about twenty minutes from you, right?"

We ended the call. There was no way he'd cracked Leonard Boggs already, and his phone call had felt engineered not to give me enough time to ask.

I set my navigation for the state police building in Port Jervis. Followed the desk jockey's instructions to Meacham's office.

He looked up from his computer and smiled. Two paper cups rested on the desk before him, as well as an assortment of pastries as big as the plates they occupied.

"Someone joining us?" I sat in the chair opposite Meacham and considered the spread before selecting a muffin.

"Nah, I just didn't know what you liked."

Sweet of him, I thought. An attentive boyfriend, probably. Meacham's desk was barren of any personal effects. No photos of children, or a lover. It did not mean there weren't any; he had said this office was temporary, a place for him to decamp while he worked on my family's case.

I watched him watching me, my tentative bite of muffin, his fingers kneading the joints of his opposite hand.

"So when did you get divorced?" I asked.

"Excuse me?"

"You're always touching your ring finger. Like you expect it to still be there."

"We've been separated since last fall," Meacham said. "I assume she'll send me the papers one year to the day."

"Ah, yes. My ex had a similar issue with New York State's divorce law."

"You were married?"

"Don't look so surprised," I said.

He'd been a college friend. We lived on the same floor freshman year, and although I suspected he always had a thing for me, we lost touch when he followed his high school sweetheart to Richmond after graduation.

When he returned a few years later, alone, we met up with some friends who were in town for the marathon. We got nearly blackout drunk at Texas Barbecue, and when we woke up mashed against each other in my bed the next morning, I was surprised that I didn't want him to leave, like every man who had come before him.

So he didn't leave, not for another two years, eight months after we got married. The last I saw him was in the lobby of the attorney's office. I hear from him maybe every eight months or so. I kept all our mutual friends, not because they chose me but because he moved to Seattle shortly after our divorce was finalized.

I knew it puzzled them all, how I continued to behave as if nothing had happened. How I accepted their half-hearted invitations to couples' game nights, how I perennially showed up dateless to their weddings, their children's birthday parties. I told myself it was because the thought of negotiating casual dating around my nurse's schedule was simply too exhausting.

"But we're not here to chitchat about happier times," I said.

"No. We are not." Meacham knotted his hands together and rested his chin on his knuckles. "I got a phone call from Karl Holcombe this morning."

"Karl Holcombe?" I broke off the outer rim of the muffin, eyes on my fingers.

"He was the lead detective on your family's case."

I sucked in a breath, trapped it in my puffed-out cheeks, before exhaling loudly. Stalling. "And what did he have to say?"

"He hadn't realized the state had boarded the Newsom investigation. He told me I could call him anytime with questions. I was obviously curious how he'd gotten wind of this, since our involvement hasn't been made public." Meacham's eyes were no longer friendly.

I set down the piece of muffin. "Can you get the wrist slap over so we can move on?"

"Sam. Everything I've shared with you has been at my discretion. Going forward, I could as easily choose not to share information with you."

"Okay," I said.

"Okay. Now that we're simpatico." Meacham reached for a chocolate croissant. "What did you think of Holcombe?"

"What do you mean, what did I think of him?"

"Just your general impressions. He seemed pretty taken with you."

I rolled my eyes, popped a piece of muffin into my mouth. "I had no idea my mom took out almost two thousand dollars the morning of the murders."

Meacham chewed his croissant and chased it with a sip of coffee.

"That's why Holcombe thinks it was drug related," I said. "He thinks she took out the money because Scott was hooked on heroin."

"When I got hired as an ADA down in Pelham, the office was tracking a disappearance. A woman went missing the night before her husband's fortieth. Just got in her car, didn't tell anyone where she was going."

"I think I remember that." Pelham was just outside the city, and it seemed that everyone knew someone who knew *someone* who knew the Missing Mom, as the media had dubbed her.

"Right, it was all over the news for a while. Anyway, bank surveillance showed her taking three grand out of her checking account before she disappeared. Stuff starts coming out that she was overwhelmed, three kids and a demanding job in finance. Nancy Grace raises the possibility that maybe she took the money and skipped town to start a new life." Meacham took another bite of croissant, swallowed. "Meanwhile, over a year has gone by with no word from her, and her family starts pushing the DA to charge the husband. Then, five years later, volunteer divers found her car at the bottom of the Hudson."

I'd known how things ended for the Pelham woman, or at least I'd clocked it mentally at the time. But I'd still wound up hanging on to every word of Meacham's story, hoping for a better ending.

"Turned out she'd withdrawn the money and driven to a specialty shop upstate, to surprise her husband with a custom racing bike for his birthday," Meacham continued. "It was still mounted to the top of the car when they found it. She didn't know the area, was a nervous driver at night. *No one* thought that she'd simply gotten into an accident."

"So now you don't put stock in someone withdrawing a huge pile of cash the day they get their brains blown out," I said. "But my parents weren't the type to surprise each other with expensive gifts."

Every morning on his birthday, my father woke up to his favorite meal—Mom's homemade waffles with vanilla ice cream on the side. Dad planted roses in the decrepit greenhouse out back so he could surprise my mother with two dozen of them on Valentine's Day.

My parents were perfectly ordinary, and their brutal ends were not an accident. The only explanation was that Scott had been the one to bring evil to our doorstep that evening.

"What about Ed Robinette?" I asked. "You said to me, after we saw Boggs, that whoever took my sister from the house cared about her. Pedophiles, in their fucked-up way, think that they love children. His victim was five years old," I said.

"Again, a nonviolent offense. And Lyndsey was only twenty months old," he said.

"So she was too young to kidnap and rape and murder?"

In my few brief months in pediatric intensive care, I'd seen enough horrors to make me consider quitting. The youngest victim of sexual abuse I'd encountered had been only five months old.

When I requested a transfer to adult intensive care, my supervisor hadn't seemed surprised. *It takes a special type of person to work here.* I was okay with not being special as long as I never had to look an abused child in the eye again.

Meacham's voice was gentle when he spoke. "I didn't say that. But the facts of this crime don't support kidnapping as a motive."

Even I had to admit it sounded too depraved to feel possible. Murdering an entire family just to abduct a twenty-month-old. If some sick fuck had seen Lyndsey from afar, wanted her, they would have known that my mother and the baby were home alone most of the time.

Chaos, Holcombe had said of the crime scene. A killer who did not show up at that farmhouse on a Saturday night planning to execute everyone inside.

Meacham's voice, gentle, drew me back. "Have you ever done a DNA test?"

"Like 23andMe?"

"Yup."

"I'm a nurse. We don't trust that shit."

"Alive or dead, there's a small chance Lyndsey's DNA is in the system."

"How small?"

"If she's alive—if she's ever been arrested for something serious, or if she voluntarily submitted it for an ancestry test."

"And if she's dead?"

"DNA testing on unidentified remains has come a really long way."

"I don't know," I said.

"What do you have to lose?"

Twenty more years, I thought. I would hand over my DNA and then I would wait, while Travis Meacham moved on to the next murdered family or missing child.

"Nothing, I guess," I said.

Meacham offered a smile, set a plastic baggie on his desk. Inside, two vials, buccal swabs. He pushed it toward me. "I'm sure you do a hell of a swab."

I sat in my car, unable to leave the state police parking lot. My head was clogged with the idea of babies stolen from their cribs, snatched from shopping carts. The possibility Ed Robinette had abducted Lyndsey, chopped her into pieces, scattered her across the state. The thought of a tiny toddler foot, sitting in an evidence locker somewhere, tagged *unidentified remains*.

It could not be that easy. A quick DNA swab, some database magic, and an answer as to what had happened to my baby sister the evening of September 8.

I pulled up the most recent address for Ed Robinette on the sex offender registry, and I thought of my mother.

If my mother had been the one to escape the carnage in our house, she would not think twice about showing up at Edward Robinette's house and shaking him by the ankles for anything he knew about what had happened that night.

I shook my head, inhaling sharply. Ed Robinette lived in Spring Meadow, a town about fifteen minutes outside Carney.

I parked alongside a sun-charred strip of grass between the street and what appeared to be a subsidized housing complex, the apartment units sectioned off by wooden fencing, its brown paint weathered and flaking.

I hewed close to the far side of the sidewalk, away from a dog straining against the rope tethering him to a pole in the ground. Its fur was the color of butterscotch, one ear partially missing. A pit-Lab mix, maybe. When it could not reach the fence, it let out a snarl that devolved into a low-pitched whine.

A voice from beyond the fence opposite the house said, "He won't bite cha. Just annoying as fuck."

Outside unit 8A, a man was seated on the steps. On his lap, a gray cat was curled into a ball.

"Are you Edward Robinette?" I asked.

Next door, the dog's whining reached a crescendo. He pawed at the base of the fence.

"The lady in 7D sneaks him grapes," Robinette said. "Says it'll kill him eventually."

I swallowed. "You're Robinette, right?"

The man peeled the cat off his body and advanced toward the gate. His skin was the color of raw meat that had begun to turn. He leaned over, peered into my face in a way that made my heartbeat stop.

"Well, shit, you're a goddamn Ginns," he said.

The stench of him—cigarettes, something fishy—sent bile rising up in me. I breathed through my mouth as I spoke again. "Have we met?"

"I know a Ginns when I see one." Robinette's face clouded with suspicion. "You're Scotty's niece."

"Samantha," I said.

Robinette glanced over at the adjacent yard, empty except for the whining dog. In the unit beyond, a man was wedged in a lawn chair, a baseball cap low over his face. I couldn't tell if he was alive or not.

"Too hot to speak out here," Robinette said, pushing his gate open. I balked at the thought of entering his home until he stepped through, shutting it behind him. "I was about to go to lunch anyway."

Robinette moved purposely, briskly, as if he'd been grinding at a desk at J.P. Morgan and not lazing on a busted porch in Section 8 housing. I followed him to the corner, where we waited for the light to change. A woman in a motorized scooter rolled up next to us. Robinette tossed a "How you doing, Bernie" her way, to which she replied with a grunt.

Brooklyn Brothers Pizzeria was wedged between a dry cleaner and a vape shop. As soon as the bell tinkled over our heads, the man behind the counter was advancing on us. "Oh no you don't. The fuck out of here."

The man's accent suggested the Brooklyn Brothers moniker was accurate. His hands were the size of dinner plates, arms coated with wiry black hair. According to Gil, half the restaurants opened by Italian Staten Islanders were fronts for money-laundering operations. Minor racism aside, I was inclined to believe it, from the looks of this man.

Next to me, Robinette lifted both palms in surrender. "Not looking for trouble, Guy."

"I can vouch for him," I said.

The man—Guy, or maybe Robinette had simply meant *guy*—gave me a wary look before sticking a meaty finger in Robinette's face. "Remember, Ed. I know what you are."

Guy kept shaking his head as we retreated, muttered "Fuckin' pervert" under his breath. I was regretting just about every decision I'd made since waking up in the morning as I followed Robinette to a booth at the back of the pizzeria. He deposited himself in the side farthest from the bathroom, folding his hands together on the table in front of him.

The booth cushion still bore ass-shaped sweat marks of the last occupant. My thighs stuck to the plastic as I sat. Next to our booth, the bathroom door banged open, blasting me with the smell of ammonia as a woman exited, retying the apron around her ample waist.

Guy or *guy* appeared at the edge of our table. "What are you having, Ed? And mind you, I still got the last bill you skipped out on."

"I did?" Robinette squinted and leaned forward, as if searching for evidence of said bill.

Guy tapped the breast pocket of his polo. "I keep it right here, close to my heart."

"I've got it," I said. I nodded to Robinette. "Just order."

"A garden salad with only the lettuce, croutons and dressing on the side," Robinette said. "And a water, no ice."

Guy's gaze lingered on me. "Anything for you?"

"I'm good."

"Blink twice if you need help," he muttered before walking away.

I studied Robinette, the storm that seemed to be raging inside his whittled-down body, the frantic movement of his eyes around the pizzeria. A swell of defeat in my gut; this man looked as if he could not tell me the current president, let alone provide an accurate account of the events of twenty years ago.

Before I could speak, Robinette's eyes focused on me. "Smarty Sam."

"What did you just say?"

"That's what Scotty called you. He was quite the braggart. Said you got the best marks in your class, that you were going to be the first lady president."

I thought of my uncle, socked feet on our coffee table, watching *Wheel of Fortune* with me while Mom fixed dinner. Turning toward me with that goofy smile every time a phrase stumped the contestants. *Well, what is it, Smarty Sam?*

Guy returned with two waters and a Styrofoam bowl of iceberg lettuce. A separate bowl housed croutons and a pot of Italian dressing. I watched as Robinette removed the lemon wedge from the rim of his glass and squeezed it into his water, oblivious to the fruit fly on the rind.

I swallowed hard to clear my throat. "Did you sell my uncle heroin?"

Robinette's fingers, still working that lemon rind, went still. "No, ma'am, I did not."

"Then why did Detective Holcombe think he owed you money?"

"I've been out of the life a long time, but back then, I had enemies. People who would have loved to see me behind bars, just to thin the competition."

"So you never, ever sold Scott drugs?"

"No, ma'am. In fact, we had a business arrangement. We'd been friendly, back when we were schoolmates. When he was injured, summer of '01, I helped him move his product." Robinette made a noise with his lips, like air releasing from a valve. "Twenty years, I never found sativa as good as Scott Ginns's."

"Clearly the real tragedy here."

Robinette didn't seem to hear me. He dumped his bowl of croutons on the lettuce. "Smoke hadn't even cleared before Holcombe dragged me in, says he has a couple questions 'bout my arrangement with Scotty. Next thing I know, he's screaming in my face that I killed them all before raping that baby and setting her body on fire."

"Did you?"

A look passed over his face that made my stomach fold like an accordion. "I've done things I'm not proud of, but I've never once harmed a child."

"What about the five-year-old back in 1998?"

"I sold ice cream at the stand at the ballfield back then. You know the one, not far from the church. No one was around that morning, or so I believed. The little girl approached the stand, and not seeing me at the counter, she went around to the back door, where she witnessed a completely consensual encounter between me and myself."

"Then how did you get slapped with bribery to commit a sexual act?"

"I offered her a treat from my wares and asked her not to tell anyone what she'd seen. Course, the child ran off to her mother, gave her quite a wild rendition of what happened." Robinette's face darkened. "Never seen a man so gleeful as Stephen Rhodes was when he booked me. He did things to me made what he did to your uncle look like a Swedish massage."

"Rhodes was the one to arrest you?"

"Yes, ma'am. Had it out for me for years, that one. I first saw him beating a perp his first week on the job. I said, 'Sir, this is state-sanctioned violence.' He pulls his gun on me, says, 'Keep moving, cretin, or I'll blow your dick off.'"

"After they took your whole family out, I bolted. I knew it was only a matter of time before Rhodes planted something to finger me for the murders, or worse."

"You think he would have killed you," I said.

"I sure would have, if I was him," Robinette said. "I was the only one who knew the real reason he killed 'em all."

"The real reason." The words were flat as they left my mouth. I was unable to tear my eyes from Robinette's beard, which was now coated with Italian dressing. "Scott was going to sue the department. That was the reason."

Ed worked at his croutons with the teeth he had left as he spoke. "Yes, Scott was suing *the department*. That means if he won, *the department* would have had to pay up. If you're Officer Rhodes, the worst you're facing is a suspension, possible termination. Killing an entire family to stop a civil suit doesn't make sense—unless, of course, you're worried what will come out in the investigation."

"Like what?"

Robinette leaned forward so he was eye level with my chest. "I do want to tell you everything, dear, but keep in mind, I would be doing so at great personal risk."

I noticed, now, that Robinette was not eyeing my breasts but my wallet, resting on the table in front of me.

I unzipped my clutch and opened the billfold. I counted out forty-seven dollars onto the table. Robinette watched me thumb through the bills, his tongue poking out the corner of his mouth.

"This is all I have," I said.

Robinette rested a paw on the pile of cash and leaned forward to glance inside my wallet. "What's that there?"

"A Dunkin' Donuts gift card with three dollars left on it."

Robinette pulsed his outstretched hand. I placed the gift card in it. Satisfied with his haul, he stuffed it into his jeans pocket, oblivious to the glob of Italian dressing on his chin.

"When Scott got out of the hospital, I asked him why he ran. He only had a dime bag on him, a misdemeanor at best." Robinette dropped his voice. "Scott said he *didn't* run. Rhodes took the pot Scotty had in his glove box. He made Scott wait in his cruiser while he searched his car. Rhodes kept saying, 'I bet I'm gonna find something good in here, Ginns.'"

"Ten, fifteen minutes go by. Scott's locked in the car, and he's getting restless. And that's when he notices the duffel bag."

"Duffel bag?" I said.

"It was on the floor, in the back seat. Scott wasn't cuffed, so he opened it and took a look-see. Next thing he knows, Rhodes is yanking him out of the car, going ballistic, asking him what the fuck he thinks he's doing. Scott says Rhodes had a look in his eyes like he was going to kill him. Rhodes shoved him and Scott panicked, thinking he'd get collared for assaulting a cop if he fought back, so he tried to run."

"What was in the duffel bag?" I asked.

"Ladies' clothes. Lacey panties, makeup."

"Why would Rhodes flip out over that? Maybe it was his wife's stuff." Or his girlfriend's, or maybe Stephen Rhodes himself likes to put on silky undies and get spanked like a naughty little girl.

"*Listen*, dear, I'm getting there."

Robinette paused. Relishing his role in the sordid tale, no doubt. "There was a passport in there, so Scott opens it up. And it's that Polish girl, gone missing from the farm a couple weeks back."

I reached back to that summer, the rumors about the missing berry picker. An eighteen-year-old girl from Poland on a work visa. Some said she'd skipped town to avoid going back to Europe, that she talked of making her way to the city and meeting a man who promised to get her work as a model. The darker versions of what had befallen her included a gang rape, a pack of migrant workers from Mexico who had burned the girl's body before fleeing south. I could not remember her name.

"And Scott never told anyone about the passport, aside from you?" I asked.

"He never got the chance. But the last thing he said to me . . ." Robinette lowered his fork from his mouth, pointed it at me. "He said, 'I'm gonna bury that motherfucker.'"

Chapter Five

Back in the Accord, the blast of the air-conditioning aimed at my eyelids. A knot of worry had been forming in me ever since leaving Ed Robinette at the pizzeria table. Had he glimpsed the address on my driver's license when I opened my wallet?

Eyes still closed, a memory came into focus. I was ten, maybe younger, in Scott's trailer, snooping through his CD tower while he played *Duke Nukem*. One of the album covers stopped me cold.

I ran back to the house, shrieking to my mother that Scott had a picture of a little boy's penis. She ran over there, ready to end his life, only to find him laughing his ass off and blocking her punches with the cover of Nirvana's *Nevermind.*

Could Ed's story possibly be true—that my uncle had seen a missing girl's passport in Rhodes's cruiser the day he was beat senseless?

I needed a name. Back at Gil's, I did some browsing on the national database of missing and unidentified persons. Only one person had been reported missing in Carney in 2001, a twentysomething-year-old army veteran named Kyle Lawson. I widened my search, balked at an entry from 2011.

Luiza Witkowski. The name lit up my brain; I was sure it was her, the migrant girl who had gone missing that summer. Why had it taken ten years for the police to start looking for her?

There was nothing else on Luiza's case, only a number for the detective at the state police troop handling the investigation. I closed the database, frustrated, and tugged on a pair of kitchen gloves.

The quiet unsettled me; I turned up the volume on my phone. I removed the grates from Gil's stove and scrubbed, my phone shuffling between nineties grunge and the Top 40 earworms my coworkers had me hooked on.

And I kept going back to that day, how my mother had reacted when I told her about the photo of the naked baby in Scott's trailer.

The memory took on a darker hue now. Ed Robinette was the type of person my uncle associated with. He was a convicted sex offender, and he sold heroin.

I'd be foolish not to consider the possibility that Ed had entirely fabricated the story about Scott being able to implicate Rhodes in Luiza Witkowski's disappearance—that far more likely, on the evening of September 8, Edward Robinette had done several lines of blow, killed my entire family, and woken up the next morning not remembering a single thing.

The setting sun leaked through Gil's kitchen window, lighting the floor in amber. The tile sparkled now, thanks to two hours of obsessive scrubbing. I stood and washed my hands, my hunger threatening to level me.

I looked up the number for the Riverhead Inn, the only decent place to eat within five miles of Gil's. Their phone rang ten times before I gave up and headed straight to my car.

I'd worked at the RI as a waitress my senior year of high school and when I was home from college, until I stopped coming back to Carney for breaks at all. The restaurant occupied an old home at the corner of 42 and a residential street. The back lot was full, so I parked on the side street before retrieving a sweatshirt from the back seat of my car.

The door to the RI was propped open, tepid air circulating in the foyer. Nothing inside had changed, albeit the linoleum floor looked a little cleaner, the wood-paneled walls a bit cheerier with the addition of a string of colored triangle pennants. One television screen over the bar still broadcast horse racing, another, the Quick Pick numbers.

The man behind the counter, however, was not Ron, my old boss. He was about a thousand feet tall, linebacker shoulders straining against the sleeves of his Tommy Bahama shirt. I ordered a whiskey neat and a burger to go, trying to disappear into myself when Taylor Edwards dropped onto the barstool next to me.

He nodded to my empty glass and said with a sheepish smile, "Next one on me?"

"Thanks, but I'm good."

"Please—it's the least I can do." Taylor took off his hat and set it on the bar, the nerviness that had plagued him yesterday evening blunted by the beer in his hand. At least his third, I guessed, from the glassiness in his eyes.

"Nah, it was my fault," I said. "I'm the bum-ass who can't drive, according to Rhi."

Taylor laughed. "Rhi is . . . well . . ."

He sipped his beer, not wanting to say *a cunt.* A glance over his shoulder, drawing my attention to the man hovering by the pool table. I looked away before CJ Ealy could tear his eyes from the TV overhead and catch me staring.

"You know Rhi's always been jealous of you," Taylor said.

I could see why people might think that, looking at me and my cousin. I'd been lucky enough to dodge the flat nose and close-set eyes of the Newsom lineage. I was prettier than my cousin, smarter, and I'd left Carney—first for college, and then for a well-paying job.

I knew better, though. My cousin wasn't jealous of me, but threatened. The two of us, after the murders, competing for Mitch's attentions.

Rhi never wanted what I had—she was only scared of me taking what little she had of her own.

Taylor grinned. His face hadn't changed a bit in fifteen years, but there was something aggressively boyish about him. Or maybe I was still seeing the Taylor Edwards of middle school Spanish class, squirmy in his seat, face red when the teacher asked if he'd taken his ADHD medication.

Taylor sipped his beer, nodded to me. "What are you having?"

"Just a water," I said, aware of the Wild Turkey sitting in my empty stomach.

"Yo, Petey," Taylor called to a boy at the other end of the bar, who was mindlessly dragging a wet rag over the bar top. The boy shuffled over, a look on his face as if he'd been caught crop dusting.

While Petey filled a glass with water from a soda gun, Taylor lifted his hat, ruffled the flattened hair on his head. "How's it going with the house?"

"Slowly but surely, I guess."

"Well, if you need boxes, hit me up," Taylor said. "We've got more than we can use at the farm."

Warm breath by my ear, the smell of hops, made my blood go still. A voice, smoother than Taylor's, the upstate twang ironed out of it: "Samantha Newsom. Holy shit."

"Hey, CJ."

CJ Ealy leaned on the counter beside me, tanned forearms on the bar top. "Mind if I join?"

"Sorry," I said. "I stole your drinking buddy."

"It's cool. As long as you're not playing any more bumper cars with my company vehicles."

CJ smiled, lifted his Budweiser to his mouth, the top still smoking. I had a flash of myself, at my father's funeral, thirteen, in a velvet black dress borrowed from my best friend Caroline. I'd grown an inch over her that summer, and the dress barely covered my ass.

Clinton Ealy Jr., home from college for the funerals. He'd done a double take before dipping in for a hug. The look on his face woke something up inside me. I thought of CJ Ealy's face and gave myself my first orgasm that night, in bed, Rhiannon snoring softly across the hall.

CJ leaned forward on the bar again, his voice softening. "I'm sorry about Gil."

"Thanks. Knew it was coming."

"Doesn't make it any easier. I know how much he meant to you."

A tug in my chest. It was impossible to quantify what Gil had meant to me. I'd never known him as anything but my uncle, despite the lack of blood relation. He was always there—driving Grandma Lynn to her doctor's appointments, in the front row at all my dance recitals. Gil yelled at Scott and me for stealing from the bank during our Monopoly games and was always the first to come knocking on my door while I lay on my bed, tear-soaked and exhausted from a spat with my mother.

Then Grandma Lynn died, and Gil's visits to the farmhouse became less frequent. Lyndsey arrived, and before her second birthday, Gil left. Swiftly, and without goodbyes. Because his country needed him, my mother had explained, while I sobbed so hard I could not breathe.

I remembered CJ Ealy beside me, and I thought of Gil's frail body on the couch. His voice, small and frightened. *I'm sorry, Marnie.*

"Had you seen him lately?" I asked CJ, keeping my voice even. "In town or whatever."

"Maybe once or twice. He didn't leave the house much."

"How did he seem to you?"

"He wouldn't even look at me." The corner of CJ's mouth tugged upward. "He never forgave my father for letting him go."

Gil had become a certified farm mechanic after his first deployment; I knew Clinton Ealy Sr. hired him on occasion to fix their equipment, even though the farm already had a regular mechanic. Ealy Sr.

was generous, but never in a way that insulted my family's pride. "How is your dad?" I asked.

"Early-onset dementia," CJ said. "Only knows who I am half the time."

"Are you serious?" Ealy Sr. would only be in his late sixties.

"He's been in assisted living over a year now."

"I'm so sorry," I said.

CJ shrugged, as if to say *What're you going to do*, and nodded to the bartender. "Another Budweiser for me. What about you, Samantha?" My name was reduced to two syllables in his mouth. *Sman-tha.*

"Nothing," I said. "Don't think I'll be able to catch an Uber around here."

CJ put a hand to his chest, as if covering a shotgun wound. "I'll have you know, we do have an Uber driver in town."

"Just one?" I asked.

"His name's Brandon," Taylor said. "Except Uber deactivated him for having a shitty rating, so you've gotta call him if you need a ride."

"I'm sure I'd be in great hands with Brandon," I said. "But I just want to get my burger and go."

A glance at the kitchen door, where there was no sign of said burger.

"Come on," Taylor said. "One game of pool?"

CJ lifted his beer to his mouth, awaiting my response, a smile prickling on his lips. The light over the pool table glinted off the smattering of gray in his hair.

"All right," I said. "But I suck."

"Tay," CJ said, handing me a pool cue. "Play the winner."

Taylor looked a bit pouty as CJ snuck behind me, fingers grazing my lower back. I bent lower, gave the cue ball a smack. It rolled lazily toward the racked balls, curved, and dropped into the corner pocket.

Taylor howled with laughter.

"Told you I suck."

Overhead, the Journey song leaking through the speakers faded to a radio spot for a cosmetic dentist. CJ aimed, took his shot. Broke the racked balls and inched closer to me.

"How long you sticking around for?"

"Are you asking on behalf of my cousin?" I asked.

CJ smiled, sank the seven ball. "Maybe."

He took his next shot with one hand, sipped his beer with his other at the same time. Cocky. When he missed, I raised my stick, pocketed my eleven ball. "Why does Rhi even care?"

"You're her family."

"Mmmm, I don't think that's it." I couldn't say I blamed Rhi for not wanting me around. Mitch and I tended to wind each other up; no doubt Rhi had already gotten an earful about my unannounced visit yesterday.

"Really, Sam," CJ said. "It hurt her that you never came to meet Kaylee."

I pocketed the cue ball and turned to face CJ. "She never asked me to."

"The two of you. Jesus." CJ examined the ball in his hand before placing it on the table. He took his next shot one-handed, sank his three.

Rhi's and my stubbornness comes from the Newsom side. The day my mother flung that plate at Scott, he was back for dinner hours later, as if nothing had happened. The Newsoms, though, tended to their grudges like houseplants. The pettiest of disagreements could stretch into weeks of the silent treatment. "If we keep talking about my family, I am going to need that drink."

CJ propped himself up on his pool cue and drained his Heineken. He set the bottle on the high-top. "Tay, get me another? And a whiskey for Sam."

Taylor, a good dog, nodded, bounded off to procure our drinks.

When Taylor was out of earshot, CJ said, "Between us, I think Rhi is concerned."

"Concerned about what?"

"She said you smelled like booze yesterday when you rear-ended the truck."

"It was a bumper tap. And I met a friend for a drink."

CJ smiled. "In the middle of the day?"

"How is this any of your business?"

"I'm just curious if it has anything to do with a rumor I heard about an out-of-town detective."

"What have you heard?"

"Just that he dropped by the police department and left with records. So is it about your family's case?"

I thought of Meacham's warning not to tell anyone about the visit to the jail, suddenly hyperaware of the fact we weren't alone in the bar. A few of the patrons had the over-sunned look of vacationers, but the Riverhead Inn was by and large a local joint.

No one seemed to be paying us any mind, but many were close enough to hear our conversation. I dropped my voice and said, by CJ's ear, "What if the state was handling the case? Hypothetically speaking, would that be a problem for local law enforcement?"

"I think the chief of police is relieved, honestly, since other crime is up and he doesn't have the resources for old cases." CJ lifted his stick, took his next shot. "Hypothetically speaking, of course."

"And what about Officer Rhodes? What's he up to these days?"

"That's Detective Rhodes now."

"Are you kidding me?"

Stephen Rhodes would be pushing sixty. The average cop put in their twenty years and cashed out at the first opportunity to take a job as a hospital security guard.

"Why the hell is he still working?" I asked.

CJ watched his ball sink into the pocket, his expression darkening. "The man loves his job, I guess."

I had pictured Rhodes in several scenarios over the years. On a boat in the Keys, enjoying his pension, pickled in Bud Light and occasionally remembering he'd gotten away with murder. Or he had died, maybe—alone, and in a manner so unremarkable that no one had bothered to post an obituary online.

Not once had I considered the possibility that Stephen Rhodes was still a cop.

"Sam." CJ's voice was gentle. "You okay?"

"Not really."

"We saw his ex-wife when we brought Kaylee to visit Pop at the nursing home. I only knew it was her because Rhi acted like she saw Hitler, alive and making balloon animals at a kid's birthday party."

Because Rhodes's wife had given him an alibi. She said he was asleep in bed by ten thirty, and according to Karl Holcombe, that was evidence enough that Rhodes couldn't have set the fire.

While I eased around the corner of the table, I was aware of CJ watching me, Heineken hovering below his chin.

"What?" I remembered the stick in my hand and rushed a pathetic shot at the cue. It rolled to the side, missing my remaining balls by a foot.

CJ shook his head. "Just be careful who you ask about Rhodes, okay? Small town."

CJ bent and took a shot, the cue connecting with the eight ball.

Taylor had returned, drinks in hand, in time to watch the cue ball follow the eight into the pocket. He howled with laughter while CJ considered the stick in his hand as if it had betrayed him.

I stayed to play Taylor, and then for another hour to nurse the double whiskey he bought me after I'd promptly lost. I thought about inviting Taylor back to Gil's, but I couldn't handle the thought of the taunting I would get when Rhi found out tomorrow.

Sex was far from my mind. After my conversation with CJ Ealy, I did not want to spend the night in Gil's house alone.

For the first time in many years, I felt scared to be in Carney.

As a kid, it hadn't taken very long for me to shed the fear that my parents' killers would come for me. It was clear from the marathon interview sessions with the police that I didn't know anything. I wasn't the target of the crime, and as long as I couldn't identify the killer, I wasn't in danger.

I was well cared for after the murders. Strangers showered me with toys I was way too old to play with, brand-new clothing that my parents never could have afforded. My teachers were lenient with me; the local church prayed for me.

Is it any wonder, then, I grew up believing that no one could ever possibly want to harm me?

A chill rose on my arms as I entered Gil's house. I'd left all his windows cracked, the AC units running, in an attempt to flush out the stench of a lifelong smoker.

I'd been very careless so far. CJ Ealy was right. Carney was a small town, and it was only a matter of time before word traveled that I was asking around about Stephen Rhodes.

Detective Rhodes.

He was still a fucking cop.

I moved from window to window, chanting the words in my head with every latch I shut. *Fucking cop. Fucking cops.*

The fucking cops killed my family.

Chapter Six

I dragged myself into Gil's kitchen at the first slice of sunlight, a headache brewing with the intensity of a hurricane. I emptied the inch of water left in Gil's Brita filter into a glass and refilled the pitcher. Ealy Farms opened to the public at 9:00 a.m.

A long strip of road, single lane, marked by side-by-side billboards advertising divorce for the low price of $399 and a chubby-cheeked baby pleading for the viewer to Choose Life. The only structures between the 42 Café and Ealy Farms were barns and silos. Every half mile or so, I passed fenced-in livestock that lay on parched grass, unmoving in the heat.

At Ealy's, Rhiannon's Tahoe was in the dirt lot off to the side of the main building.

The summer before my junior year, I'd joined Rhi picking berries at the farm for a dollar a pound, cash in hand at the end of every week. Mitch had fought me on it, even though my younger cousin had been working the blueberry fields since she was fourteen.

Mitch heard the way the day pickers talked, the men that came into the deli on their lunch breaks, dusty clothes and sun-worn limbs. Migrant workers from the South, out-hauling the local kids, laughing at the boys and leering at the girls.

I was too easily distracted by the attention of males, not like my younger cousin. I had curves in the places Rhi was flat. My aunt never came out and said it, but I knew she believed it to be true: Rhiannon could handle herself, and I could not.

I stepped out of the Accord; a man in manure-stained jeans ambled past me, pushing a wheelbarrow weighed down with sod. Inside, some touristy types dragging kids waited in line with pints of berries ready to be weighed and purchased, consumed in fistfuls that would stain their children's GapKids ensembles.

Rhi was nowhere in sight, and gone were the pockmarked twentysomethings of my day who stocked the produce bins. High school dropouts, most of them, the type of guys who my ex–best friend Dani Burkhardt used for access to booze. Once, she and I had made out for an audience of them in exchange for a handle of rotgut vodka.

Now, baby-faced teenagers in hunter-green T-shirts worked the floor, refilling cartons of produce, cleaning the fridges that held fresh cider and cheeses. One of them watched me from behind the register, her T-shirt knotted at her hip, sliver of tanned belly peeking over her jean shorts.

"Hey."

I turned to spot Taylor Edwards coming toward me. The grin on his face sent up a flare of annoyance in me. I tamped it down, returned his smile. "Hey yourself."

"Taking a break from packing the house?" he asked.

"You could say that. Hey, is that offer for boxes still good?"

"Of course. I can bring 'em by tonight, if you're around?"

I promised I would be, and we swapped numbers the millennial way so I could text him Gil's address. As I handed Taylor his phone back, I asked, "Is Rhi around?"

"In the office."

"Thanks."

I knew from my time here that the door led to a narrow hall with an employee toilet on one side and the office on the other. We would line up at the office every Friday, stinking and dust-caked, for Mrs.

Ealy to distribute envelopes of cash, our names written on the outside. I suspected, over the course of that summer, a few extra twenties had found their way into my pay envelope.

The office door was cracked open, the thrum of a fan leaking out. I half expected to find Cecilia Ealy seated at the desk, licking the pad of her thumb as she counted out a stack of cash. Instead, my cousin sat ramrod straight in her chair, texting.

Rhi looked up at my knock. She set her phone down, eyes trained on me. Tacked to the wall behind her was a yellowing poster bearing the old adage about only being able to please one person per day.

"What's up?" she asked, her tone clipped.

"I was hoping you could help me with something. But I see that today is not my day."

Rhi blinked at me. I pointed to the poster behind her. She shook her head and reached for her phone again. "Sorry. Half the seasonal workers are city kids. They want weekends off."

"Pretty cool, though," I said. "Being the boss."

Rhi shrugged, didn't look up from her phone. "The Ealys reward loyalty."

When she was done texting, I said, "Do you have a minute to talk?"

Rhi's response was cut off by her cell phone ringing. She held up a finger, answered with a borderline vicious "What *is* it?"

She ended the call and stood. "Come with me."

"Where?"

"There's a bat trapped in a port-a-potty in the fields. We can talk on the ride over."

Rhi pocketed her phone and, when she thought I wasn't looking, a pack of Parliament Lights from her drawer.

I followed Rhiannon outside to her Tahoe and waited for her to unlock it with her key fob. I climbed into the passenger seat. She didn't bother putting on her belt, so neither did I, the reminder chime from both of our seats filling the silence as she backed out of the lot and onto 42.

Rhi rolled onto the dirt shoulder by the blueberry fields and cut her engine. I followed her down a row of bushes swollen with berries, my flip-flopped feet coated in a layer of dust by the time we reached the port-a-potty.

She opened the door, stepped back, and gave the portable toilet a rattle. Manic flapping sounds, and a blur of gray flew out and into the cloudless sky.

"How fuckin' hard was that," Rhi said, shooting a look of disgust at the workers who had their heads down, oblivious to Rhi's and my presence. I remembered the focus, the heat on my back, the desperation to pull in a bigger haul than the boys whose eyes traced the hem of my shorts to my ass.

The heat shimmered off the dirt paths cutting through the rows of bushes. Even though I had asked her to talk, I got the sense Rhi had a thought of her own she was circling, waiting to share with me until we were away from any ears tuned to us.

I watched my cousin; a cigarette I hadn't noticed her slip out of the pack was wedged between her lips. "I heard you and CJ had fun last night," she said.

"It was just pool. Taylor was there too."

"Relax." Rhi cupped her hand around her Parliament while she lit it. "We're not together."

This didn't surprise me, although I still couldn't work out how Rhiannon had wound up pregnant from a fling with CJ Ealy, a man seven years her senior. A man who also happened to be her boss.

Fifteen years could alter a person, but I still sensed Rhi was the person I'd grown up alongside. She had always been committed to avoiding any behavior that might draw unwanted attention to herself. My aunt had never married, and people were open about their belief that Rhi's father was the husband of our elementary-school gym teacher.

I thought of Rhiannon on the bus to our grade-school picnic, stone-faced in her seat when Mrs. Sherman called her name at roll call. Years later, when Mr. Sherman died of a heart attack, I came home from school to find Rhi in bed, facing the wall. When I asked if she was okay, she barked at me to get the fuck out of her room.

"So what did you want to talk about?" Rhi asked.

"Gil bought a TV last year," I said. "Fifty-two inches. Practically new. It's yours if you want it."

Rhi aimed the cloud of smoke over my shoulder. "I wouldn't be able to tell Mom where I got it from."

"I know."

Rhi had not gone totally unnoticed by her employees. A girl, maybe seventeen, eighteen, was watching us from the edge of her row. She threw a skittish look at me and Rhi before bowing her head low over her crate of berries.

"Probably thinks you're ICE," Rhi muttered. "Like I'd let a pig on this farm."

"Speaking of, I heard you ran into Rhodes's ex-wife while you were visiting CJ's father."

"I wouldn't say that." The cherry of Rhi's cigarette glowed. "I recognized her, from afar."

"You know her name?"

In the distance, shouting in Spanish disturbed the quiet. Laughter, and then more silence, the hum of June bugs, until Rhiannon said, "What are you playing at, Sam?"

"I don't know. Just wondering if anyone has talked to her recently. To see if her story has changed about the night of the murders."

"And what if it has? They're never gonna have enough to put him away for it."

"Unless someone came forward. Someone who might have seen something."

"Who the fuck is going to come forward, Sam? It's been twenty-two years."

Rhi dropped her cigarette, ground it beneath her boot. "I don't wanna talk about Rhodes. I don't want to think about him. Because when I do, I feel like I'll lose my fuckin' mind. They were my family too, you know."

My dad never missed one of Rhiannon's soccer games if he could help it, especially since Michelle had to work Saturdays at the deli. He was the closest thing Rhiannon had to a father of her own, and I suspected part of Michelle's disdain for my mother was because of the time Rhi was forced to spend at my house on the weekends and after school.

Mom had been the one to guide Rhi through getting her first period while Mitch was at work. Rhi was a prickly child, and even pricklier preteen, but my mother was one of the few adults she respected.

"I just want his ex-wife's name, Rhi. That's all."

"It's Diane," Rhiannon said. "Don't do anything fucking stupid with that information."

I should have been thinking about acquiring lunch, or maybe making Gil's house presentable enough for when Taylor dropped by tonight, but I was at the kitchen table, making a list of every assisted living and rehabilitation center in the county. There were an alarming number of Dianes who worked in elder care, and so far, none of them had ever heard the name Stephen Rhodes.

I moved on to the next facility on my list, Mountain View Assisted Living. The line rang three times before an annoyed woman said, "Nursing desk."

"Hi. Is Diane working?"

"Which one? We've got three."

"I'm not sure what she goes by now. She used to be Diane Rhodes."

The line was quiet. "Can I ask what this is about?"

"My name is Samantha. I used to know her," I lied.

"This line isn't for personal calls."

My brain was lit up, but after two drinks and an hour of sleep last night, I felt myself barreling toward the point of no return. My body would give up, and I would lapse into a Rip Van Winkle coma. I couldn't afford to lose that kind of time because of a cunty charge nurse.

"It's important," I said. "Could I leave her a message so she can call me back?"

"I'll see if she's at her desk."

A click. I was being transferred.

"Diane speaking. Who is this?"

"Samantha Newsom."

"Ohhhh."

"I'm so sorry to bother you at work. I didn't know how else to get in touch."

"It's fine, sweetie. To be honest, I expected I'd hear from you someday. This is just more of an in-person conversation, you know?"

"Maybe we could meet for coffee tomorrow?" I asked.

Diane mulled this for a moment, before: "Are you in the area?"

"I'm in Carney for the next few days."

"I'm going to lunch at one. Think you could make it up here by then?"

&

I set my GPS, anxiety humming in my blood. Whatever I thought I knew about Stephen Rhodes, I had even less information about his former wife.

I parked in one of the visitor spots in front of the nursing home. In the fire zone, two EMTs were loading an open-mouthed old man into the back of an ambulance. While I watched them, a woman in scrubs stepped out from the automatic doors.

She scanned the lot, zeroed in on me. She was at my window before I had the chance to lower it fully.

Diane had close-cropped black hair and wore no makeup save for eyeliner that appeared to be tattooed on.

"I'll meet you at the Dunkin' across the street," she said before disappearing again.

Somehow, Diane beat me there. By the time I entered, her scrubbed back was to me at the milk station. She moved with a frightening efficiency that reminded me of myself at work. Most of the other customers wore scrubs, or lab coats. I suddenly felt unmoored in my street clothes.

Diane turned, wielding two coffees, an insulated lunch bag draped over her forearm. She nodded to an open table by the window.

"You're very pretty," she said, unpacking her lunch. A wilted salad, covered in milky dressing.

"Thank you," I said, taking in the woman seated before me. At her throat was a crescent of a scar. Thyroid cancer, I was willing to bet. Sounded like the radiation had done a number on her voice.

"You know, when I heard someone was on the phone asking for Diane Rhodes, a part of me hoped that he was dead," Diane said.

I took a polite sip of coffee, unsure of what to say. I settled on, "How long have you been divorced?"

"Fifteen years now. We were together more than double that. I was nineteen when we met and convinced I'd found the great love of my life." Diane offered a wry smile. On the table, her phone lit up with a message. I eyeballed the text: Everything okay?

"Hold on." Diane swiped a finger across the screen, tapped out a response I couldn't see. "That's my husband. I told him I was meeting you, and he was a little worried, so I said I'd stay in touch."

"That's sweet for him to look after you."

"He's a good man." Diane speared a cucumber. "Stephen isn't a good man. But you already know that."

"I don't really know anything about him," I said. Stephen Rhodes had been a bogeyman for most of my life, but I'd never so much as seen the man in the flesh. "All I have is secondhand information and rumors."

Diane tapped a finger to her coffee lid, mulling this. "The only thing I can tell you with certainty is that there are many different Stephens."

"What do you mean?"

"The Stephen I knew, before we got married, was attentive. He was kind. I didn't have the best childhood, but with Stephen, I never wanted for anything. A big house, vacations, jewelry. I realized too late that it was his way of distracting me from *wanting* anything, you know?"

Diane shook her head. "Stephen never wanted kids. So I decided I didn't either. I spent most of my adult life convinced I only wanted what Stephen wanted. The first time I truly felt afraid of him was when I approached the idea again after we'd been married several years. He was so angry with me—made me take my pill in front of him every morning, then waited, just to make sure I didn't make myself throw it up."

"Sounds like he was emotionally abusive," I said.

Diane slapped a hand against the table, as if spanking a child. "*Yes.* It took me years to wake up to it."

She closed her eyes for a moment, shook her head again, and shoveled some salad into her mouth. I let her be, no stranger myself to lunch breaks that passed like lightning flashes. After a moment, she looked up at me.

"Was he ever violent?"

"With me, no. I'd heard things, of course, about the things he did to people. But Stephen was an exceptionally good liar. He convinced me that people in the department had it out for him. Jealousy, because he had the most arrests. Then, a few years after the incident with your uncle, I treated this girl in the emergency room, back when I worked as an RN. Came in half-frozen to death. She told me a Carney cop picked her up for soliciting, but instead of booking her, he drove her an hour outside town. Threw her out of the car and punched her in the face when she tried to take her phone and purse back. He left her there.

"I tried to get her to file a report. She wouldn't, because he had her purse, and she had cocaine in it. She described him, and I knew. I knew the officer who assaulted that poor girl was my husband. Years later, I learned that's why they wouldn't allow Stephen to work the night shift anymore. They called what he was doing to those poor people 'taking them on a Starlight Tour.'"

My coffee had lost its taste, but I sipped anyway. The room around me had taken on a dreamlike quality. Diane, perched in that chair like Scheherazade, feeding me stories, each more unbelievable than the next.

"Is that why you left him?" I asked.

"It was the straw that broke the camel's back. Money was an issue—Steve was always giving it to his friends. So-and-so was going through a rough patch and their kids needed Christmas gifts, or his sick partner couldn't afford the copays on his medication." Diane sipped her coffee. "It wasn't until his partner died with his dick in a prostitute that I learned his 'medication' was cocaine."

"His partner," I said. "Wasn't that the guy he supposedly drove home the night of the eighth?"

Diane said nothing. My heart raced. "If Rhodes was funding his partner's coke habit, what was to stop the guy from lying about the time he got dropped off after the poker game?"

"Maybe Neil did lie, but Stephen was in bed, like I said he was. He called me when he left his poker game that evening, to see if I'd been able to get off at ten. He had off that Sunday, and the plan was that I'd work half a shift the night before so we could spend the day together." Diane closed her eyes. "There was so much I didn't know until years later, when I knew everything. But I know that he was in bed when I got home. He couldn't have killed those poor people."

"The fire started after midnight," I said. "But they may have been killed earlier. Someone saw a man leaving the house between eight and nine."

With my sister. I stopped short of saying it. Meacham had warned me not to tell anyone about the trip to visit Boggs. The killer, Meacham believed, was likely embedded in the community. We couldn't risk tipping him off.

But the look in Diane's eyes now. All my digging, prodding her—I had hit on something, long buried.

"Please," I said. "Anything you might remember, about that night, something he said about my family over the years . . ."

Diane Rhodes touched her lips, then the base of her coffee cup, a small tremor in her fingers. "I . . . I asked him, once, how he could talk about those poor people the way he did. I said, 'How could that baby possibly deserve to die?'"

My stomach bottomed out. "What did he say?"

"I remember it, because he'd been studying the Bible—it upset me, hearing him talk like that. He said to me, something like, 'Anything that can survive a fire will be clean.'"

Anything that can withstand fire must be put through the fire. And then it will be clean. Numbers 31:23, according to Google.

On the way back to Carney, I stopped to top off my gas tank, my phone pinging with a text from Taylor Edwards.

Just getting off work now. Cool to swing by with the boxes?

I shook away the thoughts of babies being fed to fire and replied. Sure. Come hungry.

The last time I'd eaten Domino's was when I was drunk and desperate in college, but it was the only pizza place that would deliver to Gil's address. I placed an order online when I got back to the house.

I dragged a chair to the fridge so I could access the cabinet above it. I'd hidden Gil's booze up there on my last check-in, when I caught him mixing it with methotrexate. I wiped the grime from the rim of a bottle of Captain Morgan, gave it a sniff. I tossed the rest of the liquor bottles in the sink and was halfway through emptying them down the drain when someone began rapping at the front door.

The Domino's delivery guy had beaten Taylor. I had no cash to tip him with, thanks to Crazy Ed cleaning out my wallet, and made him wait while I counted out five bucks in quarters from the dusty beer stein of coins in Gil's bedroom.

I snuck a Cinnastick, eyeing the microwave clock. A little after seven, and still no sign of Taylor. I was about to say fuck it and make myself a Captain and Coke when a gentle rap at the door sounded.

Taylor stood on Gil's porch, a pallet of flat cardboard boxes under one arm.

"Hey." He grinned.

"I got pizza and Cinnasticks," I said. "Want to come in?"

I already knew what Taylor's answer would be—wet hair clung to his forehead, and his face was freshly shaven. He stepped over the threshold and rested the boxes against the wall. "Shit. *Cinna*sticks."

He followed me into the kitchen, propped himself against the fridge while I scrounged up a roll of paper towels and a sleeve of Diet Coke.

"Sorry the soda's warm," I said.

"No worries."

We helped ourselves to slices of the pizza, eating between sips of Captain and Diet Coke, my long-neglected iTunes library leaking from my phone speaker. Taylor and I had been friendly in high school but not friendly enough to have anything to talk about thirteen years later over Domino's. When a Temple of the Dog song began to play, he set down the slice of pizza he'd been working on. "Man, I haven't heard this one in ages."

I tore off a sheet of paper towel and dabbed some grease from my chin. "I was obsessed with them. Still can't believe Chris Cornell is gone."

Taylor tipped some more Captain into his Coke. "Chester is the one that really got to me." He set the bottle down, shook his head. "I just don't get it."

"You don't get why someone who made a career singing about being depressed would kill himself?"

"Nah, I mean, I get being thirteen and pissed off at the world and feeling like there's nothing waiting for you. But these guys had kids is the really fucked-up thing."

Taylor sipped his drink, stopping short of saying it: His heroes were selfish. They chose to leave their children because they were weak.

I tore at a bit of crust, took a hamster-size bite. "I don't know. Sometimes I think maybe certain people were just never meant to be here."

"What do you mean?"

"You look at some of these guys, their music . . . it was there all along. Maybe it's selfish, they left kids behind, but isn't it kind of remarkable they held on so long?"

Taylor blinked at me, slowly, like a cat. I stood, my knee making contact with the leg of the table. Pain radiated through my patella as I crossed to the kitchen counter. I felt Taylor's stare on my back as I tugged open the junk drawer, emerged with the baggie of joints.

"Damn," he said. "You can take the girl out of Carney."

"That's all Gil." I tossed the bag onto the table, slid back into my chair. "Got a lighter?"

I'd spotted the outline of a pack of cigs in his back pocket the other morning, when he'd bent to examine the damage to the delivery truck's bumper. Taylor's cheeks went pink as he shifted in his chair, reached into his jeans pocket.

Mercifully, he lit the joint for me, saving me the indignity of admitting that the sight of an open flame still sent me spiraling with panic. Taylor offered me the first toke. A gentleman. We passed the joint back and forth, tearing into the remains of the Cinnasticks, Eddie Vedder moaning from my phone.

Suddenly, Taylor laughed.

"What's so funny?"

"I can't believe I'm smoking with Samantha Newsom." He rubbed his eyes, blinked at me as if trying to convince himself I were real.

I kicked his foot under the table. "What's that supposed to mean?"

"You were one of the smart kids, and I was the loser who had to sit outside in the hall."

It made me sad, hearing him call himself a loser. School couldn't have been easy for a kid like Taylor Edwards. He had that funny scar over his lip. In the cafeteria, taunts about his mother, because everyone knew Wendy Edwards was ranting-at-the-sky crazy. Taylor's father was former military, fond of rules and shame as punishment. When their mother died, Taylor's half brother, Bo, moved in with his uncle, Ealy Sr., rather than follow Mr. Edwards's rules.

I tipped some more rum into Taylor's cup. "I wasn't that smart."

"Oh, come on. You were, like, the most serious kid ever," he said. "Remember seventh grade? You were in that play."

"I was." *The King and I.* It had ruined my Christmas break that I hadn't gotten a speaking role. My mother, hissing to my father that she was sick of my sulking. Every disappointment at that age a crisis.

"Detention met in the room across from the auditorium," Taylor said. "I used to watch you and the other girls practice your dance out in the hall. You were the only one who never smiled."

"We weren't supposed to smile! We were concubines." I held the Captain bottle by its neck, added more to my cup.

"Sometimes I got detention on purpose so I could watch you."

I pointed my toes, nudged Taylor's boot under the table. "No, you didn't."

"I swear, I did. Then one day you caught me watching and gave me this *look*. It was the end of the world for me. I had such a crush on you."

"Bullshit," I said. "Didn't you ask out every girl in our grade except me?"

"You were too good for me," Taylor laughed. "I knew you'd say no."

"I was not that good." I accepted the joint in his outstretched hand. Took a hit and exhaled, the smoke cloud obscuring Taylor's face. My bad phase was fleeting, over by the end of sophomore year, around the time my guidance counselor reamed me out for showing up for the PSAT hungover and Dani stopped speaking to me.

"You don't remember my Dani Burkhardt phase?" I asked. "Sophomore year?"

"Not really," Taylor said. "But I was probably too busy sniffing spray paint under the bleachers."

I laughed, the sound coming from another dimension. I was on the way to quite stoned, the memories of that year edging through the cracks in my brain. Sitting in a bathroom stall sophomore year, listening to Caroline Mason and a new cheerleading friend at the sink. Between swipes of lip gloss, discussing a party that had occurred over the weekend, the type they would not be caught dead at.

Two guys at the same time, I heard.

The tragic orphan thing is played out. How else is she supposed to get attention?

I don't understand how she went from you as a best friend to a skank like Dani Burkhardt.

Caroline had laughed, a razor-sharp noise I barely recognized before the door thwacked shut behind them. Later that day, lying on Dani's bed, my head in her lap, I admitted how badly it hurt. How Caroline and I wore matching outfits as kids, how Mrs. Mason treated me more like family than my own aunt did.

"Fuck them," Dani had said. She bent down, kissed me square on the forehead, a display of tenderness so rare that I still felt the memory like an ache. "I'm your family now."

I thought about asking Taylor if he ever saw Dani around, what she was up to, but stopped myself. No need to start digging at long-healed wounds. I peeked in his cup, offered him the bottle of Captain for a top-off.

"Nah, I'm good," he said. "I gotta get up early and head to Gloversville."

"What's all the way up there?"

"My daughter." Taylor looked a bit bashful about it, but it softened me toward him.

"How old is she?" I asked, realizing I was still extending the bottle. I added another small splash to my own cup.

"Three," Taylor said. "I don't see her much since my ex moved them up there."

That made me sad. I'd encountered enough men in this town to know a woman could do a hell of a lot worse than Taylor Edwards.

"You got kids?" Taylor asked, eager to punt the conversation back to me.

"No," I said. "No kids."

"Boyfriend?" Taylor didn't bother hiding the hopeful lilt to his smile.

"Divorced." I sipped my drink. "Because I didn't want kids."

"Rough," Taylor said, and I shrugged. My ex knew early on that I didn't want children. He said he was fine with it, that he'd always been unsold on parenthood himself. Either he changed his mind, or he was arrogant enough to think he could change mine. The night he stopped moving against my thighs, nibbled my earlobe, and whispered, *Let's make a baby*, I froze before saying *Okay* in time for him to finish inside me.

I stared at our bedroom ceiling that whole night, trying to warm to the idea. Maybe a child would thaw the parts of me that made me difficult to love. I tried to paste my face onto the bodies of the women I saw cycling through our apartment building, infants wrapped to their chests.

By the light of morning, I was in a full-fledged panic about what might be taking place inside me. Not at the idea of becoming a mother, but at the power of my own body to bring more life onto a planet that was only concerned with maintaining balance through death.

When my husband left for work in the morning, I headed for the pharmacy a block away from our apartment. He found the Plan B box when he was taking out the trash two days later. By the end of the month, he'd moved out, the only trace of him left in our apartment a stray sock stuck in the corner of a fitted sheet in the laundry.

I sensed that Taylor was feeling awkward at my admission. I swiped a finger through the tub of Cinnastick frosting, licked it off. "What's it like? Being a parent."

He thought for a bit, sipped his drink. "It definitely changes you. I care about shit I never used to. I want to be the type of person she deserves for a dad, you know?"

My stomach swam, Captain and too much sugar. I had a flash of myself at Ealy Farms as a child, a crisp October day with my parents, before Lyndsey. We always got free admission to the fall festivities, a perk of my father's job. One year I'd gorged myself on cider donuts and got sick inside the bounce house. I'd been inconsolable at the humiliation, the way the other children had fled from me as I vomited everywhere. My mother had seemed equally mortified, but Dad had held my head to his chest, stroking my hair, murmuring, *It's all right, Baby Doll.*

I felt sick and unmoored now, relieved that Taylor was ready to head out. I didn't need him triggering more Daddy issues this evening.

While Taylor used the bathroom, I stood and grabbed a trash bag from the roll on the counter. When he returned, Taylor helped me clear the debris from the table, sidestepping the trash bags I'd filled with kitchen items.

I walked him to the door and he smiled, propped against the doorframe. "Maybe I can call you when I get back tomorrow?"

"I'm more of a texter, but sure." I cracked open the door, watched Taylor step out onto the porch. "Be careful getting home, please!"

"Don't worry, I'm an excellent impaired driver."

I gave his chest a whack with the back of my hand.

"Nah, really. I'm straight."

I had followed him out to the driveway without meaning to. Taylor paused when his truck reached the base of the driveway. He raised a hand, smiled at me before turning onto 42, his taillights shrinking to pinpricks.

I stood there, the driveway cool beneath my bare feet, the chatter of the crickets transporting me to the hill behind our house. Lying on my belly, grass tickling my shins, watching the sky for Hale-Bopp. My father next to me on the blanket, tinkering with his telescope. Scott, on his back somewhere, smoking a joint, his mind tripping through the cosmos.

This was why I didn't smoke anymore. Being high sharpened my mind too much, brought long-blurred memories into focus.

The worst is the way time slows down and everything goes still. So still that I can hear them. Lyndsey's cry, so startling and real I have to stop myself from bolting into the next room. My mother, the slam of that car door, the last words she spoke to me. *What the hell is wrong with you, Samantha?*

"I'm sorry," I said into the darkness. "I don't know what's wrong with me."

I waited for a sign she heard me, but there was no response, only the sounds of the night.

I woke with half my body off the couch, the outer seam of the cushion imprinted in my jaw. I'd gotten a bit sloppy last night. The cold blast of the shower did nothing to clear the gunk around my brain. I hadn't smoked an entire joint since college, and the blend Gil had sworn was medicinal couldn't curb the effect of that final ill-advised Captain and Coke. A blast of pain in my skull so brutal I bent over, one hand on the wall, watching a spider corpse circle the drain.

Out of the shower. I wrapped myself in a starchy towel and tugged open the drawers of Gil's vanity, rattling pill bottles and assorted detritus. I pawed through the prescription bottles—Decadron, tramadol, Zantac, Zofran. There were no over-the-counter painkillers, as Gil was more of the self-medicating type.

I popped open the tramadol, counted out the thirty pills he'd been prescribed, according to the bottle. I tipped one onto my palm, waffling. Tramadol was a narcotic—less addictive than an opioid, but people still got hooked on it. I wondered if that's why Gil refused to touch the pills.

I swallowed one with a scoop of faucet water, making a mental reminder to check the FDA's "Do not flush" list later before emptying the bathroom of the pharmacy worth of medications. I dried, dressed, and headed for the kitchen to pop a mug in the microwave for tea.

While the water nuked, I felt my will to live slowly returning, my temples quieting from the tramadol.

I was due back at work Saturday night, and I still could not get a human on the phone at the junk-removal company. Time for my plan B: attempt to donate the furniture.

I sipped my tea and put in a call to the Salvation Army, spent ten minutes negotiating with a sassy coordinator who insisted the earliest they could arrange a pickup for Gil's furniture was Monday morning.

"I can't be here on Monday," I said. "Does someone actually have to be here?"

"Yes, ma'am. Do you want the appointment or not?"

"Fine." I massaged my eyelids, the pulsing behind them cresting. I confirmed Gil's address and pried myself from the chair, considered the box of junk I'd emptied from his closet last night.

A vintage Chevy, the red paint chipped on the front bumper. I lifted the hood, let it drop with a clink. I couldn't picture it in my apartment, but it felt wrong to give it to Goodwill, let it wind up in a stranger's hands. I shot off a text to Taylor.

Does your daughter like trucks?

Hell yeah lol

A minute later, Taylor texted a photo. A little girl, no older than three, sat at the steering wheel of a delivery truck. Although she was red-haired, the Chiclet teeth in an enormous grin were unmistakably Taylor's. Her freckled face radiated delight, tiny hands gripping the wheel.

I have something for her, then, I texted back.

that's sweet of u

wanna meet up when I get back from Gloversville later?

I thought of the way he'd spoken of me last night. How he'd seen me.

Not everyone was in agreement. In college, during a late-night pity spiral, I wound up reading about my family's case in the bowels of true-crime internet. A Reddit thread floated a theory that *I* had killed my family, with the help of a coked-out older boyfriend. Never mind that I was only in eighth grade when my parents were killed.

Someone-who-knew-someone in Carney had made the post. The person hadn't named Dani Burkhardt, my best friend of less than a year when I was fifteen, but there was talk of the bad crowd I fell in with after my parents' death. Yes, Dani did drugs. Yes, I smoked pot with her. For a number of people, this was evidence enough that the Newsom family was a bunch of druggie degenerates.

Reading those things about myself gave me my very first panic attack. Part of me suspected that Dani herself had written that post. Retribution, for finding me in the back of Bo Ealy's pickup truck, two months after they broke up. Dani had dragged me to the party at the Ealys', in the farmhand cottage Bo's uncle had allowed him to move into when he turned eighteen.

A week earlier, Dani had abandoned me in the Triple Crown parking lot. That night at Bo's, I hadn't wanted to drink, nervous of how I'd fend for myself if she left me again. And she did leave me, with a girl I'd never seen before, who slipped a Molly pill on my tongue and nudged me toward Bo Ealy. *He told me he knew you'd always grow up to be hot.*

The next thing I remember is being on my back in Bo's truck. Bo Ealy, kissing my neck. I sort of said *Oh*, my body turning to a rag doll before the jolt of panic as he unzipped his pants, the weight of him pressing into me, his dick hardening in the crook of my thigh.

Hands, jamming down the front of my pants, the words never making it to my lips. *But Dani. Dani will kill me.*

As if I'd manifested her, I heard her screaming. I opened my eyes and she was there, screaming at Bo, at me.

I was fifteen years old.

Dani dropped out of school not long after that, knowing she wouldn't be able to graduate anyway. When I'm feeling particularly sorry for myself, unable to breathe under the weight of everyone who has ever left me, I think of Dani Burkhardt.

Curiosity had the best of me now, curdling with my strong urge to put off dealing with Gil's basement, which was FUBAR. *It's not cyber-stalking if it's been more than five years since you checked in on someone*, I told myself as I reactivated my dormant Facebook account.

Dani Burkhardt

My breath caught. The top result was for a page called MISSING IN SULLIVAN COUNTY

> DANICA E. BURKHARDT
>
> HEIGHT: 5'9"
>
> EYES: BROWN
>
> HAIR: DYED RED AT TIME OF DISAPPEARANCE

My heartbeat quickened. I scrolled, but there were no comments on the post, no other information. I left the Facebook page open and opened up NamUs in a new tab.

The entry had been made less than a year ago, despite the fact that her missing poster said she was last seen in 2021. All the fields were blank, except for one.

> CONTACT: Detective Stephen Rhodes, Carney Police Department.

Chapter Seven

The night I met Dani was the night my best friend since kindergarten finally had enough of me. I'd sensed Caroline's patience becoming brittle for months. I had always fallen short of her expectations, but I *technically* owed her my life, with that sleepover, and it wouldn't have killed me to perk up a bit, act more grateful.

It was the August before ninth grade, Caroline still breathless from that morning's cheerleading practice as she called to tell me she'd been invited to a party at the Ealys' place that night. *You have to come*, she'd said. *You need to get in with the right people.* Girls like the cheerleaders, who always had an in with Bo Ealy, the Gatsby of Carney, purveyor of Natty Ice and dark barn corners to hook up in.

Caroline secured us a ride. A caravan of cheerleaders, Smirnoff Ice already on their breath when they pulled up outside the Masons' house, where I told Mitch I was spending the night. I wondered aloud if the girl behind the wheel should be driving—what if we were pulled over?

The other girls laughed as if I had suggested a starship might beam us up from the road. "No one's pulling me over," the driver had said. "My godfather is the chief of police."

Caroline, who was on the lap of the girl wedged into the middle seat, tensed against my body. For a while after the murders, I survived on the kindness of strangers. If I'd been paying attention, I would have noticed how the mood in town had shifted against my family, how I was becoming a social liability.

When we arrived at the bonfire at Bo Ealy's, Caroline promptly disappeared on me. The boy who found me, unmoored and debating walking home, looked like maybe he was a senior, but I'd later learn he was in his twenties.

His smile was wolflike as he offered me a Bud Light. I don't remember his name or his face—only Dani Burkhardt, watching us, through the smoke from the bonfire. Body like a golden pear in cutoffs, D cups straining against her crocheted white halter top. When the boy left to fetch us more beers, she marched up to me, steered me away by my arm.

"His ex is fuckin' crazy," she said. "She's got a box cutter."

Dani was dating Bo Ealy, she told me, but she was pissed at him for talking to another girl. She and I spent the next few hours in the barn beyond the farmhands' cottage, passing a bottle of Bacardi back and forth. Caroline, red-faced and hysterical because the other cheerleaders had left without telling her, found us giggling on our backs on a pile of hay.

After that night, Dani and I were inseparable. She got me a job at the Wendy's drive-through, and she did my makeup in the bathroom before taking me to parties hosted by guys who were much too old for both of us. Dani was on the cusp of her senior year, although there was some talk of her having to repeat eleventh grade.

I heard the things people whispered about us. That Dani had no friends her own age because she'd cycled through them all. Slept with their boyfriends, talked shit about them, never paid back money she borrowed. I didn't care. Being in Dani's orbit afforded me the anonymity I'd been craving since the murders. I was no longer the Newsom girl but *that girl who hangs around Dani Burkhardt.*

That spring, a few weeks before the incident at Bo Ealy's, Dani's older brother left the Triple Crown and wrapped his motorcycle around a tree. I spent the night of his funeral with Dani, at her grandmother's house. After we'd drunk an entire box of Franzia, she told me Tommy had been molesting her since she was nine years old.

I thought of the last time I'd seen Dani. I was stuck at the Riverhead Inn, my last shift before I had to leave for my freshman year at Binghamton. One of my tables was lingering past the kitchen closing, and I was worried about Mitch giving me a hard time because she did not like when I came home after ten.

I'd been lurking in the hall between the bar and dining room, my eye on that table's unpaid check, when the bathroom door banged open. She stumbled out, pupils the size of dimes. It had been three years since we'd spoken, and Dani looked through me as if she did not recognize me, and for this reason I decided to be cruel.

I muttered "Fucking cokehead" before I disappeared into the kitchen. After that, I stopped searching for her face everywhere I went in town.

I'd stopped searching for her, and sometime after, Dani Burkhardt had disappeared.

❧

I was on 42, rolling past the Carney Police Department for the third time. I would have looked unhinged to passersby, had there been any. This stretch of highway was in the opposite direction of town, miles from the tourists clogging the cluster of businesses on Main Street that would shutter for the winter months.

If I kept driving, I would pass the Triple Crown, ironically placed less than a mile from the police department. The place was a no-man's-land, the type of building law enforcement stayed away from. My grandfather on my dad's side, who died before I was born, was said to have frequented the TC, feeding his paychecks to the Quick Draw machine and leaving Mitch to stuff wads of toilet paper in her panties when she began to bleed because he could not afford pads.

Dani had snuck me into the Triple Crown once. She'd told me we were meeting some guys she'd met in Fallsburg over the weekend. In hindsight, I recognized that she must have met them while buying drugs.

Dani disappeared with one of the guys while the other had me cornered by the dartboard. "Let me get you a drink."

"No, thank you."

"Honey, when a man offers you a drink, you take it."

The shots of SoCo I'd done in Dani's bedroom swirled in my gut. The eyes in the bar were yellow, wolfish. I wanted to go home. I mumbled an excuse about needing the bathroom and bust into the water closet without knocking and I found Dani, bent over the sink, snorting coke from the debit card she had used to apply my eyeliner earlier.

I bolted, and she found me in the parking lot, shivering. Behind the dumpster, wet slapping sounds and a woman's exaggerated moan.

She grabbed my wrists, nails digging into my skin, while I babbled about how scared I was, how scared I was when she left me with that man.

"Nothing was going to happen to you," she snapped, pulling me to her. The first hug she'd ever given me, and all I remembered was the violence of it, as if it were not an embrace at all but a warning. "Nothing is *ever* going to happen to you."

I shook the memory out of my head, the old vacuum repair shop across the TC coming into focus. In the window was the same AVAILABLE FOR RENT sign that had been there since I'd left for college.

I continued on 42 and turned at the brick sign inscribed with CARNEY POLICE DEPARTMENT and followed the long stretch of asphalt to the campus.

A squat brown building stood at the edge of the parking lot, which housed three cruisers and a jail transport van. I cut my engine, a high-pitched thrum in my ears.

I stepped out of my Accord, my legs wobbling as my feet met the pavement. I did not have to do this. Meacham had all but told me not to do this.

I rolled my shoulder until it cracked and headed for the entrance.

Inside, the hum of a fan. The sole occupant of the waiting room was an elderly woman in Coke-bottle glasses who wore a down jacket, despite the heat. She hunched over paperwork while the man behind the desk observed her, bored.

Underneath his polo and khakis, his body was like a Ken doll's. His sandy hair was shaved close to his head, and both cheeks bore constellations of acne. Early twenties maybe, much younger than I'd initially pegged him. He looked up at me, his jaw working to fight a yawn. "Help you?"

"I was hoping to speak with a detective," I said. "About a missing person."

"Okay. Has it been at least forty-eight hours?"

"She's already been reported missing. She's a friend of mine, and I wanted to know if there have been any updates to her case."

"What's her name? I'll see who's handling it."

"Danica Burkhardt."

The kid typed, eyes on his screen, devoid of any indication Dani's name meant something to him. His gaze flit up and down his computer screen. "Looks like you'd have to talk to Detective McElhenny."

A pinprick of panic that I'd missed him, that Rhodes had put his retirement papers in this morning. "The last time I checked NamUs, it said the detective was named Rhodes. Did he retire or something?"

"No, Steve is still here." A question was brewing in the kid's eyes.

I tried to keep my voice even, uncurious. "Is there a reason he'd be taken off her case?"

"One detective used to handle missing persons and narcotics. Now there's a detective assigned to each."

And the man who was suspended for planting drugs on a suspect now worked in narcotics. "Is Detective Rhodes here?" I asked. "He was the one who originally had Dani's case. I'd really like to talk to him, if possible."

The kid looked over his shoulder. "I could see if he's at his desk—give me a minute."

The kid rose, wincing, kneading his knee as he headed down the hall off his desk. Above his computer was an IRQ sticker. Honorable discharge, I'd wager. Probably came home too fucked-up to be allowed to hold a gun.

Silence, except for the hum of the fan, punctuated by the old woman's phlegmy cough, reminding me I was not alone. The urge to flee rose up in me. I'd imagined coming face-to-face with Rhodes before, usually out of nowhere. While rounding the pharmacy aisle in Walmart, thinking, *What if he's right there, buying Tums?*

What would I say?

Banter, in the hall, a booming voice that drained the blood from my head. The desk boy had returned, and he wasn't alone.

Rhodes had put on weight, and his head was bare and shiny as a cue ball. His face was the same, a permanent crease in his forehead the only evidence of the years that had passed since the only photo of him that existed online was taken.

Stephen Rhodes didn't offer me a hand. He barely seemed to register my presence at all, his voice affable as he said, "Let's go talk in my office."

I followed the man who killed my family to a room at the rear of a building, the door wedged between a water cooler and an anemic-looking fan palm. I lingered at the threshold while Rhodes dragged a chair from the corner, plunked it opposite his desk.

I swallowed my heartbeat as I sat, eyes on Rhodes. I searched his face for any trace of humanity. Any indication he was the sort of killer to spare a small child who could not identify him.

He knotted meaty fingers together, leaned back in his chair. "So. Danica."

Dani had hated her full name, even though it had an otherworldly quality, an exotic bird among dozens of Katies and Ashleys and Jessicas.

"She was a good friend of mine," I said, when I found my voice. "I saw her missing poster on Facebook this morning."

Rhodes spun a small semicircle in his chair, giving me a look that read, *Can't be* that *good of a friend, then.* After a beat, he said, "You're from Carney?"

"Spring Meadow," I lied. "We worked at the Wendy's together. I guess I'm just confused why it took over a year for her to be reported missing."

Rhodes sighed. "Danica, Danica. I don't know what to say, except some people don't want to be found."

"Who reported her missing?" I asked.

"Some distant cousin noticed she hadn't been posting on Facebook for a while. She got on us to file a report, and it turned out no one had heard from her since summer 2021."

"And why do you think she disappeared on her own?"

"Danica was bipolar, already had a bunch of rehab stays under her belt. She'd just been fired, and several of her coworkers said she'd relapsed."

Rhodes cocked his head. "You didn't know she was an addict?"

I never knew if her brother's death was the catalyst for Dani's drug use or simply an excuse to stop hiding it, but she wasn't the same after his funeral. I thought of the scene I'd busted in on at the TC, what I suspected Dani had done to score drugs from the Fallsburg guy.

"Her brother's death was hard on her," I said to Rhodes. "And her grandma got cancer not long after."

Rhodes gave me a sad little smile. "Dani first used drugs when she was twelve years old. She gets mad at her grandmother one day, runs away from home. Her mother was out of prison at the time. Dani tracked her down to some hovel, and they smoked together."

I said nothing, my pulse gaining momentum. *Dani.* Rhodes had insisted on calling her Danica at the beginning of the meeting.

Rhodes turned to the AC unit below his window, cranked the power. "She stole Oxy from her sick grandmother, and when the pills ran out, she stole her money. She's an addict. Eventually addicts get tired of disappointing the people who care about them, and the only way to break the cycle is to disappear."

"Dani didn't have anyone left who cared about her," I said.

Rhodes smiled. "Yet here you are."

Gooseflesh rippled over my bare shins. "I just want to know someone is looking for her."

"We did what we could. Talked to all her coworkers at the strip club," Rhodes said. "Dani had been fired for stealing before she was reported missing, and she was seen at the bus stop in Port Jervis after her cell phone was turned off. If I had to guess, she was spooked about her boss pressing charges, so she skipped town."

"So you think she's alive."

"I think she was. But it's been a couple years." Rhodes held up his hands, palms to the ceiling. "There's a sickness in this town. Not everyone can escape, even if they leave."

He was staring at me now, a question forming in the crease between his eyes. "You still live in the area?"

I shook my head. "Left after college."

"Good for you." Rhodes nodded. "Good for you."

Chapter Eight

I was bent over in the parking lot of the Spring Meadow Rite Aid. One final adrenaline-fueled heave, and nothing. I was too empty. I went inside the drugstore, purchased a ginger ale and a water. I alternated baby sips of each, tormenting myself by looping the conversation with Rhodes.

The former Diane Rhodes had said her ex-husband had brutalized a sex worker after picking her up for a Starlight Tour.

I thought of the way Detective Rhodes's mouth curved around Dani's name, his confidence she had left town of her own accord. The mention of her coworkers at the strip club.

He targeted people he knew wouldn't report him—people no one would look for, in the event they didn't make it back to Carney alive.

I was across the street from Cloud 69, the only strip club within a fifteen-mile radius. I'd never had the privilege of visiting, but I'd heard you could buy anything there from a blow job to a horse tranquilizer. In high school, there was no greater insult to a classmate's mother or sister than to suggest she worked at Cloud 69.

Cloud 69 opened at 1:00 p.m. The venue was sitting at a solid three out of five stars on Google, with the top commenter lamenting the "50/50 ugly-to-pretty dancer ratio." I scrolled through the other reviews.

Don't even LOOK at the girls unless you want the psychotic bouncer to drag you out back and curb stomp you some skank stole my buddy's card and charged $400 to it when we went back the owner threw us out . . . STAY AWAY

great buffalo wings!

The neon signs in the blackened windows were the standard fare—busty effigies of women and Budweiser logos.

At ten minutes to one, a cherry-red Mustang peeled into the parking lot. A girl climbed out, lifting a vape pen to her lips. She wore a black dress wrapped around her body tight as gauze. A big girl, substantial chest.

The Mustang revved out of the lot, drawing the girl's attention to my car. Her face was pretty, tanned, heavily made up.

She headed for me. I sat, pinned to the driver's seat, wondering what I had possibly done to deserve such a swift confrontation. A moment later, the girl was tapping at my window with nails filed to stiletto points. I lowered the window.

"Samantha?" she said.

I blinked at the girl, trying and failing to place her. There was something familiar about the roundness to her face, her sleepy brown eyes.

"You don't remember me," she said.

"I'm sorry," I said. "You look so familiar."

"Brenna. Erin Corbin's sister." Brenna drew from her vape. The smell was a sticky fake strawberry, reminiscent of a lip gloss lost to the grime of my sixth-grade backpack. "You used to play at my house."

"God, right," I said. "Hey."

My voice betrayed how thrown I felt. Our third-grade teacher had caught Caroline Mason passing me a note mocking Erin Corbin's weight. A phone call home had led to a playdate being arranged between Erin and Caroline. Somehow, I had gotten roped into being there at the Masons' house. Renee Mason, Caroline's mother, had arranged a spa day. Cucumber sandwiches, manicures.

Caroline was forced to accept the fact that chubby little Erin Corbin was actually a suitable playmate. Eager to please, loyal and funny. The three of us were inseparable for the next couple of years, until we finally secured an invitation to Erin's house.

She had twin siblings, grimy-faced little girls who were too big for the Pull-Ups they wore. Brenna and another girl, her name forgotten to me. Caroline, an only child, might have been able to get past the annoying sisters, but the animals did her in.

There were so many. Guinea pigs that let out incessant squeals, as if they were being drowned. A bullmastiff that drooled on Caroline's lap while we watched *Ever After*. In the backyard, a shit-crusted chicken coop.

Caroline began quietly telling everyone at school that Erin's house smelled like a zoo.

I looked into Brenna Corbin's eyes and felt a blast of shame for how Caroline and I had treated her family. "How is Erin?"

"She's in South Carolina," Brenna said, as if that explained everything. She ran her hands over her bare arms. "Not to be rude, but, like, what are you doing here?"

I pointed to the strip club. "You work there?"

"I'm a cocktail waitress." Brenna's tone was neutral, but a muscle in her jaw pulsed. Daring me to suggest she did anything else but serve drinks within Cloud 69's walls.

"Did you work here at the same time as Dani Burkhardt?"

She shot a glance back at the club. She rounded my car, let herself in the passenger side. "Yeah, I worked with Dani. Why?"

Brenna was studying herself in the flip-down mirror. Long brown hair with honey highlights, well-maintained pillow lips. Pretty enough to net good tips. I wondered why she'd been saddled with a day shift until she swiped at her eyeliner, drawing my attention to the creases at her eyes. Pushing thirty, which would make her a dinosaur in strip club years.

"She's missing," I said. "We used to be friends, and I'm worried about her."

"Right," Brenna said. She kneaded her wrist, exposing a black tattoo. A crescent moon symbol, either a star or flower over it. "I mean, no one has heard from her, but she got into a huge fight with Billy before she left."

"Billy?"

"The owner. Dani kept coming to work high, and someone had been stealing from the till, so I guess Billy accused her, and she got pissed and said she wasn't coming back."

"I heard she got fired."

"Who fuckin' knows," Brenna said.

"What kind of drugs was Dani doing?" I asked.

"Whatever she could get her hands on." Brenna examined her nails, the smattering of gold glitter painted over the polish on her ring finger. "She got hooked on Oxy after her car accident."

"When was that?"

"Five, maybe six years ago? Dani was driving—her grandma was killed, and Dani needed neck surgery."

"I had no idea her grandma died," I said.

Dani's grandmother was a leathery-skinned woman who cleaned rooms at the Best Western in Birchwood Glenn. She was in her fifties, and although they fought like animals sometimes, Dani had been inconsolable when her grandmother was diagnosed with lymphoma.

"Do you know if she's tried to contact anyone since she was last seen?"

"She definitely wouldn't have tried to contact me," Brenna snorted. "Maybe one of the dancers, I don't know. They all liked Dani, 'cause when she was straight, she watched the customers like a hawk. They're not allowed to touch the dancers, but of course they do. None of them tried any shit when Dani was working."

Brenna looked down at the phone in her lap, slid a finger across the screen. "We open soon."

"One second." I pulled up the photo on my phone of Stephen Rhodes. "Have you ever seen this guy?"

Brenna was quiet for a beat. "Yeah, I know him. Like, I don't *know* him, but I know who he is. We all do."

"Does he ever come into the club?"

"Hell no." Brenna ran her hands down her arms, despite the heat. I waited for her to bring up my family, the rumors Rhodes had murdered them. She was young when it happened, but surely she must have heard at some point.

"You know he was the detective assigned to Dani's case, right?" I asked.

Brenna reached for the passenger-side door handle. "Why would I know that? I told you, we weren't friends."

"Wait," I called, but Brenna was already outside the car. I leaned over, caught the passenger door before she could slam it. "Do you have any idea where she might have gone if she left town?"

Brenna poked her head back in. "No. But she knows never to show her face here again."

I was mounting my phone to the dash when my screen lit up with an incoming call. Meacham. I let my finger hover over the answer button, pulse ticking, thinking of my visit to the police department this morning.

"There you are," he said.

"Where was I again?"

"I called you about fifteen minutes ago."

I glanced at my screen, the missed call in the bottom corner. "Sorry. I was catching up with an old friend."

"Where are you right now?"

I looked up at the blackened door of Cloud 69, the one Brenna Corbin had disappeared behind. The neon outline of a woman was rubbing her comically large ass up and down a pole. "Walmart."

"Want to meet at the 42 Café?" Meacham asked. "Couple things I want to go over with you."

My heart plummeted. Meacham's voice was even, empty of any indication of what he could want to talk about. He could have been calling to ream me out for going to talk to Rhodes this morning, or because my DNA sample had pinged a hit.

"Sure," I said.

Cloud 69 was another ten minutes east of Walmart, the opposite direction of Carney. I floored it back to town, parked in the lot of the 42 Café in time to spot Meacham beside a planter of marigolds outside the restaurant. He checked his phone, frowned, before bending to swipe a spot of dust from his shoes with the pad of his thumb.

"Sorry," I said, when I caught up to him. "Got held up at checkout."

"No worries."

Inside the 42 Café, a chalkboard sign invited us to seat ourselves. We grabbed a booth, the paper placemat menus on the table warped from the moisture in the air. The only waitress I could spot was occupied with a child who sat at the counter, an iPad propped in front of him.

The waitress caught me staring and hurried over, spilling apologies. A tag on her blouse read JULIE, the *J* partially blocked by a schoolkid's gold-star sticker. "What can I get you folks?"

Meacham smiled at her. "Any specials today?"

Julie hiked up her shoulder, wiping away the trail of sweat by her ear. "I've got Italian wedding soup, linguine with clams in white sauce—"

At this, Meacham lifted his eyebrows at me. I shook my head at him, as if to say, *Don't order seafood here.*

When she was finished rattling off the specials, Julie lowered her notepad with a wheeze. Meacham ordered a tuna melt and a seltzer, while I requested an unsweetened ice tea and a chicken sandwich.

"Be right back with those drinks." Julie plunked wrapped sets of silverware on the table and disappeared.

Meacham sighed heavily, unspooling the paper wrap from his silverware. "Samantha. You're killing me."

I pled the Fifth for a beat, until Meacham looked up at me. "I spoke with Diane Tomlinson this morning."

"Who?"

"Rhodes's ex-wife."

So, then, this wasn't about my drop-in at the police department. Still, Meacham looked pissed, and the thought of him learning how I'd spent *my* morning had me praying the booth's cushions would consume me like a Venus flytrap.

Meacham shook his head, clearly disappointed in my silence. "You're killing me," he said again. "Absolutely killing me. You're god-damn lucky his ex-wife didn't call Rhodes up."

I should have groveled, maybe, because I really did want him to keep me in the loop, but I could think of nothing but Diane telling me about the prostitute Rhodes had assaulted and left for dead. Brenna Corbin's reaction to Rhodes's photo. Her reluctance to talk about Dani.

"Diane is afraid of him," I said. "Everyone is, and that's why he gets to keep hurting people."

Meacham was quiet, knocking his straw against the table until the wrapper came off.

"Did she tell you about the Starlight Tours?" I asked.

"I spoke to the former chief of police back when I inherited the case." Meacham plunked his straw into his seltzer. "There were enough rumors that they eventually barred Rhodes from working the night shift, but none of his victims ever made a formal complaint against him."

It unsettled me, the casual way Meacham said *victims*. As if victims were a perfectly normal thing for a police officer to have. "What about Luiza Witkowski?"

Meacham took a pull from his seltzer, his eyebrows lifting.

"She was a migrant worker who went missing in '01. There's rumors Rhodes killed her." I halted short of telling Meacham about the passport, the duffel bag Scott had allegedly seen in Rhodes's cruiser the day of his assault. I didn't want to tip him off that I'd spoken to Ed Robinette.

I knew how it sounded—that he'd cleaned out my wallet and given me some crackpot story in exchange. I knew I was coming across as obsessed with Stephen Rhodes.

If I were being honest with myself, sure, I was obsessed with Rhodes. I'd told myself the visit to the police station was out of concern for Dani, an estranged friend I still cared for, but I had wanted to look the man in the eye.

I had hoped, I realized now, that he might recognize me. That after twenty-two years, he might finally feel the fear that he would not get away with killing my entire family.

Meacham was still silent, studying me over the mouth of his straw, as if I were an inscrutable painting.

I swirled my own straw through my ice tea. "Was Luiza Witkowski ever mentioned in any of the Starlight Tour stories?"

"Even if she was, I wouldn't be able to discuss other investigations with you."

"Then what about the cops Rhodes played poker with?" I said. "Diane basically said his partner was a cokehead."

Two angry cops on a Saturday night, wallets cleaned out, maybe a few drinks deep. Talking about how to make the Newsom family pay for threatening to sue the department.

"The poker crew all sat down with Holcombe in '01," Meacham said. "Everyone's story matched: Rhodes got knocked out of the game around nine, threw a fit about it, and left with an officer who lived across town. The timeline is just too tight for him to have been at the farmhouse between nine and ten thirty."

"*If* he drove his partner home like he said he did. A guy who conveniently died of a drug habit Rhodes helped fund."

"Sam." Meacham's voice was algebra-tutor patient, as if I just weren't *getting it*. "The other men at the game had no reason to lie. To pull off a cover-up of that scale—it doesn't make any sense."

Because you weren't fucking there, I thought. I was there, in the car that afternoon, with my mother and Lyndsey, when the police cruiser appeared in her rear window, closer and closer until whoever was driving had run us off 42, Lyndsey thrashing and screaming in her car seat.

I had crawled into the back to soothe her while my mother bent her head to the steering wheel and screamed. A primal, awful sound that I still heard in my dreams sometimes. The sound of a mother who had realized she was powerless to protect her children.

I set my glass down, loud enough to startle the child sitting at the counter.

"The police *hated us*," I said. "You know what it's like to be afraid to leave the house because cops want you dead?"

Meacham's smile, patient, placating, never made it to his eyes. Blood flowed hot to my cheeks.

"I'm sorry," I said. "That was a fucked-up thing to say to a Black man."

"Samantha, I know you didn't mean any harm."

"I just get defensive about my parents." I was nervous-babbling now. "The police basically ran a smear campaign, saying we were trash. But they were good people."

It was important to me that Meacham knew it. I had no idea what was in those interviews he'd pored over, but I knew the sorts of things people said about my family. My mother, in particular, was the target of judgment among those who believed the murders were drug related. Marnie Newsom knew Scott was growing pot on the property. She lied to her own husband about how much her brother was selling, because the extra cash meant she didn't have to pick up extra shifts at the Walmart.

Everyone knew the Ginnses were a lazy bunch. It began when my grandfather, who had managed a local stable, broke his back after being thrown from a horse. My mother and Scott were still in diapers, and Grandma Lynn had never worked. The disability checks weren't cutting it, so my grandparents began fostering children. In the photos I remembered, the ones that hadn't survived the fire, my mom always had a baby at her hip, even as a young girl.

Before she graduated from high school, Grandpa Ginns died, along with my mother's dream of attending veterinary school. Medicaid barely covered the surgeries and care Scott needed after he lost his eye. Grandma Lynn was sickly, unable to take in more children. They would have lost the farmhouse as well if my mother didn't stay in Carney after high school to work.

"Samantha, I have to ask," Meacham said. "How did your parents get along?"

They were happy, I thought. Happy enough, at least. I had been a surprise, the result of a summer dalliance not long after my mom graduated. My parents had married at the town hall shortly after my mother learned she was pregnant.

My father used to joke that he had snagged the prettiest girl in Carney, but on some level, he must have known. Even I noticed it as a child. The way he would sneak up behind my mother at the sink, the way her body tilted away from his while he kissed her neck.

My mother didn't love my father, but her commitment to him, the father of her children, a man she felt no passion for—in some ways, I thought their marriage was the most romantic thing I'd ever witnessed.

"They were happy," I said finally. "But after my grandmother died and Lyndsey was born, my mom was pretty depressed, I guess."

"Was she excited about the pregnancy?" Meacham asked.

My mother, at the table with Mitch, head in her hands. *What am I going to do?* I tamped the memory down; after all this time, I was still programmed to protect my mother's secret. She had not wanted another child.

"What does any of this matter?" I asked. "My mom was the least likely person in that house someone would have wanted to murder."

I sounded like one of those women interviewed on *Dateline*, pink-nosed, drunk with denial. *My loved one who was brutally murdered was loved by everyone, I swear.* "My mother was a cashier at Walmart, for Christ's sake. My father was a farmhand. My uncle was a drug dealer who pissed off a sociopathic cop. It's Occam's razor."

I quieted as Julie returned, arms weighed down by our meals. Neither of us moved to touch our plates.

"Where are you at with my DNA sample?" I asked.

"Samantha. You need to trust I have a handle on this investigation."

"How? If you're not up the only viable suspect's ass, if you're not out there *looking for her* . . ." I grabbed a grease-heavy french fry, petulantly shoved it in my mouth.

"I'm up the DA's ass about Boggs," Meacham said. "Every night, I spend hours rereading the interviews from '01, hoping there's something I missed. A clue to the car, someone who warranted another look and never got one."

"You're not going to find the car unless Boggs talks," I said. "He's not going to talk unless he gets something out of it."

"We don't know that. With time, and pressure, he may do the right thing."

I crushed an ice cube between my back teeth. I thought of March 2020, working in the ICU. Watching people die, alone, gasping for air, their family members cursing me out over the phone for telling them they could not come to say goodbye. Waking up every evening to do it all over again, knowing it didn't have to be that way. Knowing that people were incapable of doing the right thing unless it benefited their own interests.

"Samantha," Meacham said. "Even without the car, I'm not going to stop looking for who did this—for her."

I said nothing as I sipped my ice tea. I thought of Dani, of Luiza Witkowski. Of the hundreds of thousands of people who go missing every year, each with better odds at being found than a little girl, lost to either fire or the night, over twenty years ago. Of all of them, why had Lyndsey captured Meacham's full attention?

Chapter Nine

I wanted nothing more than to knock out when I got back to Gil's, my inedible chicken sandwich heavy in my stomach, slowing me down. But the bagged fridge detritus by the front door was going rank in the heat. I hauled the bags outside, the sun sinking lower with each trip to the driveway.

In the early evening, Taylor Edwards pulled into Gil's driveway as I battled with a trash bag threatening to bust at the seams. He killed his engine, a smile blooming on his face.

"Hey." I dropped the bag as Taylor held out a white paper bag spotted with grease. I took it and peeked inside.

"From the farm," Taylor said, although the bag's contents needed no explanation. Ealy's pies were too dry for my taste, the crusts overbaked, but their muffins were to die for. On the rare days where some remained unsold at the end of the day, Rhi would bring them home for Mitch and me.

Before I could protest, Taylor was lifting the trash bag I'd abandoned by the porch. "Jesus, what's in here?"

"Besides every issue of *Playboy* printed since '89?"

Taylor laughed, even though I was serious. I had a flash of myself, wandering the detached garage behind our property, where my mother had banished the shit she'd cleared from Gil's and Scott's old rooms in the farmhouse. I'd gone snooping inside a water-stained box, saw a magazine with a naked woman on the cover, shaving her pussy.

How sad, I thought, *that the nudie rags had survived while the dollhouse my grandfather had built my mother had burned.*

"You got someone coming to pick up all this trash?" Taylor asked.

"I was just going to drive it to the dump."

"In that tiny-ass car? It would take you ten trips."

"If only I knew someone with a truck," I said.

Taylor grinned. "And I thought I was here because of my charming personality."

"I'll buy you dinner," I said, but Taylor was already tossing the trash bags into the bed of his truck.

"And you are very charming," I added.

"It's okay." Taylor grunted. "I'm used to girls ditching me for CJ."

"I'm not interested in my cousin's baby daddy," I said.

Taylor laughed. "Well, CJ and the baby mama are not together."

"Were they ever?" I snuck a hardened drizzle of cinnamon frosting from one of the muffins, let it dissolve on my tongue.

"No one really knows."

Since puberty, my cousin had hewn close to my aunt's philosophy about men. They could not be relied on for anything, from staying sober to giving orgasms to cutting a support check on time. The only good men who had ever existed had been my grandfather and my father.

When he was finished, the tailgate secure, Taylor wiped his brow.

"I really appreciate this," I said. "And I was serious about dinner."

"There's a Sonic on the way home from the dump."

"Cheap date."

Taylor grinned as he opened the passenger door for me. "That's what this is?"

When we hit the highway, Taylor lowered the windows, raised the volume on the radio. I tilted my head back, let the setting sun turn the insides of my eyelids pink. I felt like I'd lived half a dozen lives since this morning.

My thoughts kept circling my conversation with Rhodes. I waited until the bags were unloaded at the dump, until Sonic was consumed, and Taylor and I sat, full and greasy fingered, in the parking lot.

"Do you remember Dani Burkhardt?" I asked. "She dated your brother back in high school."

"Dani. Wow." Taylor took a pull from his soda. "I saw her a couple years ago, tending bar."

"At Cloud 69?"

Taylor flushed. "I was there for my buddy's bachelor party."

"You don't have to be embarrassed you went to a strip club," I said.

"Well, I mean, *that* strip club." Taylor thought for a beat, lowered the radio volume. "What made you think of Dani?"

"Did you know she's missing?"

"Missing? Shit. I mean, I can't say I'm surprised. We had a whole conversation, but I don't think she even remembered who I was."

In the cupholder, Taylor's phone started to ring. He dabbed his lips with a napkin, checked the caller.

Taylor swiped at the screen, stuck his phone between his ear and shoulder so he could use both hands to stuff his trash into the Sonic bag.

"Hey." He listened, nodding, even though CJ could not see him, before ending the call with a curt "Okay."

"Some of the kids are drinking down at the orchard," Taylor sighed. "I've been summoned to go break up the party."

"CJ can't do it?"

"He's out of town, and Rhi's putting Kaylee to bed." Taylor's voice had gone flat, maybe at the prospect of our night being cut short.

"You want backup?" I asked.

"Are you sure?" A goofy grin spread across his face as he shifted the truck out of park. "These kids know how to cut to the core. Apparently my using emojis means I'm old and uncool or something?"

"Tay, a patient tried to choke me last week. I'm not afraid of a bunch of teenagers."

He laughed, and I couldn't help myself from reaching for the back of his neck, trailing my fingers across the smooth skin there.

Taylor drove past the farm, long closed for the day, and made a right onto the road with signs pointing to the U-Pick orchard. His truck lumbered over the dirt path like the ones I'd walked as a child, paper bag filled to bursting with Pink Ladies. At this time of year, the fruit on the trees was unripe. Music leaked through them, guiding us to a clearing marked off by a wooden split-rail fence.

Eight or so bodies were gathered by the fence, some of them perched atop it. Taylor looked at them, shook his head. Despite his warning, I couldn't help feeling like a relic. My shirt was twice the length of what was in style. The girls were all tanned, with bee-stung lips. One of them lowered her White Claw from her mouth and shouted, "Uh-oh, Daddy's here!"

"Hailey wishes he'd be her daddy!" said a tiny blonde in itty-bitty jean shorts, a gauzy peach top that matched the color in her booze-warmed cheeks.

"Get fucked." The third girl, Hailey, I presumed. She'd been the only one to clam up when we arrived. Pretty eyes, meticulously winged with black liner, kept finding Taylor.

Some snorts from the guys, all of them with their eyes cast downward as the blonde in the peach shirt hopped off the fence. "Want a beer, Tay?"

"What? No, I do not want a beer." Taylor gestured to the set of iPhone speakers, the music pulsing from them. "What is this garbage?"

The girls erupted in laughter, the one holding a White Claw shouting over the others. The tallest, and loudest, and also the homeliest.

"Billie *Eilish*!" She wore a Led Zeppelin crop top and sat in the lap of one of the guys. He had a hand over her flat, tanned tummy, his thumb hooked in the waist of her denim cutoffs. He eyed me curiously, and I realized how I knew him. The boy behind the desk at the police station, with the empty eyes and a fucked-up knee.

"Who's your friend, you big slut?" Peach Shirt nudged Taylor with her elbow.

"None of your business," Taylor said.

Peach Shirt looked me up and down, blinking feathery lashes. These were not the city kids Rhi had complained about. I ventured that many of them had been conceived in this very orchard. The girl in the peach shirt, in particular, screamed Carney-bred through and through, a natural boldness aided by whatever had shrunk her pupils to pinpoints.

The shyest girl, Hailey, kicked her cowboy boots against the fence rail. "Rhiannon's cousin, right?"

Before I could open my mouth, Peach cracked another beer, shouted over the foam spurting out of the can. "Fuck Rhiannon!"

"She signs your shitty paycheck, so watch your mouth," Taylor said.

"Who invited Grandpa?"

The voice came from beyond the apple trees. A skaggy-looking kid emerged, adjusting his zipper. His dirty-blond hair was slicked down his forehead, a silver chain around his neck.

Taylor's jaw hardened. "What're you doing here, Cory?"

The kid sipped his beer. "Was invited."

"The fuck you were. CJ told you what would happen if he ever saw you here again."

"So he sent his bitch boy to handle me?" Cory smirked.

Taylor took a step toward Cory, lightning fast, and swatted the beer can out of the kid's hand.

Cory's expression shifted. The kid from the police station hopped off the fence, joined one of the other guys in taking a step toward Taylor. My breath stalled.

"Oh my God, chill!" Peach Shirt shrieked.

I took in the boys' faces, the dots of acne along their jaws. They were older than I'd initially pegged them, probably old enough to buy the girls beer. No doubt they had also supplied whatever drugs were making Peach Shirt sweaty around the lips. Cory looked Taylor up and down, shook his head. "Yo, fuck this. Let's go."

Taylor killed the music. "Party's over."

From the girls, a chorus of "Come on" and "Noooo, pleeease, Tay!"

"Y'all are being way too loud," Taylor said. "And get rid of those cans unless you don't want a job when you wake up."

"Stay and help us drink it!" said the girl in the Led Zeppelin shirt. Their male companions were already retreating. Cory, the one who had gotten Taylor so riled, stuck his tongue between his fingers at us as a parting message.

Taylor let out a beleaguered sigh and looked at me. "Ready to go?"

The girl in the cowboy boots' face fell. I felt for her; I remembered being that young, that crushing sense of longing for men too old for me.

"Stay for Hailey!" Peach Shirt shouted again. "She wants you so bad!"

Taylor looked like he wanted to die, as did poor Hailey, who was suddenly consumed with the screen of her phone. Taylor lifted a hand over his shoulder but did not turn around. "Go home! And quit hanging out with shitbags who are too old for you!"

We headed back down the path, their hollering petering out.

"Who was the Eminem wannabe?" I asked.

"Cory?" Taylor shoved his hands in his pockets, gaze flitting up to the moon. "A huge pain in my ass."

I could tell he didn't want to expound on the matter, so I nudged his arm, playful. "Seems like you have quite a fan club back there."

Taylor finally said, "What they were saying—they were just messing around."

"You don't have to explain yourself."

"What Tori said when she saw you—I don't . . ."

I thought of Taylor's admission the other night, how he'd always had a crush on me. Something primal flared in me. I halted on the path. When Taylor stopped, a question forming on his face, I grabbed the loop of his jeans and pulled his hips to mine.

"Here? Really?"

"Stop talking, slut."

His mouth was warm, his tongue sloppy and roaming. I did not need him to be a good kisser. I tugged the zipper of his jeans down and reached inside, feeling him turn hard in my hand.

Fingers, at the hem of my shirt, pulling it over my head. Taylor ran his thumbs down my bare stomach.

"Holy shit," he murmured. He grabbed me by the hand, guided me to a tree at the edge of the path. He leaned against it and I fell into him. Taylor rubbed a thumb over my right nipple, moving his opposite hand down my stomach and to the button on my jeans.

I tugged down his boxers until he was exposed, erect, and while I guided him into me, I had to stop myself from laughing because of what he'd said the other night. *I can't believe I'm smoking with Samantha Newsom.*

Thankfully, Taylor did not say, *I can't believe I'm fucking Samantha Newsom.* He said nothing at all, his face tilted to the moonlight, lips parted, eyes closed. Once I could tell he was about to come, I moved his hand lower, his fingers frantic as he brought us both to the brink of climax.

"Sam," he gasped. "I gotta come out."

He came, hot and quickly on my pelvis, as I finished myself. Taylor stripped his hoodie off, wiped himself from my skin, the look on his face tender.

And I saw his half brother's face. I felt the crush of Bo Ealy's body on mine, a girl screaming, *Are you serious?* And then I saw her, face bathed in moonlight. Dani Burkhardt, my best friend, angry enough to kill me.

Bo had scrambled off me, muttering that he was looking for his keys.

In her twat?

I couldn't look at Dani. I pulled my pants up and I ran because I knew it was already too late. I was dead to her. I did not stop running until I reached my aunt's house, limbs numb with the cold by the time I arrived.

Taylor sighed, heavy, content, drawing me back to the orchard. The moon was garishly white, blinding. I reminded myself that I had enjoyed it, wanted it this time. Taylor was gentle in the ways his brother was not. He pressed his lips to my forehead, and even though they were warm, I was cold.

Chapter Ten

After the farm, a trip to the gas station convenience store for chips and beer. We drank in Taylor's truck, made out for a bit like a couple of high school kids. He had me back at Gil's by ten, as he had to be on a delivery route early in the morning.

"That was fun," Taylor said, engine purring beneath us.

"It was."

"I'm off Sunday," he said, twirling a bit of my escaped hair around his finger.

"Any fun plans?"

"Want to grab breakfast?"

"I'm leaving next week, you know."

"It's just breakfast, Sam." Taylor smiled, but there was a question in his eyes.

"Sure. Just breakfast."

I waited by the front door, watching him loop around Gil's driveway, his truck lights fading after he turned onto 42.

Inside, I brushed the taste of corn chips and Bud Light out of my mouth, thinking again of Dani.

She could be alive. If Stephen Rhodes had taken her on a Starlight Tour, maybe she'd simply opted not to come back to Carney. What was left for her here anyway? She'd lost her job at Cloud 69, and according to Brenna Corbin, she'd lost the only person Dani had ever cared about disappointing.

I'd only met Dani's grandmother a few times. She was rarely home, between her job at the Best Western and dates with the elderly widowers she met there. I realized now that I did not even remember her grandmother's name.

I searched *Carney fatal accident* and found an article from 2017.

> The identity of a woman killed in a collision this weekend has been released. Nina Pollack, 53, was the passenger of a 2001 Nissan Sentra that crossed a guardrail. The driver of the Nissan was taken to Catskills Medical Center for minor injuries. Drugs and alcohol were not a factor in the crash. Weather is believed to have caused the unnamed woman to have lost control of the vehicle.

Brenna was right: the crash hadn't been Dani's fault. She'd been sober.

I opened Facebook and searched for Nina Pollack. The top result was a woman with an overlay on her profile photo of a peace sign. Dani's grandmother smiled in the photo, not showing her teeth, just like Dani refused to do for pictures.

I always felt ghoulish when I happened on a dead individual's Facebook page. I was guilty of seeking them out every so often when I lost a patient, when I felt myself on the verge of disassociating. It was wrong; it was digital grave robbing. But sometimes I needed to know, especially when there had been no family there at the end, that a person had been cared about. Sometimes it helped fend off the creeping darkness, the worry that there wouldn't be anyone there in my own final moments.

The latest post Nina Pollack had been tagged in was dated over a year ago. A glittering explosion of flowers surrounding Happy Birthday in Heaven.

I kept scrolling through the tribute posts until I found a photo that made me freeze. A much younger Nina Pollack had her cheek pressed to a little girl's. The image had a grainy quality, as if it had been scanned from an older photograph. The child was blonde, freckled, and missing her two front teeth.

Can't believe it's been a year without you

Dani Elise.

I clicked on her name, my insides going hollow. My senior year of high school, when I got a job waiting tables at the Riverhead Inn, I found myself on high alert after 10:00 p.m. Always eyeing the bar, especially if I saw a younger blonde seated there. Waiting, always, for glimpses of the faces that were never Dani's, imagining what I might say.

I'd explain myself, that I never wanted her ex-boyfriend. I'd tell her off for abandoning me at the Triple Crown, and then again at Bo Ealy's.

I'd beg her to take me back, because I could not walk through a CVS without smelling her cotton-candy perfume and remembering the last time I felt like I was home.

In the Facebook profile photo, Dani was no longer blonde. Her hair was to her shoulders, dyed a head-turning shade of red. She was looking backward, over her shoulder, smirking. Dani's face looked round, healthy. In one hand was a Solo cup, a paper bracelet around her wrist.

Her most recent activity was the addition of this profile picture, five years ago. Either Dani had updated her privacy settings or she had not used her Facebook account since 2019, almost two years before she'd last been seen in town.

There were several posts before 2019. That tribute to her grandmother, a photo of a truck with monstrous wheels taking up two spaces in a parking lot, with a caption: Someone's got a tiny winky dink

Her posts had very few likes, save for one in November of 2016. If you voted for Trump fucking unfriend me. Thirty likes, and nearly a hundred comments. For days, Dani had sparred back and forth with names, mostly male, that I did not recognize.

Talk to me when you've actually BEEN raped, asshole

I knew what her brother had done to her and how she never told her grandmother because it would kill her, another hit to their already fractured family. It made me sick to think of it, but something told me Dani's Facebook comment about being raped had not been about her brother at all.

In any case, I did not get the sense the people who had commented on this post were friends of Dani's in any sense. I scrolled back up to her profile photo and loaded the comments.

Hottie 😉

Someone named Jay Matera. It was the only comment Dani had "liked."

I followed the link to Jay's profile. His privacy settings were locked down tighter than Fort Knox, and I wasn't able to message him since we had no mutual friends.

I googled *Jay Matera New York*. The top hit was a wedding website for Jason Matera and Arianna Towsen.

I scrolled through their engagement photos, their Bed Bath & Beyond registry filled with pricey china. Jay Matera had gained a few pounds since his Facebook profile picture, but the faces matched. Dark hair, blue eyes, Mediterranean complexion. Good-looking guy. Some more poking around and I found that Jason Matera was an adviser at Wells Fargo in Narrowsburg, New York.

I brewed an undrinkable cup of coffee and resumed emptying Gil's dresser. Clothes, bagged, to be dropped at Goodwill. Sneaking glances at the microwave clock between trips to my car.

An hour or two of sleep, interrupted by staccato bursts of panic, turning over in my head what I might say to Jay Matera.

At 9:00 a.m., I dialed the number for Wells Fargo and asked to be transferred to his office. The overly peppy receptionist didn't ask questions. A millisecond on hold, then: "Jay speaking."

"Hi. My name is Sam Newsom. Is this a good time?"

"It's always a good time to plan for the future." Matera sounded affable, ready to pitch me on term life insurance.

"I'm actually trying to track down an old friend. I saw you commented on a Facebook post she made. Dani Burkhardt?"

Matera's end went quiet. Then, the click of a door shutting. "I'm sorry, what did you say your name was again?" Stalling.

"Sam," I said. "I went to high school with Dani."

"Sam, right. I have no idea what Dani is up to these days. You said you found me through her Facebook?"

I detected what sounded like the furious clicking of a mouse. I guessed Jay was deleting his *hottie* comment from Dani's Facebook before the future Mrs. Matera could see.

"You left a pretty friendly comment for her," I said.

"We were friendly, yeah. But I haven't heard from her since I broke things off."

Matera was picking his words carefully. Making sure I knew he and Dani hadn't been serious, that the relationship ended on his terms. Interesting.

"You didn't hear that she's missing?"

"I honestly don't know what to tell you. We broke up, what, three years ago? I wasn't interested in keeping in touch."

"Because she was using drugs?"

Matera's voice was softer when he spoke again. "Look, there's shit in my past I'm not proud of. I mean, I met Dani at Narcotics Anonymous. My fiancée knows all this, but her family—her dad is my boss. We agreed my history was my business."

So then, Jay Matera was an addict too. I wasn't surprised. In our brief time as friends, I'd seen Dani cycle through a series of boyfriends who shared her propensity for self-destruction. Speed demons who crashed their parents' cars, petty thieves. Even a boy who had slit his wrists and wound up in a coma after Dani dumped him.

"Is that why you broke up? Because she started using again?" I asked.

"I was already sober two years when we met," Matera said. "She'd just gotten out of rehab, and she was serious about staying off Oxy. We eventually moved in together. Things were great, until they weren't."

I knew the hurt, like a knife between the ribs. One moment we were curled against each other in Dani's bed, her secrets warm at the back of my neck, and the next, I was alone in the Triple Crown parking lot.

"What made her relapse?" I asked.

"She was working in this vet's office, and she loved it. But she wouldn't drive after her accident. She was late too many times because she couldn't find a ride, and they eventually fired her."

"So she got a job at Cloud 69."

"I told her it was a terrible idea. I used to score there. You go to that place after ten and the girls are practically snorting coke off the stage. I told Dani she wouldn't be able to stay sober there. She swore to me she only drank a little during her shift.

"One night she comes home with a fucking tooth knocked out. She's covered in blood, probably concussed. She tripped in the parking lot, and instead of bringing her to the emergency room, the bouncer dumped her on our doorstep and left. And Dani was *laughing* about it." Jay Matera sighed, and I imagined him kneading that baby-smooth face of his. "I told her to get out. I was done. She left and crashed with a friend from the club."

"Did you see her after that?"

"I called her all night to make sure she got to her friend's okay. She wouldn't answer her phone, so I stopped by the club the next day. She had the bouncer throw me out. Told him I was harassing her."

"I'm sorry," I said. "That's brutal."

"Yeah, well. That's Dani."

I still felt the memory of rejection, like someone pressing down on a bruise. Say the wrong thing and Dani would look at you in a way that made you wish you'd never gained the ability to speak. Betray her, and she would excise you like a tumor.

"The friend from the club she stayed with," I said. "Do you remember their name?"

"I don't know her real name. She was a dancer. Went by Harmony." Shame had crept into Jay Matera's voice. I was willing to bet he'd had some one-on-one time with Harmony back in his clubbing days.

"Listen, I really hope she's okay. I'm sorry if I sound cold or like I don't care. I really did," he said.

I thanked Jay Matera for his time, ended the call.

Harmony. Dani had crashed with a friend from the club named Harmony. I typed the word in my phone browser, scrolled until I found the symbol for harmony. A crescent moon on its back, a star above it. Just like the tattoo on Brenna Corbin's wrist.

Two p.m. on the dot. The air was thick with the threat of rain. I was in the parking lot of Cloud 69, psyching myself up to take another run at Brenna Corbin.

She knew more about Dani, about Rhodes, than she offered to me in my car yesterday. I'd been inclined to think it was because Brenna had no reason to want to help me.

Inside the club, I blinked, my eyes transitioning to the darkness. The stage at the center of the room was awash in green and blue. I made my way to the bar, aware of the lone dancer in the club, her tattooed arms wrapped around one of the poles. A dishwater blonde in a black bikini, bony, back arched like a cat. Stretching, bored.

The bouncer, an enormous bald man dressed all in black seated in a folding chair by the stage, disregarded me. Probably pegged me for a desperate day drinker.

Behind the bar, a door thwacked open. Brenna Corbin barreled out, carrying a crate of clean glasses. The sight of me sitting at the bar nearly sent them crashing to the floor. Brenna was quiet as she composed herself, but I detected the tremor in her fingers as she stacked the glasses under the bar.

"I can't talk while I'm working," she said.

"Okay. Do you think they'll talk to me about Dani?" I made a show of looking around the club. "Think the bouncer knows something?"

Brenna rounded the bar. I flinched, as if she were about to slap me, but she waved over the bouncer. He lifted his head, curious.

Brenna said, "Watch the bar for a sec."

She took off toward a curtained room labeled PRIVATE. I assumed I was meant to follow. Down a grimy tiled hall occupied by an ATM and two toilets. Brenna held open a door that led to a locker room.

The space smelled of sweat and hair spray, but Cloud 69's strippers were a tidy bunch by the looks of the dressing tables. Hair straighteners with the cords wrapped neatly around the handles, lip glosses arranged by color.

Brenna shut the door behind me. "What the fuck do you want from me?"

"Did Dani stay with you when her boyfriend kicked her out?"

"Yeah, for like a week. What does it matter?"

"You said you weren't friends."

Brenna turned her back to me, strode over to a locker marked by a holographic sticker in the shape of a lotus blossom. "We weren't. But she had nowhere else to go, and I wasn't gonna tell her no when she showed up at my house at two a.m. tweaked out of her mind."

"Brenna. What are you too afraid to tell me?"

"*Nothing.* I just don't fucking feel like talking about her, okay?" Brenna used the open door of her locker as a shield, blocking out her face, but she couldn't hide the tremor in her voice.

I closed the space between us. "Why didn't you want to talk about Rhodes?"

Brenna slammed the locker. She shut her eyes, palming the door, as if in prayer.

"He killed my family, Brenna. You've heard that, right?"

Brenna did not turn to face me. "One of the dancers saw Dani at a gas station. Couple days before she was reported missing. Dani was in the passenger seat of a car, and she looked beat up," she said to her locker door. "When Jada went to tap on the window to ask her why she hadn't been in to work, she said Dani gave her this look. Like she had no idea who Jada was.

"And then the man finished filling the car and got in and drove them away. It was the same day she stopped answering her phone. Jada said the man was Rhodes."

"And she never reported it?"

"Who the fuck would she report it to? Don't you get it? He's a fucking *cop*."

Brenna took a step away from the locker.

"Wait," I said. "Would you be willing to talk to the investigator working on my family's case?"

"I don't talk to cops."

"He's not a cop—"

"It doesn't fucking matter what he is, Samantha. There are people—if they knew I was talking to you about Dani, they would fucking kill me."

Brenna pushed past me, her shoulder colliding with mine. "Don't come back here. I'll have you thrown out."

Before I could form a response, she grabbed a bag of trash and barreled into the crash bar of the exit door, sunlight flooding the locker room. By the time I followed her out to the back lot, shouting her name, Brenna was gone.

I had no doubt she would make good on her promise to have me ejected if I went back inside the club. I turned to head back around the building, and I spotted her by the dumpster.

The dancer with the tattoo sleeves. She stuffed something in the bra of her black bikini top, started making her way back toward the club. Beside her stood Ed Robinette, who was staring at me, stricken.

"Hey!" I shouted as he bolted.

Ed was much faster than he had any right to be. He darted across the side street, narrowly missing the hood of a sedan that screeched to a stop.

"Fuck." By the time I made it to the edge of the lot, Ed had disappeared behind the strip of businesses on the other side of the street.

I jogged back to my Accord, my thoughts chaotic. Ed, darting in front of that car. Dani, inside Stephen Rhodes's car.

Robinette's housing unit was only a few blocks away from the strip club. I headed west, catching every red light, unable to shake Karl Holcombe's words. Ed Robinette is the type of man who couldn't tell the truth if his life depended on it.

I parked in the space directly outside Ed's apartment. Ed Robinette had told me he'd quit selling heroin, but there was no mistaking the baggie the dancer had slipped inside her bikini top. I would wait, as long as I had to, until he came back so he could tell me what else he had lied about.

In Ed's window, the curtains moved.

I stepped out of my car. Forced some air into my lungs, inhaling the stench from the dumpster carried over on the warm breeze. In the unit adjacent to Ed's, the half-eared dog was losing its mind, quieting only to turn his head and gnaw a hot spot on his haunch.

I depressed Crazy Ed's doorbell. Once, twice, three times before I slammed my palm against the doorframe. "Ed! I know you're in there."

Silence. I cupped my hands over my mouth, shouted, "Open up! I'd like to buy some heroin!"

The storm door creaked open, and Ed's face appeared behind the screen still dividing us. "Are you out of your goddamned mind?"

I stuck my phone in his face. I had Dani's Facebook profile picture pulled up. "Do you know this woman?"

I heard the click of a latch sliding into place. "Oh no. I want no part of this."

"You sold to her, didn't you?"

Robinette watched my fingers move across the screen of my phone. "Who are you calling?"

"An anonymous tip that someone is selling narcotics in the Cloud 69 parking lot."

Robinette's tongue flicked over his bottom lip. He looked for a moment as if he might launch himself through the screen door and attack me. I exhaled as Robinette unlatched the door, shuffled backward to let me in.

An AC unit rattled the vertical blinds above the living room window. While Robinette shut them, I braced myself against the smell of ammonia and days-old kitchen waste and took in my surroundings. I spotted at least three cats in the kitchen alone. One watched me from the counter, its limbs tucked under its body, one eye yellow, the other sealed shut with gunk.

Ed wore flannel pajama bottoms, tanned belly stretched and swollen over the band. Cirrhosis, I guessed. Likely from chronic hep C, judging from the array of prescription antivirals on his counter.

"What's her name?" Robinette asked. "I knew her as Ariel. None of the girls use their real names."

"Danica," I said.

"Mind if I sit?"

I remained standing as Ed slid into the single chair at the card table. Beside it was a rolling cart with a microwave and a caddy holding various packaged silverware from fast-food places.

"When was the last time you saw her?"

"A while back. The other girls, they said she'd come to work high. That was Billy's one rule—you don't come to the club high." Robinette moved to the fridge, retrieved a can of a generic brand of cola. "Then about a year later, one of my regular scores tells me she thinks Ariel is dead."

"Why?"

"She told me she went on a date with a customer. Retired cop, real loudmouth. He paid her to come to his motel room after the club, and while they're partying, he tells her one of his old cop buddies confessed to Ariel's murder. His friend told him that he picked up a redheaded junkie, and she promised to have sex with him if he let her go. Last minute, she changed her mind. That made him real mad, so he strangled her and dumped her."

I slapped the can out of his hand. "You're a fucking liar, Ed. You told me you stopped selling drugs. Why should I believe a goddamn thing that comes out of your mouth?"

Robinette picked up the soda, examined the dent in the can. "Well, now I can't open this."

"Who told you that story about the cop?" I asked. "Does she still work at the club?"

Ed's eyes widened, as if I'd finally said something to surprise him. "Yes, dear. She was the girl you were shouting at in the parking lot before."

Chapter Eleven

I headed back to Gil's. I thought of calling Meacham, telling him that Stephen Rhodes was a serial killer. Then I thought of his face when I told him I'd obtained this information from a strip club waitress and a heroin-peddling sex offender.

Rhodes was a police officer. I let the thought loop in my head, as if I had only just learned it. He was a cop, and that's why he had gotten away with it. The murders, the drug planting, the Starlight Tours.

And Lyndsey. Why would he go through the trouble—why would Rhodes risk getting caught for the murders—to make sure she was safe?

He targeted people he believed were disposable. Addicts, immigrants. People who broke the law. People who deserved what was coming to them. Scott, who sold drugs, who resisted arrest. My mother and father, who let him grow weed on their property, who supported him when he wanted to sue the police department.

But my sister—maybe Rhodes believed she did not deserve to die.

Maybe it had not been a coincidence at all that I was at Caroline's the night they were murdered.

Could Rhodes have known that I wasn't home that night? Is that why he chose that evening, out of all the others that had passed since war broke out between the police and my family?

I locked and bolted Gil's door when I got back. My heartbeat was as wild as a lab rat's.

I needed to do what Meacham had begged of me: let him handle the case. I had a job, friends, a life waiting for me back in the city.

I googled the number for the local junk-removal company as I pushed my way into Gil's bedroom. The line rang five, six, seven times before I gave up and waded into the bedroom closet. I'd been putting it off, the mildew smell inside nearly unbearable.

Breathing through my mouth, I ducked, the ceiling angling down to a crawl space.

On the floor, beside stacked see-through storage tubs, was a metal lockbox. The sight of it drew my breath away. I knew what would be inside before I engaged the key, popped the top.

A pistol. I picked it up, my body going still at the gun's weight in my hand.

You could have done it yourself, I thought. *Why did you need it to be me?*

I considered the question for a long while, the only noise in the room the rattling inside the AC wall unit. All I could come up with was that Gil, who had spent the entirety of his adult life single and childless, had not wanted to die alone.

It sucked the wind from me, how badly I wished I hadn't done it. I could have made him stay longer, until my questions were answered, until I'd said what I needed to. That I wished we hadn't lost each other.

I tossed the gun on the bed, turned my sights on one of the storage tubs. The ammunition should have been nearby, if Gil had any in the house.

I lifted the lid off the storage tub. Inside were photos. Gil, in full fatigues and a helmet, kneeling in front of an armored vehicle with four other men in uniform. Gil, crouched on a cinder block, mid-chew, a plate of mealy stew in his lap and a stretch of desert behind him.

Gil and me, at my elementary-school graduation, my lips slick with Dr Pepper Smackers. My father had had to miss the ceremony—he was a driver for Ealy Farms, and one of the farmhands had gotten his fingers crushed in a piece of machinery. Gil had come to the ceremony in his place.

Beneath the photo of Gil and me was an envelope, my handwriting blasted across it.

A flash of myself that summer, hunched over the Lisa Frank gel pens I'd received for my birthday. There were twenty-four of them, nearly enough to write each letter in a different color. *Dear Gil, Please be safe in Afghanistan.* I'd had to look up the proper spelling in one of Dad's encyclopedias, had still gotten it wrong and had to wedge an awkward *h* between the first few letters.

I swiped at the area under my eyes. I folded the letter and put it in my pocket. There were others in the tub, written in a scrawl I did not recognize, some of them still carrying the scent of perfume. Old lovers, maybe.

I junked them all, my throat sealing up at the one at the bottom of the tub. The same faded lilacs that matched the pad I used to steal from the kitchen counter while Caroline was over. Shut in my room, giggling, trading written messages, nasty things we'd never say out loud. *Mr. Simons has a tiny little cock. Anna Mulligan is a lard ass WHORE.*

We'd forgotten to tear off the top sheet once, before I replaced the notepad. My mother said nothing, and I never saw the notepad again.

I sank to my ass, back against Gil's bed frame, the stationery shaking between my fingers.

> Dear Brother,
>
> I feel cowardly writing a letter instead of picking up the phone. I told myself it's no different than how I wrote to you when you were deployed, even though you feel farther from me now than you were then. I barely remember what those letters said, although I'm sure you saved them all. You were always better than me at protecting what's important.
>
> This summer seems endless, without you here. The girls are miserable. Jack doesn't see this side of them. The crying, the screaming, the slammed doors.

They're so happy to see him when he gets home, only because he's not me.

I sound terrible. You know what's even worse? I would kill for my daughters, I really would. But sometimes, I hate being a mom. I hate how my daughter lies to me, and I hate lying to her about where you are. I can tell how much it's hurting Sam, you not being here, but I'm afraid the truth about why you left would be just as painful. She wouldn't understand. I don't either, Gil. I only hope that you will give me the chance to make things right. I hope you know you are family, and you always will be.

Love,

M

I set the letter on my knees, a tremor forming low in my gut. Proof that she had existed, that the fire had not erased her completely. I read her words over and over, burrowing into the folds of my brain where I knew they would live forever. The things she thought about me, how my sister and I had drained her until she had nothing left for herself.

I heard that car door slam, Lyndsey waking and wailing, the last words my mother had spoken to me. *What the hell is wrong with you, Samantha?*

I pressed the heels of my hands into my eyes, the noise in my head reaching a crescendo. Uneasiness hit me like a slap to the face, waking me up. There was no date on this letter, no envelope to accompany it.

I fumbled for the envelope I had trashed, the one that held my letter to Gil, that desperate appeal. *Please be safe in Afghanistan.*

The envelope was postmarked to Verona, New York, which was less than four hours from Carney.

People lie. I knew this; I dealt with it every day in my line of work. And yet, every now and then it got under my skin in a way that lit my nerves on fire. That flash of violence, in Ed Robinette's apartment, the way I'd knocked the soda can out of his hands.

At my core, I loathed people like Robinette, who lied like they breathed. And as it turned out, Gil might have been the biggest liar I knew.

I was in the living room, pacing, considering the text to Rhiannon I'd composed.

Hey. What are you doing tonight?

I sent it, slipped a ragged thumbnail in my mouth. Ellipses showed that Rhi was typing, briefly, before disappearing. There was no greater conversational snare trap than *What are you doing tonight?*

I have a toddler. I'm going to bed at 8

I was wondering if we could talk. Maybe grab drinks

I needed to find out what my cousin knew. Mitch had to have known that Gil was in Verona, in America, when my parents told me he was in Afghanistan. It was a whopper of a lie, designed to quash my questions about why Gil had abruptly stopped coming by to see us.

After a few minutes, Rhi responded.

I have a roast in the crock pot already. Come 4 dinner

Are you sure that's a good idea?

As long as you don't antagonize Mom. We eat at 6:30

It was already after five, and the only bakery still open was all the way in Spring Meadow. A single gluten-free chocolate torte remained in the display case when I arrived. Thirty bucks charged to my card later, I was en route to Mitch's.

I thought of Mitch ignoring the puppy I'd brought for Kaylee. I thought of Lyndsey, pictured Uncle Scott dangling her upside down over the couch by her feet. Her body convulsing with laughter as she hit the cushions when he dropped her. Gil coming into the room, slapping Scott upside the head. *What if she breaks her neck?*

Then, Meacham, across the table from me at the Neversink Lodge, telling me that whoever had taken Lyndsey from the house had probably cared about her.

What did Gil drive in 2001?

Mitch's front door was shut, TV leaking from the other side. I depressed the doorbell button, the torte box heavy on my forearm. The door creaked open, and from behind the screen, my aunt stared at me in a way that made it clear I was as welcome as a Jehovah's Witness.

"Am I early?" I asked.

While Mitch frowned, CJ Ealy appeared behind her, Kaylee at his hip. "Samantha's here," he said, surprised.

My aunt pushed the screen door open, disappearing from view the moment I stepped inside the house. I waggled my fingers at Kaylee, who responded with an eardrum-piercing wail and a panicked stare up at her father.

CJ whisked Kaylee to the couch as I stepped aside, like an asshole, waiting for Rhiannon to show up and explain everything. She'd invited me; I hadn't randomly stopped by to terrify the child.

I remembered the pastry box in my hands and started for the kitchen. Over the sounds of Kaylee's cries, Rhi yelled, "Is Sam here?" Then pots clattering, and: "Goddamn it all to hell."

The racket made Kaylee shriek louder. CJ reached into the playpen for something to soothe her. He passed over her puppy and handed her a pretend cell phone that played "Oh! Susanna." Kaylee quieted at the sound, pursed her rosebud lips at the reflective mirror while CJ bounced her on his knee.

I shrugged at CJ and headed into the kitchen. At the counter, Rhi had her back to me. With two forks, she poked at a roast in the Crockpot, peeling back pieces of meat as if performing an autopsy. "It's not wired right," she said to my aunt. "The low setting gets hotter than high."

"Funny how it's wired right when I use it." Michelle dropped into her seat at the table. She kneaded her knee. *Nervous.* The word rose in me out of nowhere. I had seen my aunt in pain for nearly twenty years. I knew how it manifested on her face, like she was holding back rage.

The door had been closed when I arrived, the AC unit humming under the window, which meant her joints could tolerate the chill. She was having a good day, until I arrived.

"That won't fit in the fridge." Rhi nodded to the box, which seemed comically large in my hands.

I left the torte on the counter. "What can I do to help?"

"Nothing." Rhi's voice was crisp, absent the congenial tone she'd developed toward me this week. "You're a guest. Sit."

Michelle avoided my eyes as I slid into the seat across from her. CJ wandered into the kitchen, Kaylee's arms looped around his neck like a monkey's, as he attempted to thread the child's legs through her high chair. At the thought of detaching from her father, she began to scream again, thrashing as if her tiny body were caught in a rip current.

"You have to remove the tray," Mitch said. CJ did not seem to hear her, or he was too focused on his daughter, who was now stuck between the tray and seat. When CJ's brow began to glisten, I rose from my chair.

Rhi swooped in, popped the tray off the chair, and set it on the table in a single motion before returning to her roast without a glance at CJ.

"Can never get the hang of this damn thing," CJ said, fastening the buckle across Kaylee's lap. Rhi had set the tray in front of me; I passed it to CJ, who snapped it into place. Satisfied with his handiwork, he turned and opened the fridge door. "What are you drinking, Sam?"

A whine from Kaylee preempted my response.

"Overtired," Mitch said, but I got the sense it was my presence that was agitating the child, that I'd disturbed the balance in the house. I suspected this was the first time all week Kaylee had even seen her father.

"Whatever is fine," I said. Mitch rolled her eyes and rose from the table, as if she had urgent business she'd just remembered.

Rhi plunked a platter down in the center of the table. What she'd salvaged of the pot roast lay alongside carrots and potatoes in oily pools of gravy.

CJ returned from the fridge with a pitcher of Crystal Light. "How's it going at the house, Sam?"

"Going, I guess. Gil had a lot of useless shit."

"Tay said you cleared out a ton." Rhi did not look up from her plate. She speared a piece of meat while Mitch returned to the table with utensils for the toddler.

"Still got to clear the basement and get a Realtor in." I sipped the Crystal Light, diluted to the point of tastelessness.

"Must be nice," my aunt said. "To be able to take so much time away from work."

Something in me fractured. "Yeah, I just fucking love being here, Mitch."

Rhiannon's eyes dropped to the piece of meat she was sawing at, as if she had not heard me at all. Blood pooled into my aunt's face, a tremor in her voice when she finally spoke. "There's a child here."

CJ snorted behind the lip of his glass. Rhi looked up from trying to coax a piece of roast into Kaylee's mouth. "Something funny?"

CJ set down his glass. "She can't even say *mama* yet and y'all are worried about her walking around saying *fuck*."

Rhi's grip on the toddler fork tightened. Kaylee, who had been stubbornly shaking her head, lips sealed shut, slapped the fork out of her mother's hand.

"We don't *do* that." Rhi grabbed Kaylee's wrist, delivered the message at eye level.

"Come on, Rhi, chill," CJ said over Kaylee's wails, but my cousin was already standing, the legs of her chair squealing against the linoleum.

"Bath time." She scooped Kaylee out of her high chair. "I hope you all enjoy the rest of your evening."

CJ stabbed a piece of meat, chewed, while Mitch and I stared at each other.

She was the one to break the silence. "Something you need to say to me?"

I was aware of CJ, in the chair beside me, sipping his Crystal Light, eyes darting between Mitch and me. I unfolded the letter in my pocket, passed it to Mitch.

"I don't have my reading glasses," she said.

"Was he ever in Afghanistan in 2001?"

Mitch said nothing as she refolded the letter. She shoved it back at me, as if it were a bill she planned to contest at some later date, and resumed eating.

Anger building in me, like a heat-seeking missile. "Why the *hell* would they tell me he was deployed?"

"Because your mother didn't want you to know they'd had a falling-out."

"He didn't come back for the funerals," I said.

"Because I asked him not to, out of respect for my brother."

She'd barred him—Gil, the person I needed most—from returning home to bury my mother and Uncle Scott. Worse, the doubt germinating in my brain.

He was only three hours away when they were murdered.

I pushed my chair from the table. "I think I'll head out."

My aunt snapped to attention. She dropped her fork, a shred of meat still speared to the tines. "You'll keep your ass there until I've said something."

CJ cleared his throat. "Michelle—"

My aunt held up a hand, and even though her gnarled fingers trembled, CJ said nothing more. Shame burned in my face. I was eleven again, waiting at the register at Ealy Farms. My overtired mother snapping at me while Lyndsey fussed in her stroller, all because I'd asked for a honey stick when she told me we were only stopping for green beans. CJ Ealy was behind the counter, within earshot, and I thought I'd die from the embarrassment.

I stared at my aunt. "What is it?"

"You come back here after all this time, after running from us like we're diseased, and *you* accuse me of hiding things. Why, Samantha?" My aunt's voice warbled on my name, as if I had stabbed her.

"I just want to know who killed them, Mitch. I know you don't think it matters—"

"You want to know what I think? If your father hadn't met your mother, he'd be here right now."

Mitch returned to her dinner while CJ watched her, agape.

"Okay," I said. "I'm glad to know you feel that way. It makes a lot of things clear to me, actually."

I left without clearing my plate, a punishable offense fifteen years ago. I did not stop in the bathroom to apologize to Rhiannon. I would text her later, when I'd talked myself down.

I shut myself in the driver's seat, holding in a sob that I felt might split my body in two. I was fumbling to fit my key in the ignition when a rap at my window nearly sent me out of my skin.

CJ Ealy ducked so he was eye level with me, palming the roof of my car. I opened the window, my voice still lost to the void.

"I could use a drink," he said. "How 'bout you?"

"God, yes."

CJ climbed into the blue Silverado parked at the curb. I flipped on my radio and followed his taillights, the blinkers, which I gathered he was only using for my benefit.

He passed the Riverhead Inn, the Triple Crown, until we were on the entrance ramp for 42, heading toward Fallsburg. CJ signaled for the Birchwood Glenn exit.

I recognized the town name. Birchwood Glenn had become a hot weekend getaway spot for city singles due to its proximity to the Poconos and the Delaware River. I followed CJ into a municipal lot, parked alongside his Silverado. He propped a hand against his SUV, shifted his weight to his hip as he dug in his pocket for change for the meter.

"Sorry for all of that back there," CJ said. "I didn't help by riling them up."

I joined him on the sidewalk, jamming my parking receipt into my shorts pocket. "They were already riled."

I was aware of CJ's proximity, the heavy notes of sandalwood and bergamot on his body. CJ's fingers barely connected with my lower back as he guided me into a bar. I followed him to an empty table in the corner, watched him settle into the cushioned seat as if it had been waiting for him.

Almost immediately, a young guy in Dahmer glasses descended on us. "What can I get you folks?"

"Whiskey neat for me." CJ nodded across the table, but the waiter barely seemed to notice me. CJ was striking, even in a place like Birchwood Glenn, where the median age of the bar patrons was significantly lower than in Carney, the haircuts more expensive.

I grabbed a cocktail menu off the table, pointed to the first item on the list without reading what was in it.

"Great choice." The waiter was looking at CJ as he said it. "I'll get those going for you folks."

"Thanks, bud," CJ said, his eyes tracking the waiter to the bar, where he blushed. When CJ met my eye again, I lifted my eyebrows. He shrugged, as if to say, *Can you blame him?*

"The Bank," I read off the menu on the table. The adrenaline from Mitch's was leaving my body, but I still felt wobbly, nerves alight. Alone with CJ Ealy.

CJ tilted his head to the vaulted ceilings. "Because it used to be a bank. Get it?"

"Very hipster."

"Figured you'd feel at home. You still living in Brooklyn?"

"Queens."

"Same thing."

"Don't say that to a Brooklynite."

The waiter returned with our drinks. I picked the foliage from the surface of mine and took a sip of what tasted like lavender-infused lighter fluid.

"Why'd you come back here?" I asked. "After school."

"You mean, why did I take over a business that's been in my family for over fifty years?" CJ blinked at me.

"You had a college degree. You could have done anything you wanted."

"Tell you the truth, I had no choice. Mom got sick and was gone a year later. Pop took it real hard and couldn't manage the farm on his own."

"I had no idea about your mother. Did her leukemia come back?"

"Nah, secondary lymphoma. Sixty percent curable. I think she didn't have it in her to fight again."

"That's awful," I said. "I'm really sorry."

"Yep. Sometimes I don't know what's worse—a parent losing a child or a child left alone in the world."

I thought of Kaylee on his hip, the panic in her body when CJ set her down. I wondered how he could possibly say such a thing now that he had a child of his own. I sensed that it was for my benefit, that he considered us the same and needed me to know it.

"I don't think there's anything worse than losing a child," I said.

"Probably. But then you look at someone like Mitch, what it does to someone." CJ shook his head. "What kind of life is that, you know?"

I knew what CJ meant. Most people Mitch's age had something to live for—hauling their ass to the elementary school to vote for whichever candidate promised to defend their social security checks, their homeland from the illegals. I could not be fucked to come up with a single reason my aunt had to get out of bed each day.

CJ shifted in his seat, propped his ankle on his opposite knee. "You want to talk about what happened back there?"

I commanded my brain to send the words to my lips. The thing I was too afraid to say out loud, because it felt like a betrayal. Because I was terrified of what it might mean.

"If Gil wasn't in Afghanistan, he might not have an alibi for my parents' murders," I said.

"The police must have checked him out."

"Maybe not."

Maybe the cops had heard Gil was deployed and hadn't bothered to verify he was in Afghanistan. A note slipped in the file, *Foster brother out of the country*, never questioned by the detectives that passed the case around like a fussy infant. *Here, you take it, I've tried everything.*

Could they have fucked up that badly?

I turned over the days after the murders in my head, itemizing each fuckup. Karl Holcombe, proclaiming Scott was the killer, only for his body to be found a day later, under a pile of debris the searchers had trampled.

I closed my eyes, my heartbeat rolling like a snare drum, my memory coming full circle to that night at the Riverhead Inn, playing pool with CJ. His offhand comment that Gil had never forgiven Ealy Sr. for letting him go.

"When did your father fire Gil?" I asked.

"Jeez, it was ages ago."

"Were my parents still alive?"

"Yeah." CJ shifted in his seat. "Your dad was the reason Gil got fired, actually."

"What?"

CJ let out a low sigh. "Gil and your dad got into an argument at work, and Gil took a swing at Jack. My dad told Gil not to come back."

"Wait, Gil punched my *dad*?"

CJ shrugged. "They were both hotheads."

My father, I knew, had bursts of violence in his past. There was the fight with the boys in the locker room who had insulted my grandmother, murmurs he'd broken the nose of one of the same kids years later during a scuffle at the Triple Crown.

But I'd never seen Gil lose his temper. As a kid, I'd witnessed my mother fling a dinner plate at Scott during an argument. A shard had ricocheted off the stove and embedded itself in Gil's arm; I watched in horror as he calmly plucked the ceramic from his skin with one hand and shoved Scott out the back door with the other.

"What were they arguing about?"

"Don't know," CJ said. "Pop said they'd always butted heads. Gil wasn't used to someone else being the man of the house, once Jack married your mom and moved in. When your grandma died, they asked Gil to move out."

I stuck the tip of my pinkie in my drink, sucked lavender sugar off the tip. I grasped for memories of Gil and my father together, some simmering tension I hadn't picked up on.

"I don't remember any of that," I said darkly. "They did a great job hiding all the bad shit from me, I guess."

CJ's eyes hooded in the dim light of the bar. "Sam. You know it was mostly good, right?"

I said nothing, knocking back what was left of my cocktail.

"After my aunt Wendy died and Bo came to live with us, he and Pop got into a fight so bad that Bo took off," CJ said. "He made it to a truck stop an hour away before your father tracked him down. He gave Bo a ride home, talked sense into him."

"I had no idea," I said. My father had never said anything to me about this.

"That's just who he was," CJ said. "He'd drop everything for a person in need."

I waved the waiter over, held up my empty glass. "What was in this?"

"Vodka—"

"I'll take a vodka neat, please. A double."

The waiter nodded and disappeared. A question was forming on CJ's lips, one I hadn't quite worked out the answer to myself: *Why was it driving me to drink, hearing his memories of my father?*

I plucked a piece of bullet ice from the empty cocktail glass the waiter hadn't taken. I crushed the ice between my back teeth. "You remember a girl from Carney High named Dani Burkhardt?"

"I was friends with her older brother Tommy in elementary school. Rough family."

Dani and her brother had lived with their grandmother since they were kids. Their father was not allowed to see them, per a judge's order, and Dani's mother was a nonentity. "She and I were friends for a bit, but I never met her parents."

CJ shook his head, as if holding back something impolite. Finally, he said, "Some people just shouldn't have kids."

I heard this all the time in my line of work. I didn't bother challenging the other nurses on it, but for some reason, the judgment chafed coming from CJ Ealy. "Well, we can't all be born into a family like the Ealys."

I reached for the vodka that had appeared on the table. I took a healthy sip while CJ studied me.

"You know my aunt didn't die of cancer?" CJ said. "Liver failure, and not from the booze. She had too many infections over the years, from needles. She poisoned herself to death."

"I had no idea," I said. "Do Taylor and Bo know?"

"Tay's father didn't want him to know the truth. But Pop told Bo and me. He always said the one rule in our house was no secrets." CJ blew out a heavy sigh. "Pop blamed himself, even though he did everything in his power to help her. Some people are just born in pain, I think."

I took a long draw from my drink, the previous one already humming in my blood. Careful, or I'd get sloppy, too chatty. *Maybe that's why he invited me here.*

"Carney, I think, is diseased." I didn't know where the thought came from. I set down my drink, unnerved, because I remembered. Rhodes.

CJ gave me a wry smile, lifted his glass toward mine. "To being immune."

I cocked my head. "You think we're better than people like Dani and your aunt."

CJ smiled. "You don't?"

I did, didn't I? I could have stayed away from Mitch, but I wanted her to see my $300 highlights, hear the shift in my accent. When I applied to colleges out of state, Mitch had snorted and pointed out that my mother had done the same. My mom had thought she was too good for this town too, and look where it had gotten her.

"We're not better than anyone," I said.

CJ's smile didn't waver. "Why not?"

"We're both alone."

The waiter was back, eyeing my empty vodka glass with a look I interpreted as judgmental. "Another round for you folks?"

"Just the check, thanks," CJ said.

I downed the dregs of my drink, grateful the lighting concealed the disappointment in my face. CJ handed the kid an AmEx while I circled the questions I hadn't gotten to ask, the possibility that hung in the air. I'd drunk too much, too fast, and my brain was at war. Did I want to go home with CJ Ealy, or did I want him to keep talking? There was something simmering at the back of my memory, the thing he had said about my father bringing his younger cousin home when Bo ran away.

Before I could connect the thoughts, the waiter was back with a receipt, which CJ signed, the whole transaction frighteningly efficient.

"You okay to get home?" he asked, stuffing his wallet back in his jeans.

"I think I'll hang here a bit."

"Careful," he said, in a way that made me question which way he meant it. He stood, bent to me, lips brushing the area between my cheek and my ear. "Good night, Samantha."

Dahmer Guy was hovering, and I was aware of the bodies in the corner, balancing martinis and eyeballing my empty glass, the prime real estate I was squatting in. I stood, asked the bartender to point me to the restroom.

The bathroom was single occupancy, mirrored, and over-perfumed with candles. I settled down to pee, my reflection judging me from across the room. *Why the mirrors? Who wants to look at themselves while peeing?*

I washed my hands, gave my cheeks a quick slap, occupied with thoughts about white-knuckling it back to Carney at a steady twenty miles per hour.

I could not go back to Gil's house. Not until I knew.

I called Travis Meacham.

"Sam." He sounded surprised in a way that made me feel like a needy first date calling too soon. "Everything all right?"

"Yeah. Sorry. I was going to ask you something, but now I feel stupid—"

"Hold up. Where are you?"

"Please don't make me admit I'm hiding in a bar bathroom trying to sober up."

"Which bar are you at?"

"The Bank, in Birchwood Glenn."

"What?"

"It's a bar. Called the Bank."

"Send me a pin."

Meacham ended the call, and I was still working out how to send a pin when an annoyed fist rattled the bathroom door. I slipped out of the bathroom and found an empty stool at the bar, the girl behind the counter visibly annoyed at my request for an ice water, nothing else.

I'd sucked down two glasses, shivering at the bar, by the time I felt a tap on my shoulder. Behind me, Meacham was in jeans and a zip-up hoodie, a North Face backpack slung over his shoulder. I was so struck by the sight of him in street clothes, the shape his muscles cut against the sleeves of his hoodie, that I stared dumbly at him instead of returning his affable "Hey."

Meacham hopped up on the barstool next to me and took in my glassy eyes, pink cheeks. He rearranged his expression to look properly scandalized. "My, my."

"Gil wasn't in Afghanistan in 2001," I said. "Did you know?"

Meacham's smile fell. "He was in Verona. Who told you otherwise?"

"My mother." All of them had kept up the lie, but she'd been the one to tell me he'd had little notice, he was so sorry he couldn't say goodbye, as I soaked my pillow with tears.

What if he gets killed? I'd asked.

He's not going to.

I could not form the follow-up question around my sobs: How could she possibly know that? Apparently, she did.

"She lied to me," I said.

Meacham blew out a sigh. "I'm not a parent, but I guess she didn't want to hurt you with the truth."

"You can be pretty patronizing," I said. "Is that why your wife left you?"

"No." An awkward pause, a flash of something in Meacham's expression as his eyes searched for the bartender. She moseyed over, plum-matte lips proffering a smile.

Meacham ordered a seltzer, and I scrambled to find my footing on the barstool, my legs turning to globs of Jell-O. Meacham's hand found my shoulder. "Easy, Sam."

"Gil was pissed at my parents, and he didn't have an alibi."

"He did, Sam. Gil clocked out of a job an hour outside of Verona at seven," Meacham said. "He called his girlfriend when he arrived home around eight, from his home phone. He says he showered after, watched some TV, and then called his *other* girlfriend around eleven p.m. Phone records confirmed his story. There was no way he had time to make the three-and-a-half-hour drive to Carney by the time the fire was set."

Another gulp of water, washing down the sour taste in my mouth. "But he fought with my father, at the farm. Ealy fired Gil over it."

"Yeah, that came up in interviews. No one overheard the argument, but by all accounts, Gil was the one who got aggressive."

"No one thought to ask Gil what they fought about?"

"Holcombe had a tough time with him. Couldn't get him to come back to Carney from Verona for a formal interview. He'd only say it was a family disagreement."

A flicker of a memory, one of the only times I could recall my father raising his voice at my mother. Both of them in the kitchen, Mom in defensive position by the sink, arms folded across her chest, Dad red-faced and spitting. *If I catch him selling that shit anywhere near this house or the girls again, I'll call up Rhodes and invite him here myself.*

An unforgivable threat; my father had spent nearly a week on the couch for it. Had Gil caught wind of the threat? He had always been his younger brother's protector, even going so far as to chase a troublesome customer off our property with a hammer.

I swallowed hard. "It might have been about Scott."

"What do you mean?" Meacham asked.

"After his arrest, Scott promised my parents he'd stop selling. But he still had people over, when my parents were at work, or in the middle of the night."

Meacham was quiet.

"What?" I asked. "What is it?"

"Boggs. He said he was supposed to meet Scott at eight. Risky move, unless your uncle didn't expect your father to be at home that evening."

"Didn't he get called in to work?" I kneaded my eyelids. "That's what my mom told Mrs. Mason when she asked her if I could stay the night. She felt sick, and my dad wasn't around to help with Lyndsey, so she needed me to stay over at Caroline's."

"Clinton Ealy Sr. says he never called your father and asked him to come in that day." Meacham sipped his drink.

"So my dad lied to my mom about having to work?"

"That's the thing. Two employees *did* report seeing Jack Newsom at Ealy Farms the afternoon of the murders. A produce stocker said he saw Jack on the phone in the office, and he seemed upset, so he stayed out of his way."

"Maybe something happened at the farm that day, then. The phone call that upset him—my dad was pretty senior. Maybe an employee with a grudge had threatened him."

"All of the full-time employees sat down for interviews. No one at the farm had a single bad thing to say about your father. They couldn't have been more shocked about what happened."

"And you don't think that's strange that they were shocked?" I pinched the tip of my straw between my fingers. "Everyone knew my uncle started a war with the cops."

The more time had passed, the more everyone seemed in agreement over this point. That no matter who had pulled the trigger, the violent end my family met had been inevitable. Because if it wasn't Rhodes, it was someone else my uncle Scott had crossed. Eventually the motive for the murders didn't seem to matter to anyone. Carney slept soundly without triple-checking door locks, confident that the crime had not been random.

"You said full-time employees," I said. "What about all the migrant workers and seasonal ones? There's no way they were all interviewed."

"And there's no way to track them down, unfortunately. Ealy kept decent-enough records, but it's been twenty years. A good amount probably left the country." Meacham sipped his seltzer.

"Where was Ealy Sr. the night of the murders?"

"His wife underwent a bone marrow transplant in Manhattan that morning. He was at her side in the hospital all weekend."

I felt crazy for even suggesting it. My father had worked for the Ealys since he was fifteen. Ealy Sr.'s parents had looked out for my father and Mitch through their teenage years, making sure my dad always went home from the farm with a box of imperfect produce, the morning's crop of muffins that were too brown at the edges to sell. Ealy Sr. had promoted my dad to farm manager when he took over the business. He'd paid for my parents' funeral, pledged to fund a cash reward for the killers after the murders.

So who, then? If not Stephen Rhodes, if not Gil, then who hated my father enough to put him down like an animal?

Chapter Twelve

I woke with the sun, my eyeballs starchy, my tongue heavy despite the water I'd downed at the bar. The previous evening came to me in a steady drip-drip of shame. Calling Meacham from the bathroom, that snide comment about his wife leaving him. The scene at my aunt's house, CJ telling me that Gil had taken a swing at my father weeks before the murders.

I swished some Listerine and wiped the grime from my eyes and headed outside.

My aunt was stooped over the lawn mower when I arrived at her house. I waited by the edge of the driveway until she turned, spotted me leaning against my driver's side. Her forehead scrunched, but she made no motion to stop mowing until she had completed her strip of grass.

Mitch killed the engine, leaned into the handle, trying to conceal her labored breathing.

"You should have told me about Gil," I began.

"He should have told you," Mitch said.

"Why did they have a falling-out?" I asked.

"What does it matter, Samantha?"

"Because it may have had something to do with why they were all killed."

"We know why they were killed," Mitch said. "And we know who killed them."

"But what if it wasn't him?"

Mitch gave me a look that would have made me evacuate my bowels were I still a child, were I still afraid of questioning her, making a thoughtless comment that might make her love me less. But that scene last night, at her dinner table, had finally put the issue to rest. My aunt did not love me.

"There was someone at the house that night," I said. "He says he saw a man leave the house with Lyndsey."

"How much did this guy sell you that crock for?"

"It's not a crock. He saw her wrapped in her Mickey blanket."

Mitch shook her head stubbornly, the scrunchie holding up her ponytail slipping. "No, he didn't."

"Would you fucking listen to me, Mitch!" I shouted.

"No, *you listen*." Mitch's index finger was inches from my face. I took a step back, heart hammering, wondering what I might do if my aunt struck me.

Mitch set off for the house with impressive speed for her condition. Still, I was faster and caught the door. Mitch hooked a hard right for the basement, letting the door slam behind her. I froze, sure the sound would wake the baby, but nothing. After several minutes passed, I tugged open the door, picked my way down the steps.

A single fluorescent bulb dangled from the ceiling. I tracked the sound of rustling to the corner, where Mitch was elbow-deep in a plastic storage bin.

My breathing stalled as she straightened. In her hands, Lyndsey's Mickey Mouse blanket.

I lifted my eyes to meet hers. I imagined grabbing her ponytail, slamming her body to the concrete.

"Where did you get that?"

"It was in your mother's car," Mitch said, a wheeze creeping into her voice. "They boxed everything up, turned it over to me. Wasn't much."

Wasn't much. A piece of my sister had survived the fire, her favorite possession in the world, and all these years it had been left to rot in this dank basement.

"How could you keep this from me?" I asked.

Mitch seemed to be thinking hard about this. She backed up a bit, parked her ass on a storage bin. On the side, "XMAS" scrawled across a slash of masking tape. "I thought I might give it to you someday, when you were ready to start a family. But you never came back."

And there it was. My crime and my penance. "So you kept it. To punish me for leaving, you held on to the only piece left of my sister."

Mitch sighed. "Sure, Samantha. That's it. If you're finished, I've got things to do."

I let myself out the basement entrance. Up those concrete steps, around the side of the house.

I ground my gas pedal all the way back to Gil's, filling my car with angry, indulgent sobs. I couldn't bear the thought of that empty house, but I didn't want to return to the city, my own pathetic, empty apartment.

I wanted to be left alone, but I didn't want to be alone.

I wanted my mom.

The force of the wanting was so powerful it zapped the oxygen from my bloodstream. *I want my mom.* I slumped into a chair at Gil's kitchen table, and I thought of my ex-husband, his devotion to his own mother, the way I recoiled when he insisted, *She wants you to think of her as your mom too.*

It unsettled him how little I shared about my parents, my mom especially. I imagined calling him now, saying the words *I miss my mom. Is your new baby asleep, your wife at work? Because I'm ready to talk about my mom.* The thought was laughable.

I scrolled through my contacts until I found Nancy's cell number. She wouldn't be at work for another several hours, if she was even on tonight, but I craved a familiar voice on the other end. A reminder that I had a life waiting for me. People waiting for me, expecting things of me.

"Sam?" The line crackled for a beat. "What's going on? You okay?"

"Yeah, fine, Nance. I wanted to know how it went with that patient's family. Mrs. Reitman."

"Hell if I know. They sent someone from days to meet with them. Sam, you sure you're all right?"

I was the farthest thing from it, but admitting it would be opening a door I might not be able to shut. I'd been down this road with friends, coworkers, my allergist. Reveal too much and the next thing you know, they're pitching you a meeting with their murder-obsessed boyfriend or cousin who really wants to start a true-crime podcast.

I pinched the skin between my eyes. "My uncle died the other night."

"Oh, sweetie. What do you need?"

"More time off. He left everything to me, and this house is a mess."

"I'll run a leave request by HR for you," Nancy said. "What else? You need me to send David up there to help?"

Nancy's son was a real estate agent that brokered $5,000-a-month rentals in Manhattan. I was sure David would pass away at the mere sight of this house, but Nancy's kindness, despite me keeping her at a distance about my family, made pressure build behind my eyes. "Thanks, Nance. But it's fine, I just need like three more days here."

It had to be. I needed to finish what I had come here to do. Let Meacham do his job so I could return to mine. "Thanks, Nance."

"Of course. Samantha?"

"Yeah?" My throat knotted up. I eyed Gil's ashtray, finger-traced the outline of a bird I did not remember painting.

"Take care of yourself, please."

What if I wanted someone to take care of me? Tuck me in, make sure I got a full day's sleep. I thought of my sister's Mickey Mouse blanket in Mitch's hands. I should have taken it from her.

My dead sister's blanket.

Lyndsey was dead. It was the only conclusion I could reach after seeing that blanket in Mitch's hands. My sister was dead, and Leonard Boggs was a liar, just as Meacham had warned he might be.

Why, then, did Boggs want me to believe my sister had left the house alive? If he only wanted to get out of jail sooner, why not simply dangle the detail about the vehicle he'd seen and be done with it? Unless, of course, he was lying about seeing a vehicle outside the house too.

Except you, sweetheart. Come back anytime.

I grabbed my phone, looked up the number for the Cayuga County jail, feeling that I was certainly crazy for thinking Boggs had been trying to send a message that he wanted to speak to me alone.

Two, three rings. A female voice, maybe the chatty guard who had checked us in the other day.

"I was wondering how to schedule a visit with an inmate."

"Are you on their list of approved visitors?"

My heart sank. "I don't know. I've visited before."

"Hold on. What's the inmate's name?"

I spelled it for her, waited for the sound of a keyboard clacking, before: "And what's your name, hon?"

"Samantha Newsom."

"Yep, you're here. Looks like you've already cleared the background check. Visiting hours are from eight to four. First come, first served, or we take reservations."

"Can I make one?"

"Sure. When did you want to come in?"

"Is today good? I mean, if he's available."

"Hon, he's locked up. He's always available."

"Right. Okay." I did a quick calculation as to how fast I could make it to Cayuga. "Is noon okay?"

"Sure." Some more clacking, and then: "Arrive fifteen minutes prior. Make sure to have your ID."

A quiet day at the jail today. I'd convinced myself on the drive up that I might run into Travis Meacham here, and I eased a bit at the empty lobby.

My breath caught when the guard scanned my driver's license. I did not release it until he passed me back my ID and instructed me to step through the metal detector.

Another guard gave me a half-hearted pat-down. She waved me into a room marked VISITORS. There were rows of chairs bolted to the ground. One guard stood propped against a vending machine in the corner. A woman patted the back of a baby draped over her shoulder, a formula-stained burp cloth slipping off her back.

I picked it up, handed it to the woman, who thanked me with a nod. The guard by the vending machine watched us for a beat before looking away, detecting nothing improper about the transaction.

At ten to noon, the door opened, and a guard ushered in two inmates in handcuffs. Slow day for visitors.

Leonard Boggs blinked at me as if I were the sun. He poured himself into the seat opposite me, and I found myself wishing for the Hollywood version of a jailhouse visit. Boggs, seated across from me, where he could not escape my gaze.

"You lied," I said.

Boggs looked like shit. He wiped his nose with his cuffed hands, the capillaries in his nostrils broken.

"You never saw my sister's Mickey Mouse blanket," I said. "My aunt has it."

Boggs said nothing, a sheen of sweat coming to his upper lip.

"How did you know she had a Mickey blanket?" I asked. "Lucky guess?"

When he spoke, I braced myself against the stench of his breath, old cheese and gingivitis. "No, I saw it. Just not that night. That spring,

I went to pick up some weed. Scotty wasn't at his trailer, so I went up to the house. He said his sister got called into work. The little girl was on the blanket, watching TV. You were at the table, doing homework."

"Were you even there the night they were killed?"

"Yes. It all happened like I said."

I closed my eyes. "Tell me again. Tell me the truth this time."

"I got there at eight. Scott didn't answer the door, so I sat on that bench he had, figuring he'd be back soon. I heard a door slam, up at the house, and I thought it was Scott. Then I heard the crying."

"But you didn't actually see her."

"It was getting dark, but the man put something in the truck. She was screaming so loud, I thought they'd hear her all the way in town."

I swallowed hard. "It was a truck you saw."

Boggs nose twitched, but he offered nothing more. My mind swam. "Why didn't you just say you heard the crying? Why lie about the blanket?"

"Because I needed you to believe me. That detective didn't, even though I remembered what Scott's trailer looked like. If you believed me, maybe you'd be willing to help me."

"Help you with what?" I asked.

The hair on the back of my neck lifted as I saw the man sitting beside me, really saw him. The room was a comfortable sixty-nine degrees, but Boggs's shirt sleeves and collar were marked by sweat.

"You're an addict," I finally said.

"For months, I been going to a methadone clinic up on State Street," Boggs said. "They won't give it to me here. I'm sick, and they don't care."

"If you want methadone, you should probably tell Meacham. Maybe they'll give it to you instead of a deal."

"He can't know I'm in withdrawal. He won't give me the time of day until I'm straight."

"Then maybe you should get straight."

"I can't take it anymore," he said. "I'm sick all the time. I can't sleep. Methadone was the only thing keeping me well."

"I can't get them to give you methadone," I said.

"You can get me something else. You can sneak it in. Once I'm straight, I'll tell you about the truck."

My eyes flicked to the guard standing by the vending machine. He fed himself Doritos, his empty gaze moving between the visitations and his watch.

I closed my eyes. This must have been Boggs's plan from the moment he saw me in that interview room. Get his hooks into me. Use my baby sister to leverage his next fix.

I dropped my voice to a whisper. "You know this is extortion, right? If I called Meacham and told him about this, you'd never see the outside of a prison again."

"They got my DNA. I'm never getting out. But I can't suffer while I'm here."

"You're afraid of suffering," I said.

When Boggs offered no reply, I held his gaze. "My sister was twenty months old. If she's alive, she wouldn't even remember me. If the man who took her eventually killed her, she probably suffered."

Boggs offered nothing. I watched the sweat germinating on his face.

"I just need to get well," he said. "Then I'll help you."

"Even if I could get my hands on something strong enough for you, how would I even get it inside?"

Boggs dropped his voice to a whisper. "The families here, they do it all the time. The guards don't give a shit. The ladies put it in the babies' diapers, or in those cups they wear when they're bleeding."

In front of us, the baby began to wail, the touch of the man beside the woman foreign. The mother took the child back. It settled down, cheek to her shoulder, tiny mouth smushed open into an O.

"I'm not getting my sister back," I said, so softly I did not even know Boggs heard me until he said, "What?"

I closed my eyes. Even now, when I pictured Lyndsey, I saw her dragging around that blanket, giggling at Penny trying to grab the other end. Arms wrapped around my mother's neck, her mouth and bare chest spaghetti-sauce stained. Even if she'd survived, even if Boggs could tell me right now who had taken her, she would never come back to me the way I remembered her. Nothing Boggs could tell me meant anything, because I was never getting my sister back.

I stood, my heart a battering ram in my chest, drawing the attention of the guard, his fingers Dorito stained. I dropped my voice so only Boggs could hear.

"I hope it gets worse," I said. "I hope every minute of it is hell."

I hightailed it back to my car, not pausing to start the engine and the air before I covered my mouth with a fist. I screamed until my throat turned raw.

Fucking piece of shit. Fucking junkie piece of shit.

The thought rose in me out of nowhere, until I was screaming it. Hateful, ugly words that left my fingers trembling around my steering wheel. *Fucking junkie piece of shit.*

This was not me. I'd been dealing with people like Leonard Boggs for years at work, and I considered myself more empathetic than many of my colleagues. I tended to addicts as they returned from the dead, held their hands when they were removed from their ventilators. I served as audience to their promises they didn't want to die again, and I told them I believed them, because no one else in their lives did.

I hated Leonard Boggs for using my sister as a bargaining chip, but I also hated the voice he'd put in my head. *Fucking junkie piece of shit.* I sounded like Mitch when she'd heard that Dani's brother, Tommy, had been high when he drove his motorcycle into a tree.

This town was poisoning me.

❧

I was not alone when I returned to Gil's. Rhiannon's Tahoe was in the driveway. Beside her vehicle, my cousin stood facing the house, hands shielding her eyes from the sun.

"Shit," I said, throwing the Accord into park. Gil's TV. I'd forgotten I'd offered it to Rhi, that she was off today, and I'd told her to come by.

Rhi turned around at the sound of my wheels on the gravel.

"Sorry," I said, locking the car.

Rhi wordlessly moved to the back of the Tahoe and unbuckled Kaylee from her car seat. I took the porch steps two at a time, busted into the house, and shoved the pile of dirty clothes I'd accrued at the foot of Gil's couch into my work backpack.

Mitch kept a pristine house, and although we hadn't cohabited in over a decade, I still felt ashamed at Rhi seeing how I'd been living the past few days. I was stuffing the forgotten to-go container from my burger into the trash when Rhi let herself in.

Rhi stood in the living room, her daughter now nuzzling into her neck. Kaylee wore a blouse with ruffled sleeves, her hair sprouting in a Pebbles ponytail. I could not picture Rhi at Walmart picking out such a girlish outfit.

My cousin said nothing as she placed her daughter on the living room carpet. Kaylee began to fuss, arms stretched up toward Rhi. She handed the child her phone, "Baby Shark" playing on the screen.

Finally, Rhi faced me. "Last night was really fucked-up, Samantha."

"Maybe we can try again before I leave. Just you, me, and Kaylee."

"You think I give a fuck about dinner?" Rhi's eyelids were waxy, her liner hastily applied.

"I'm really sorry, Rhi." My patience was thinning. *I'm sorry for upsetting your goddamn liar of a mother.*

"Right," Rhi said.

I gestured to the TV. "Well, there it is. I think it's a smart TV."

Rhi cocked her head, considered the television mounted to the living room wall. Having found nothing objectionable about it, she said, "What do you want for it?"

"Nothing."

"We don't need charity."

"Then don't take it, Rhiannon. Help me bring it to the street; someone will take it."

A muscle in Rhi's jaw pulsed before she turned to help me lift the TV off the wall mount. Rhi stood at the helm. I thought of Kaylee, alone in the house, as we placed the television into the trunk of the Tahoe, atop a blanket she had laid down. I felt an urgency in my blood, a need to return to the house to check on her.

But Kaylee had not moved, her eyes still glued to the phone.

"Ready to go, *chica*?" Rhi said.

"She seems very sweet," I said. My thought sounded unfinished, which did not go unnoticed by Rhiannon.

"What?" My cousin looked from me to her child.

"It's just—Kaylee Ealy? It rhymes."

"No shit," Rhiannon said, scooping up her daughter. "She's a Newsom."

Interesting. Kaylee's father had the type of last name that could open doors for her, while ours would get you refused service at the shittiest eatery in town.

"It's weird," I said. "You having a kid."

"Yeah, I know." Rhi looked down at her daughter, who had hooked a finger in her mouth, eyes still on the screen of the phone in her opposite hand.

When Rhi spoke again, her voice sounded far off. "I didn't want to keep her."

"What changed your mind?" I asked.

"CJ. His mom's gone, and his dad barely knows him most days. I think he liked the idea of a family of his own."

"And you didn't like the idea of having a family?" *Because ours wasn't.* Rhi frowned at me, hearing the unspoken part. I knew she and I always differed on this point. It didn't matter that she never knew her father, that Mitch treated her more like a colleague than a daughter, that duty, not love, had been why Mitch had taken me in after the murders. Blood mattered to my cousin; she wouldn't have been here right now otherwise.

My cousin's gaze dropped to her daughter's head. "I thought there were too many ways I could mess her up. Too many ways she could get hurt."

Rhi met my eyes. "The world is a fucked-up place for kids." I couldn't think of a response. I could think of little else but the sweat beading on Boggs's face when he insisted that he had seen a man take my sister away.

I wanted to collapse into my cousin, to tell her everything. I wanted her to tell me that the world wasn't actually *that* cruel to children, that someone wouldn't save Lyndsey from the fire only to put her through unimaginable horrors.

"Well," Rhi said, shifting Kaylee to her opposite hip. "We'd better go."

My heart sank, even though it was silly to think they'd hang around in this near-empty house that I was beginning to suspect had black mold in the walls, judging from my headaches and postnasal drip. "See you," I said.

From the entryway, I heard Kaylee protest, then Rhi's voice. "Samantha. What the fuck is he doing here?"

The alarm in her voice sent me running to the front door. Rhi stood bolted to the porch, her daughter whining in her arms. At the edge of Gil's lawn was a black Ford Edge, its undercarriage splattered with dry mud.

Stephen Rhodes advanced up Gil's driveway. I thought of Gil's gun, the empty magazine, in his bedroom.

Rhodes stopped within ten feet of the porch and nodded to my cousin. "Nice to see you, Rhiannon. You still running the farm?"

"Sure am," Rhi said, pulling her daughter closer to her body. "You still planting dope on people to make your arrest quota?"

Rhodes smiled. I positioned myself on the steps, between Rhodes and my cousin.

"What do you want?" I asked.

"You know, the other day in my office, I *thought* you looked familiar." Rhodes dipped his head to me in a bow. "Nice to officially meet you, Samantha."

Rhi stared at me, a question blazing in her eyes: *What the fuck were you doing in his office?*

"*What* do you want?" I asked Rhodes again.

I flinched as his hand dipped to his pocket. He smiled, producing a Life Saver mint. He tore the wrapper open, nodding to Gil's house. "So Ramos is dead, huh?"

"I didn't know you knew my uncle." I folded my arms across my chest and took a step back, angling myself so that Rhi and Kaylee were in my periphery.

"We were roommates at the police academy in '97, before he dropped out to go kill hajis." Rhodes slipped the Life Saver into his mouth. "I heard he had six months left."

"Well, God isn't always fair."

"But he's merciful," Rhodes said. "Ramos wasn't the type of man to die pissing into a catheter in hospice, you know?"

I couldn't tell if he was fucking with me, if he knew what I did for a living. I thought of Gil's body, still in the queue for cremation, I assumed, since they hadn't called me to pick up his remains yet. "Tell me why you're here, or I'm calling the state police."

Rhodes hooked a thumb through his belt loop, rocked back on his heels. "You paid a visit to Cloud 69 Friday afternoon, correct?"

"No," I said, "I did not."

Rhi's arms curled around Kaylee, who was now in a full-on tantrum.

Kaylee's shrieks seemed to activate something in Rhodes. His body had stiffened, his hands moving to his waist. While Rhi hoisted Kaylee up on her hip, he said to me, "Perhaps we could have this conversation somewhere quieter."

"I think out here is fine, considering our history," I said.

"Sam," Rhi said over Kaylee's cries.

"Go home, Rhiannon."

"The fuck I will."

"Go," I said. "If you don't hear from me in the next fifteen minutes, call the state police. Ask for Travis Meacham."

I watched the war waging behind Rhiannon's eyes. She hurried down the steps finally and stuffed her flailing child into her car seat, throwing glances back at me.

When she was gone, I forced myself to look at Rhodes. The corner of his mouth tugged. "You're just the spitting image of your mother, aren't you?"

I said nothing, thinking only of my mom's last moments. The terror she must have felt, knowing she could not save my sister.

Rhodes was still smiling. "When she used to work at the farm, we all had a bet. Twenty bucks to whoever got Marnie Ginns to crack a smile."

"I'll ask one more time before I call the state police," I said. "What do you want?"

"Brenna Corbin's car was found abandoned this morning."

My blood flowed to a stop. I thought of Brenna throwing me out of the club Friday afternoon. The disdain in her face. *Don't you get it? He's a fucking cop.*

I found my voice long enough to croak out, "Who?"

Rhodes cracked his mint between his back teeth. "You're not familiar with Brenna Corbin?"

"I think I went to high school with her older sister, now that you mention it." I wrapped my arms around my middle. "I haven't seen Brenna since she was a kid."

"Interesting. The club's bouncer says a woman was harassing Brenna minutes before she left work with no explanation. A woman that looks an awful lot like you."

"You have security footage to prove it?"

"She hasn't been seen since Friday afternoon, Samantha. Her car was running, purse left behind. I'm going to ask you again. *Were* you at Cloud 69 yesterday?"

"I'd be happy to discuss it at the station. With the detective who is handling Brenna's case."

"You're looking at him, sweetheart."

The sound of tires on gravel drew my attention, and Rhodes's. Travis Meacham's Mazda stopped at the foot of Gil's driveway.

As Meacham exited the car, Rhodes's hands moved to his belt, inches from his holster.

Meacham's gaze moved from the police cruiser to the man pinning me to Gil's porch steps. Meacham, who did not carry a gun.

"Can I help you, son?" Rhodes asked.

Meacham's entire being seemed to shift at being addressed in such a manner.

"Is everything all right here?" Meacham put a hand at his hip, and panic split through my body. *Don't move. Don't reach for your phone.* The thought was swift, a pulse in my rib cage. *Tell him you're police.*

"Of course." Rhodes's hand remained at his weapon. "Detective Rhodes, Carney Police. Samantha and I are having a chat."

"Travis Meacham, New York State Police. I was hoping to chat with Sam too." Meacham had gone still.

The hum of gnats by my ear, reaching a crescendo as Rhodes's hands finally slid away from his holster. "I think Samantha has given me all I need anyway."

I allowed myself to breathe as Rhodes nodded to me, then Meacham. "You all have a nice day."

Chapter Thirteen

In Gil's kitchen, I was aware of Meacham's footsteps, in search of a place to settle, as I watched coffee spit into the pot. I was stooped over the counter, elbows holding me in place, trying not to vomit or shit myself or otherwise collapse on the floor.

The coffee maker beeped, signaling that its job was done. I willed my heartbeat to steady and poured the coffee into the single piece of glassware I hadn't dropped off at Goodwill—a mug bearing the name of the BMW dealership where Gil had worked as a mechanic until his cancer diagnosis.

I turned to face Meacham. "Did my cousin call and tell you he was here?"

"No." Meacham rested a hand on the back of one of the kitchen chairs. "I was in town, and you weren't answering your phone."

The question hung in the air: What would have happened if he hadn't shown up?

I slumped into a chair, set the mug on the table.

"I thought he was going to shoot you," I said.

"For a second, I thought he might as well." Meacham made no motion to sit. "What the hell was he doing here, Samantha?"

At my silence, he dragged a hand down his face. Blinked at me, as if I'd dropped from the sky into Gil's kitchen. "I quit being a prosecutor because I hated having to lie to the victims. To apologize for the shitty police work that meant someone's rapist would be out in six months.

At least in this job, I can be honest when it matters. I can be open with families, and if I'm lucky, it means they don't have to go another twenty, thirty years without answers."

Meacham dropped into the chair across from me, shook his head. "I haven't once regretted my decision to leave that job. Until you."

We sat in silence as he noticed the mug of coffee, dragged it to himself, and took a sip. He winced. "And you can't even make a damn cup of coffee."

I kept my mouth shut, because he seemed genuinely distressed about this point in particular, and I didn't want to make it worse. I made my way to the counter and retrieved the spoon I'd earmarked for my morning cereal and presented it, along with Gil's sugar bowl, to Meacham. He added a teaspoon to the coffee, stirred. "I can't help you if you pick a fight with Stephen Rhodes."

"You really think he'd hurt me?"

"I don't know what the hell is going through his head right now, Samantha."

He's scared, I thought. I scared him, first by showing up in his office and asking about Dani, then by going after Brenna Corbin.

Brenna Corbin, who was missing. Brenna, who had four siblings and tons of animals. Brenna, who went by Harmony at the club and who obviously knew a lot more about Rhodes than she was willing to tell me.

I relayed everything to Meacham, his eyes unblinking. When I was finished, he said, "I'll see what I can get out of the Carney PD about Brenna Corbin and Dani Burkhardt. But I need you to do something first."

"What?"

"You need to go back to Queens."

My heart sank at the swiftness of the command. He didn't want me here. And I couldn't blame him.

"I can't," I said. "The Salvation Army is coming for the furniture, and I haven't gotten a Realtor in yet, or cleared the basement."

Meacham stood. "Call a damn junk-removal company, Samantha. Thanks for the coffee."

❧

Meacham had cased Gil's property before he left, saying nothing except that I needed to put a lock on the cellar door.

When I heard the sound of his tires leaving the driveway, I reached for the gun on Gil's bed.

Gil was the one in the army, and Scott was the drug dealer of the family, but neither of them liked guns. It had been my father who had taught me how to handle one. It was necessary for us all to know, he argued, living up on Sunflower Hill Road. It would take the state police nearly an hour to get to us in an emergency, and the Carney Police wouldn't bother showing up at all if the Newsom family called for help.

On top of how isolated we were, my father had developed a fear of an intruder cutting our phone line in the wake of Scott's encounter with Rhodes and the cop who had run my mother off the road.

My father had woken me one morning and driven us nearly to the creek on our property, bales of hay loaded into the bed of his truck. Scott had even left his trailer for the occasion, having been given the task of spray-painting a bull's-eye on each hay bale.

The butt of the shotgun was heavy on my shoulder and my father's earmuffs were too big for me and I could not stop fiddling with them and he barked at me to focus, to never take my hand off a loaded gun. My father was so rarely gruff with me that I felt myself disappear under the weight of the gun. When I finally pulled the trigger, the recoil nearly took me down.

His hand, on my shoulder. When I admitted I was scared, he cupped my face in his hands. "You control the gun. Do not be afraid of what's under your control."

When I finally hit Scott's bull's-eye, exploding the bale of hay, my fingers had gone so numb from the cold I could not even feel the trigger.

My father shouted with approval, but Scott looked ill, taking in the sight of me, a child armed with a deadly weapon. I understood, then, that the purpose of the exercise was not to prepare for rogue hitchhikers. It was about Officer Rhodes.

My father brought me out to that spot every week until he was killed, memories I'd kept private ever since leaving Carney. I agreed with the other nurses at the hospital when the topic turned to a need for more gun control, usually in the wake of the latest mass shooting. I donated to Everytown for Gun Safety, and I mourned with the rest of the country, and I did not think again of those rides at dawn, the anticipation in my belly.

If I had, I would have had to contend with the fact that staring down the barrel of my father's shotgun, my finger creeping to the trigger, hitting my target, was the last time I truly felt in control of anything at all.

I popped the empty magazine out of the grip of Gil's gun. Safety on, I raised the gun with both hands, aiming it at a spot on the wall where the paint peeled from the Sheetrock.

I set it on the coffee table and began to load the magazine, rain landing on the roof like bullets.

❧

My phone alarm entered my dreams. Outside, the sky had not lightened, and I reached through the fog in my brain, tried to remember what sort of malfunction had prompted me to set an alarm for five in the morning.

Narcotics Anonymous. The Potter Beach Early Risers met every Sunday morning at six, and I wanted to make sure I arrived in time. Potter Beach was the only meeting on the county's website that fit the description of the one Jay Matera said Dani had been attending.

I was out the door by 5:10, although Potter Beach was in Spring Meadow, less than twenty minutes from Carney. I stalled at a gas station in town, filling the Accord's tank and nursing a cup of burnt coffee.

At 5:57, I rolled into the lot at Potter Beach. A playground and park sat at the edge of the lake, the rising sun turning its surface into a mirror. From my car, I watched the grassy picnic area fill with people, many looking overly chipper, considering the hour. They arranged themselves in a circle. Some in lawn chairs, others on blankets. I could not make heads or tails of who ran the group, if anyone did.

At 6:03, a Datsun came to a stop beside me, a harried man exiting the driver's side, yoga mat tucked under his arm. His legs moved like a pair of chopsticks under his knit shorts; he took his place in the circle, pulling the focus of the group. I found myself scanning their faces—young, old, brown, white—for Dani's. Foolishly, hopefully.

Although the Potter Beach Early Risers could not see me, I felt like an intruder. I had no idea what was being discussed at the meeting, but I found myself enraptured with the scene all the same. I thought it was remarkably brave, the act of baring their souls to total strangers, to share the things that had happened in their lives that left them beholden to a molecule.

I turned on my air-conditioning. The meeting was running over an hour. Finally, the group members began to stand, one by one. Some hung behind, linking up with other members, shooting the shit. The leader made a beeline for his Datsun. One of the participants followed, caught him before he could shut himself in the car. He nodded, listening dutifully, arms crossed over his chest, as I snuck out of my car.

Among the handful of members that chose to hang around, the mood was congenial. Two women sat side by side in lawn chairs, cackling. The larger woman paused, called out to me. "Meeting's over, honey."

"I'm looking for my friend. She used to come to these meetings."

"Baby, what do you think the *A* stands for in *NA*?"

Her companion, a Black woman holding a Dunkin' cup, gently smacked her on the wrist. "Well, if it's you we're talking about, it stands for *asshole*."

The white woman howled with laughter, and I allowed myself to unclench a bit. She lit a cigarette and nodded to me. "Never mind Rhonda here. Who's your friend?"

"Her name is Dani."

"Oh boy." Rhonda shook her head and bummed the lighter off her friend, whose jaw had set, eyes focused on me.

"You two know her, then?" I asked.

"Dorothy does," said Rhonda.

She pronounced it *Darthie*, who, I assumed, was her companion. The woman whose face had taken on an unpleasant pinch since I'd said Dani's name. Her eyes were focused on me, assessing. Dorothy needed to be disarmed, quickly.

"I'm not looking to cause trouble," I said. "I'm just worried. One of her friends from the club is also missing."

Dorothy and Rhonda exchanged a look. As Dorothy's eyes found me again, she lifted her cigarette to her mouth, the cherry glowing orange.

"Been at least two years since I seen Dani," Dorothy said. "She stopped coming round here once she got back with King."

"Who's King?"

"Her ex's street name. He's the one got her hooked on dope, long time ago."

"Dani was dating a drug dealer?"

"I wasn't going to stand for that shit," Dorothy said. "After all I done for her, let her stay with me—I told her to get her skinny ass out when I heard she went back to King."

"Where can I find him?" I asked.

While Dorothy let out an indignant "Hell no," Rhonda piped up, spoke over her friend. "There was a scrawny guy who drove her to a few meetings. Dirty blond, tall. They got into it once in the lot, real big scene. Ray saw it all, told Dani she wasn't welcome at meetings after that."

"And this guy was King?" I asked.

"Nah, he just worked for him," Rhonda said. Dorothy shushed her friend, aimed a filthy look at her before addressing me again. "Ray's daughter overdosed on a bad batch of King's fentanyl. He's bad fuckin' news."

"I'm not looking to score," I said. "I just want to know who he is."

"Don't know his name and wouldn't tell you if I did." Dorothy lifted her chin, stubborn. "But the times he dropped Dani off here, he was driving a delivery truck for that farm down in Carney."

Outside Gil's house. My chest rose and fell violently, the oxygen in my blood never making it to my brain. If I did not bring myself down somehow, I would be flat on the pavement the second I stepped out of the car.

Taylor Edwards.

I knew he could not be the only driver for Ealy Farms. But he fit the description of the man who had dropped Dani off at Potter Beach. And the other night, when I'd asked him about Dani being missing, all he could offer was, *I can't say I'm surprised.*

Daytime running lights in my side mirror. My breath caught as Taylor's pickup pulled in the driveway behind my Accord.

I lowered my window, heart battering my rib cage. "What are you doing here?"

Taylor cocked his head, gave me a funny smile. "Seriously?"

When I said nothing, Taylor picked over the words slowly. "It's Sunday. Breakfast?"

"Right."

"You forgot."

"I'm sorry. I had to do something this morning." I swallowed hard. Of course he hadn't followed me to Potter Beach.

It was Taylor Edwards. I'd known him since we were kids.

But how well did I really know him?

"Let me go change quick," I said, aware I was still in the terry shorts I'd slept in.

Taylor followed me into the house. I made for the bedroom and shut the door, pushing the gun under Gil's pillows. I shrugged into one of Gil's flannels, rolled the sleeves to my elbows. I stripped out of my shorts and into a clean pair of jeans and met Taylor in the living room.

He nodded to the couch. "You got someone to take that?"

"Salvation Army is coming this week," I said.

"They're real picky about what they take. I can get a guy from the farm to help me bring it to the street. Someone will take it in five minutes."

"I'm sure it'll be fine."

Taylor eyed me as I grabbed my keys. "I'm blocking you in."

"I'll follow you there." I nudged him out the door. "I've got a couple errands to run right after."

The Carney Diner was crowded. I wedged into a spot beside the dumpster, a small army of cats scattering as I stepped out of my car.

Taylor was waiting behind me, eyeing my parking job. "Gonna be fun getting out of there."

I followed him up the steps, into a foyer packed with claw machines and stale Runts candy dispensers. We said nothing while we waited for the attention of the host, the same hulking Greek man we all used to give a hard time to in high school.

He seated us in a booth wordlessly. My pulse was a time bomb in my ears. Taylor. Dani. Rhodes.

"So," Taylor said. "What did I do?"

The pit in my stomach pulsed. "What are you talking about?"

"Come on, Sam."

I closed my menu, looked up. "Okay."

"Okay," he said.

"You're sure the last time you saw Dani Burkhardt was when she was working at the strip club?"

"We're really gonna talk about Dani again?" There was something sulky in his expression, as if I were being unreasonable, a jealous lover.

"She's missing, Taylor," I said. "And people saw her arguing with a guy who sounds a lot like you."

Taylor rubbed the back of his neck with his palm. "What the fuck? Where?"

"An NA meeting at Potter Beach. Dani was arguing with a blond guy who drove an Ealy Farms truck."

"And you just assumed it was me?" Taylor kneaded his chin, the day's worth of stubble there. "Christ, Sam. No, it wasn't me." He blew out a heavy sigh. "It sounds like Cory."

"Cory. The kid from the orchard?"

"He's my brother's nephew."

As far as I knew, Bo didn't have any siblings other than Taylor, his half brother.

"How?" I asked.

"His real dad," Taylor sighed. "He had another kid, skipped out on him too. Couple years ago, Cory's mom tracks Bo down. Says Bo was her husband's half brother. He and Bo never knew about each other, and the guy died before Bo could meet him. Bo wound up taking Cory in because the mother is a real piece of work."

"You don't sound like a fan of Cory's either."

"The kid is bad news. Bo convinced CJ to give him a job. I had to fire him after two months."

"Was he Dani's drug dealer?"

"I don't know, Sam. I haven't been in touch with him or Bo in years."

"You don't talk to your own brother?"

"I have a daughter. I told Bo if Cory was in his life, he couldn't be in Ellie's," Taylor said at the same moment our waitress appeared, chirping, "Coffee for you folks?"

"Could you give us a few minutes, please?" Taylor snapped.

The waitress scurried away, the bloom of red in her cheeks matching Taylor's. He thumbed his jaw, his eyes avoiding mine.

"Cory might know something about what happened to Dani," I said. "Right before Brenna Corbin went missing, she told me that a stripper from the club saw Dani in Stephen Rhodes's car."

"Hold up. What do you mean Brenna is missing? Erin Corbin's little sister?"

"Yes, Taylor. Right after she suggested Rhodes murdered Dani, she disappeared."

"Sam, Rhodes didn't murder Dani."

"How do you know?"

"Because no one murdered her. She split because her lifestyle caught up with her."

"What do you mean by that, Taylor?" My voice had cooled, and for the first time, I saw something like anger flash in Taylor Edwards's eyes.

"She's a fucking drug addict, Samantha."

I stood, swiftly, and left Taylor in the booth. *Fucking drug addict.* The words lit up my skin, made me think of CJ Ealy telling me how his aunt had died. Taylor's mother. Bo Ealy's mother.

I went straight to Gil's, grabbed the gun. I didn't plan to use it, but I had come to accept that it was necessary to have it on me at all times going forward. And then I set off for Ealy Farms.

Inside the main building, I paused by the fridge units, pretending to consider the apple cider pints while a boy and a girl in Ealy green bantered over produce boxes. The girl was familiar to me, although it took me a minute to place her. Hailey, the girl from the orchard party. The girl who had immediately identified me as Rhiannon's cousin, the one who had seemed lovesick over Taylor. Shy girl with a mouthy friend.

I grabbed a cider and uncapped it, took a sip while I watched Hailey return to the cash register. She undid her bun, combed manicured fingers through her long brown waves. Eyes cast to the side, doing a poor job of pretending she hadn't been staring at me.

I approached the counter and set the cider down. "Hi."

Hailey wordlessly entered the price into the register and looked up at me. "It's two fifty."

"Is it?"

The cider, not the time, I realized at her empty stare. I opened my wallet. "You and your friends have a good time the other night?"

"Fine," Hailey said.

"That guy Cory," I said. "What was his deal?"

The girl's fingers went still as she slipped the bills into the till. "What do you mean?"

"Does he sell drugs?" I slipped a twenty from my wallet, passed it to her.

Hailey considered the bill for a beat before slipping it in her pocket. "Yeah. Everyone knows that, though."

"Where can I find him?" I asked.

Hailey looked up at me sharply.

"Just curious," I said.

"He works at the TC," she said. "Bo owns the place."

I thought of the last time I'd seen Bo Ealy. On his way out of the Turkey Hill in town, as I was heading inside to pay for my gas before heading back up to Binghamton for college. He'd nodded at me awkwardly.

Hailey's gaze shifted to something, or someone, behind me. "Do you need anything else?"

"No." I took a swig from my cider. "Thanks."

Her eyes lingered on me for a moment before she turned back to her register, bored. "Have a good day."

When I turned around, I spotted Rhiannon, her hair in a ponytail, low beneath her Ealy Farms baseball cap.

She met me on the way out of the main building. "Is there a reason you're chatting up my employees?"

"I don't want to do this right now, Rhi."

"Samantha." She grabbed my shoulder, yanking me back toward her. "You don't get to fucking do that. Not after the other day."

Rhiannon released me, and my fingers found the tender spot on my skin where she'd gripped me. She was younger than me, but she'd always been taller, stronger. "What did Rhodes want?" she asked, her voice low.

"Exactly what he said. To talk about Brenna Corbin."

"Why did he want to talk to *you* about Brenna Corbin?"

"I saw her the afternoon she went missing," I said. "At the club."

"And I'm sure you had a real innocent reason to be in a titty bar in Spring Meadow in the middle of the day."

"Rhi, it's probably better if you don't know why I was there, okay?"

"I have a family, Samantha," she snapped. "We live here. We don't get to fucking leave like you did."

I thought of the offers to visit me at school that went ignored, and then to my apartment in the city. Rhi had told me Mitch would not let her, but I could see it now, on my cousin's face, that Mitch had been an excuse. She was too angry with me for leaving.

"Maybe you should, Rhi," I said. "I honestly mean that. Get Kaylee out of this fucking place."

"Go to hell, Samantha."

❧

I was in the parking lot of the Triple Crown.

Bo Ealy had cleaned up the TC, or at least it seemed so from the outside. The front window sparkled, a sign advertising half-price wings on Monday nights. Back when Dani and I came here, the kitchen was permanently shuttered, a place for the dishwashers to do blow.

My heart fluttered as I popped my glove box. I could not help but check on the gun every five minutes, as if it were a sleeping newborn. Despite the face-lift the Triple Crown had undergone, I suspected I was not the only individual on the premises who was packing without a carry permit.

It was risky—a felony gun charge could end my nursing career. But Rhodes had caught me unprepared once, and I didn't plan on letting it happen again.

I suppose I never stopped being scared of the police, of the people who had killed my family. Years ago, when I told my therapist I still had nightmares about being trapped in the burning house, unable to save my baby sister, she told me to imagine my younger self beside me. *How would you speak to her? What would you tell her? A ridiculous exercise*, I thought. She'd coaxed it out of me, gotten me to address Little Samantha.

You're safe, Sam.

You're not, though, I thought. *No one is.*

The lot of the TC filled as the sun sank lower behind the mountains. The rev of an engine drew my attention.

A red Mustang, leaving the side lot. Just like the one that had dropped Brenna Corbin off to work last week. The license plate read THAK1NG.

The decision to follow the Mustang was so swift, it barely qualified as a decision at all. Pure id, foot to the gas, thinking of nothing but identifying the driver.

On a stretch of road like 42, it would not be unusual for the same car to be behind you for several miles. Still, I kept back as far as I could, in the rare chance the driver might catch a glimpse of me in his side mirror.

The driver exited toward Monticello. I slowed at the traffic circle, feigning the cluelessness of an out-of-towner, so I could yield my right-of-way to another driver, put some distance between my Accord and the Mustang.

He signaled and turned into the parking lot for Resorts World Catskills.

I'd lost the Mustang.

I locked my car, heartbeat quickening, and headed for the casino.

Outside, in the valet area, coach buses belched black smoke, unloading both day gamblers and suitcase-dragging vacationers. The casino and hotel had only opened a few years ago, promising a glamorous getaway for young Manhattanites and an infusion of cash and jobs into the beleaguered town of Monticello.

Inside the casino, I saw neither glamour nor Manhattanites. At this hour, many of the patrons were hooked up to oxygen tanks. They sat slack-eyed in front of the slots, feeding the machines their social security checks.

Adrenaline hummed in my veins. I camped out at a row of penny slot machines. That Mustang—the license plate. THAK1NG

The King. Dorothy had said Dani's ex called himself King. He was one of the hundreds of people in this casino at this very moment.

"How long are you going to just *sit there*?"

I looked up to a wild-eyed woman with silver hair. She gestured to the machine in front of me. The adjacent slots were occupied.

I evacuated my seat, the woman barking an aggressive "Thank you" at me. I felt a blast of foolishness, at how stupid it had been to follow King here, if the Mustang driver even was the King that Dorothy had spoken of.

I headed for the escalators down to the parking lot. Some cheering by the roulette table drew my attention.

And there he was, eyes connecting with me, a question parting his lips.

I thought of the taste of Fireball, his stubble rough on my neck, the kisses I hadn't wanted.

I was fifteen again and I was staring at Bo Ealy, eyes black under the light of the moon, at the end of the dirt path leading up to the farmhand's cottage.

His hands in me, Dani screaming. Me, running, through that orchard, all the way back to Mitch's.

ॐ

Of course King was Bo. Bo Ealy, who had dropped out of high school and moved into the farmhand's cottage on his uncle's property. No one could control him. Not Taylor Edwards's father, Bo's stepfather. Wendy Ealy-Edwards had left Bo in her husband's care before her death, but Mr. Edwards ran a military household, and Bo Ealy did not like rules.

After he dropped out, no one ever asked what Bo did all day. There was talk of him acquiring a commercial license, becoming a driver for his uncle. I felt foolish that I hadn't seen it then, at those parties where Dani and I never wanted for anything. Xanax, booze, Ecstasy. I didn't question where it came from. *Bo knows people*, Dani had always said.

I put two fingers to my wrist, willing my pulse to slow. Bo Ealy. Dani had gone back to Bo Ealy. How many times she'd gone back to him, I didn't know, but according to Dorothy, she'd been seeing him at the time she disappeared.

I navigated back to Gil's, daylight vanishing completely as I reached the border of Carney.

As I approached the house, my side mirror lit up with blue.

Not me, I thought. I'd been doing the speed limit, hadn't crossed out of my lane at all.

Not me, I thought again, the lights drawing closer. I glanced at my rearview mirror, expecting to see the white body of a police patrol car.

Rhodes. I could not see his gaze, only the dome light strobing in the windshield. Behind his SUV, nothing but the dark and empty stretch of highway.

Don't panic. Don't hit the gas. Call for help.

I reached for my phone, clumsily knocked it off the dash mount. My body entered free fall as my phone dropped in the cavity between the center console and the seat.

Behind me, the lights persisted.

I sped up. Sixty, seventy. *Get to a well-lit area.*

Seventy, seventy-five miles per hour, and the Accord began to shudder beneath me. A transmission problem my ex-husband had warned me about, and I'd laughed it off because I never drove at high speeds anyway.

"Fuck!" I screamed into the void. I eased onto the shoulder of the highway, engaged my locks, and put the overhead light on. Before I could excavate my phone, a tap at the window.

Stephen Rhodes watched me, my hand wedged in the no-man's-land that had swallowed my phone, my lifeline. I thought of Gil's gun in the glove box, the magazine I'd put in my center console, because it was irresponsible to travel with a loaded gun.

I lowered the driver's window an inch.

"Engine off," Rhodes said. "Window down all the way."

I depressed the window button with one hand, used the other to fumble blindly between the seat and console for my phone.

"Hands where I can see them," Rhodes said.

"Since when do detectives do traffic stops?" I asked.

"We do when a missing person is involved. Hands where I can see them, Samantha."

I rested my hands on the steering wheel. "What do you want from me?"

"You keep looking at the glove box. What's in there?"

The thump of my pulse in my ears crested. Rhodes's next words were warbled by the time they reached me.

"Out of the car."

The fear gripping my body was foreign to me. I was eight years old again, the bar of a roller-coaster restraint pressing into my stomach, a scream lodged at the back of my throat as the car teetered at the top: *Let me off.*

"Samantha. I asked you to step outside your car." Rhodes's voice was calm. This was business as usual for him. I released my seat belt, the ground outside my car unsteady beneath my feet.

Rhodes looked me up and down, from my flimsy T-shirt beneath my flannel to my formfitting jeans. Detecting no place to conceal a weapon, he said, "Back of the car."

I stood by my trunk while Rhodes jerked open the passenger-side door. The breeze picked up, lifting the hem of my shirt. Overhead, the lights of a jet blinked against a moonless sky. By the time Rhodes emerged from my car, holding Gil's gun, my teeth were chattering.

"This registered to you?"

I said nothing as Rhodes examined the empty chamber, turned the pistol over.

"Where's the magazine?" Rhodes asked.

I swallowed hard, but my voice still quavered. "Center console."

Rhodes ducked into the car again. Through the back window, I watched him paw through the flotsam of my console. Old sunglasses, half a roll of Mentos, gas station and pharmacy receipts. After a beat, the passenger door slammed shut. Rhodes met me at the rear of the vehicle, stuffing the magazine in his back pocket.

"What do you want from me?" I asked when I found my full voice.

"I want to know what you discussed with Brenna Corbin Friday afternoon."

"I don't remember."

"All right, I'll give you an easier question. Where were you coming from?"

"None of your fucking business. Are you going to arrest me or not?" My fingers had gone numb. I wanted to warm them, but I was too afraid to make a movement that might prompt Rhodes to reach for his gun.

He stepped toward me, his hand moving to his pocket. When I flinched, he stopped moving, cocked his head. "You think I'm going to hurt you."

Rhodes's voice held no assurance that he wouldn't. I thought of the gun from the glove box, the bullets in Rhodes's pocket. How easy it would be for him to leave me slumped over my steering wheel somewhere off 84, make it look like I'd finally had enough and decided to put a bullet in my head.

"You're a nurse, right?" Rhodes removed a tray of nicotine gum from his pocket. "I saw the sweatshirt in the back seat."

A hoodie, gifted to the staff by the medical conglomerate that bought my hospital. My mouth went sour at the thought of Rhodes finding a window, however small, into my life outside Carney.

"My wife was a nurse." Rhodes popped a piece of gum in his mouth. "She would always say the worst part of her job was the people who kept coming back to the emergency room. People making the same mistakes over and over until it eventually kills them."

I thought of a boy I'd treated, in critical condition after a drive-by shooting. A funny kid, not even sixteen yet. He'd opened up to me that he knew the rival gang member who'd shot him, despite what he told the police. Months later, while buying a coffee, I saw his face on the TV behind the bodega counter. Gunned down on a sidewalk in the Bronx.

"Policing in a town like Carney is similar." Rhodes slipped the gum package back into his pocket. "You can't save people from themselves."

"Please don't compare what I do to what you do," I said.

Rhodes tilted his head, one half of his mouth quietly working the piece of gum. "What is it you think that I've done, Samantha?"

"I know you bashed my uncle's face in so bad he could have lost the eye he had left."

"Your uncle was almost twice my size," Rhodes said, searching my face. "He went for my gun."

"Bullshit," I said. "Why did you really do it? What did he see in your cruiser?"

"Scott was never in my cruiser." His face was curious as he shifted his weight, hands at his belt loops. "I told him to wait next to his car while I searched it. He ran when my back was turned."

"No." My teeth chattered. "He was in the back seat—you caught him looking through the duffel bag. It had Luiza Witkowski's passport inside."

"Oh yeah? Said who?"

"Ed Robinette."

Rhodes laughed. "I see what's happening here."

"What are you talking about?"

"Tell me something. Where did you go earlier, when you left the Triple Crown?"

"Monticello."

"The casino?"

I nodded.

Rhodes shook his head. "You don't know what you're getting into, sweetheart. You pick a fight with the wrong people, and even your handsome friend from Port Jervis won't be able to help you."

Meacham. I would have called him and not 9-1-1 had I been able to access my phone when Rhodes pulled me over. I clamped my jaw down to suppress the chattering in my teeth. I wanted my sweatshirt. But the urge to flee, to get help, had ebbed slightly.

I wanted Rhodes to keep talking, to tell me why he had laughed when I said Ed Robinette's name.

"Brenna," I said. "On Friday, before she disappeared, she told me that you killed Dani Burkhardt."

Rhodes blinked, as if I'd finally said something that surprised him. His eyebrows lifted as he said, "So Brenna told you I killed Dani, and Ed Robinette told you I killed the Polish girl. Jeez, apparently I'm responsible for every single murder in Carney."

"What about my family?"

"What about them?"

"Did you do it?"

"You've been waiting a long time to ask me that, haven't you?" A slow smile spread across his mouth. He may not have murdered my family, but he was enjoying this moment.

"I didn't kill your family," Rhodes said. "Why are you crying?"

Stop crying, I thought. *Why are you crying?* I swiped at my eyes, and I begged the higher powers that I would not fall apart in front of Stephen Rhodes.

I was crying because I believed him. I knew in my entire being that this horrible, cruel man had not killed my family. He had not kidnapped my sister and housed her with a loving family who wanted her.

He wouldn't be toying with me like this if he had. It was too big of a risk, especially now that he knew I was in contact with Meacham. If he'd killed my family, he'd be loading my body into the trunk of his car by now.

No—Rhodes wanted something else from me, and it had everything to do with Brenna Corbin.

I thought of the Mustang, the license plate. THAK1NG. Two missing women, both in Bo Ealy's orbit. Two missing women who possibly had nothing to do with my family's murders at all, except for the fact that someone wanted everyone to believe all the crimes had been committed by Officer Stephen Rhodes.

Rhodes took a step toward me, placed a hand to my bicep. "Go home, Samantha. Not Carney. Wherever you were before all this."

I shut my eyes, gave in to the tears, the body-racking sobs. When I caught my breath and opened my eyes, Rhodes had retreated to his SUV.

I threw myself into the Accord and locked the doors. I waited until Rhodes's taillights disappeared before reaching for the glove box.

Rhodes had put the gun back where he had found it. I threw open the center console, even though I knew the magazine would not be there, that it was in Rhodes's pocket when he walked away from me. That his last interaction with me had been to leave me completely defenseless.

Chapter Fourteen

I began the drive to Queens, not because Stephen Rhodes suggested I leave town, but because I didn't know where to get a replacement magazine for Gil's gun at this hour. I didn't feel safe sleeping in that house without one.

I made it as far as Birchwood Glenn before remembering my apartment key was in the front pocket of my backpack, which was still in Gil's house. I followed the signs for a Super 8 and spent the night in a dank-smelling yet clean room with a dead bolt, overlooking a well-lit parking lot.

My eyelids, numb with exhaustion, lowering until there was nothing but darkness, and the rumble of my cell phone vibrating.

I elbowed my way to sitting up. The hotel alarm clock said it was ten minutes to nine. The screen of my cell lit up with an unfamiliar number with a Sullivan County area code. I thought of declining it, turning my phone off, before the first three digits of the number pinged something in my brain.

"Fuck," I muttered before answering.

"Uh, hi, this is the Salvation Army driver. You have a pickup scheduled this morning, and no one is at the residence."

I scrambled out of the bed, feet meeting unfamiliar carpet. "Sorry. I can be there in twenty."

I ended the call before the driver could tell me I had to reschedule. I flung a five-dollar bill on the bed for housekeeping and hauled ass to the Accord.

Half an hour after the scheduled pickup time, I stood at the threshold between Gil's kitchen and living room, watching the Salvation Army guys carry out his kitchen table and chairs.

From the living room, the man I assumed was in charge flagged me over.

"Can't take the couch," he said.

"What? Why?"

He scribbled something on his clipboard. "It's in poor condition."

"Who decides that?"

"I do." He handed me his clipboard. "Need you to sign this."

"What is it?"

"Paperwork acknowledging that we are not taking the couch."

I gritted my teeth, made an angry slash on the signature line. "Then what the fuck am I supposed to do with it?"

"Put it at the curb. Someone will take it."

You were right, Taylor, I thought bitterly.

I called the Realtor in town, was transferred to a woman named Donna Dolce, who was more than happy to come see Gil's house tomorrow morning.

"Do I have to be here?" I asked, phone tucked between my shoulder and cheek as I shoved my dirty clothes into my work backpack. "I actually live in Queens."

"We can do it over FaceTime! Are you comfortable leaving me a key to the residence?"

I looked around the empty living room. Gil's entire life, reduced to a shitty couch and a basement of worthless crap.

"Yes," I said.

I looked up the number for We Haul Junk N' More again, ready to make a second attempt. I made my way downstairs while the line rang and rang. When I was connected with an actual human voice, I nearly fell down the last two steps.

"Hello?"

"Hi. I've been trying to get in touch with you about clearing a house in Carney?"

"We've been on vacation."

Some back-and-forth about pricing. I would have emptied my checking account just to be rid of all this shit. I listened to the man drone about dumpster sizes, inquiring about the weight of the items.

"I don't know." I eyed a clear storage tub stacked against the wall. "It's a lot of old newspapers and comics and stuff."

"And about how many boxes?"

Pressed against the side of the storage tub was a cardboard box, warped from the weather, the tape yellowed. MARNIE NEWSOM was scrawled on the side in faded black marker.

"Hello? You with me?"

I ended the call, my phone slipping from my fingers.

I had no nails left with which to pry away the tape. I punctured the seam with a pen, careful not to disturb the contents.

The box smelled of mildew and cigarette smoke. There was a plastic caddy with deodorant, a Maybelline lipstick, and a bottle of naproxen. I felt certain I was staring at what had been in my mother's work locker when she died.

At the bottom of the box was a letter-size envelope, the corners soft and yellow with age. Inside, I counted exactly $1,800.

I slumped to the floor.

The cash, I thought, *was undoubtedly the money she withdrew the morning of the murder. Why did she stash it in her work locker?*

The groan of metal, from the other side of the basement.

I stood, my knees cracking. Someone was down here. I backed up slowly, toward the stairs.

I flew up the steps, two at a time, and shut the basement door, heart pounding. Meacham had insisted on the lock on the cellar door. Whoever was down there would not be able to escape. They'd come in by the front door, maybe a window.

I grabbed Gil's gun from the backpack, thinking of the magazine Rhodes had taken. I cursed under my breath, and I heard it again, through the basement door. The cellar doors, rattling.

I padded down the steps, aimed the empty gun at the dark corner of the basement. With one hand, I fumbled for my phone, readied 9-1-1 on my keypad.

"Who's there?" I called, my voice adrenaline-warbled.

Silence.

"I've got a gun," I said.

Some scrambling, and a man's voice, muttering, "Fuck me sideways." Ed Robinette stumbled out of the shadows, hands up in surrender.

"You weren't supposed to be here," he said. Sweat poured down his face, and at his feet was a trash bag.

"What the fuck do you think you're doing?" One hand aiming the gun at Ed, I lunged forward and grabbed the bag at his feet. Inside was Gil's coin collection, an assortment of yellowing comic books, a broken lamp.

"Please," Ed begged. "I don't like guns."

"What are you doing here, Ed?"

"He said you'd gone . . . I thought—"

"Thought you'd fucking rob me? Who is *he*?"

"Please, dear, get the gun out of my face." A tear, or maybe it was more sweat, leaked down Robinette's cheek. The basement flooded with the smell of urine; Ed Robinette had pissed his pants.

"Who sent you here?" I asked, lowering the gun.

"He didn't send me—he said the man who owned the house collected coins. Said I might be able to pawn 'em for something."

"Who?" My stomach buckled, thinking of the short list of people who knew about Gil's hobby.

"It was King."

"Bo Ealy."

"If that's his real name, yes. Big fucker, runs the TC now."

"How do you know him?" I asked.

"'Bout two years ago, maybe, King corners me at the TC. Says I can't sell there no more, but I can keep the strip club, parts of Spring Meadow. In exchange, I have to move *his* product instead, and I'm to go straight to him with any relevant chatter."

"What the fuck is 'relevant chatter'?"

"He wants to know what his enemies are up to. And Ariel. He's very, very interested in anyone who has anything to say about her."

I swallowed hard. "You tipped him off the other day. After I confronted you about Dani."

"He already knew, dear. He's got ears everywhere. His new girl, the one who serves drinks at the club—he didn't like that she talked to you about Ariel."

I thought of that bouncer, eyeing me going into the locker room with Brenna. My heart moved into my guts. It had been me, after all, then. I'd gotten her killed.

I thought of Brenna Corbin's face when she said she and Dani were not friends. I thought of Dani, screaming at Bo Ealy and me that night in the apple orchard.

My heart began to race. "Did Scott really tell you he saw Luiza's passport in Rhodes's car?"

Ed shook his head. I felt a swell of rage so intense that I may have actually shot Ed had Gil's gun been loaded.

"Then why would you tell me you did? Who the fuck lies about something like that for forty-seven dollars and a Dunkin' Donuts gift card?"

"I didn't lie! Scott wasn't the one who told me, but everyone knows Rhodes picked that girl up and killed her and burned her body."

She had been burned, the only consistent detail amid the rumors about Luiza Witkowski. In every version, she'd been burned. Maybe because that was the only detail that was true.

I dragged Ed Robinette out of Gil's house by the collar of his T-shirt, tossed him onto 42. I thought about calling the state police to report the break-in, but I couldn't lose time to all that paperwork.

I drove to the Triple Crown, scanned the parking lot for the red Mustang.

I headed inside the building. Bo Ealy held court at the bar, laughing at something that pleased him. When he saw me, he hid his evaporating smile behind a sip from his highball glass.

I took a seat at the bar, watched Bo wave off the men who had been talking to him.

Bo Ealy had been one of those boys who seemed to spring from the earth a fully formed man, sweating, with a hairy upper lip. He used to be taunted for it, that chode-like body, until he went through puberty and joined the wrestling team. Between his size and his last name, he acquired a small but loyal following of the type of boys who would be dead or in prison by their eighteenth birthdays.

Bo had shredded the remainder of his baby fat. He still had the boyish face, the lack of a neck, and now a fade haircut that made his head look bigger. He deposited himself on the stool next to me, the highball glass in one hand, studying me over the rim.

"I'm old enough to remember when they served shots in mouthwash cups here," I said.

Bo Ealy smiled at me. "How you doin', Samantha?"

"Not great, to be honest."

Bo chewed the end of his cocktail stirrer. "Heard about your loss. I'm sorry."

"Yeah, you know, it's been a shitty week. I came home today and found Ed Robinette in my basement."

"Who?"

"Crazy Ed," I said. "I thought he was infamous around these parts."

Bo snapped his fingers at the barkeep. "Get the lady a drink. On the house."

"Water is fine," I said.

"Don't insult me, Sam. What do you like?"

"Water," I said.

The barkeep looked from Bo to me and ducked behind the bar, glasses clinking.

"So Crazy Ed and I got to talking, after he tried to rob my uncle's house," I said. "He had a lot to say about Brenna Corbin."

Bo swizzled his stirrer through his drink, sucked some booze off the end. "Brenna who?"

"Corbin. She's a waitress at Cloud 69."

"Right—Brenna. She used to date a buddy of mine. Haven't seen her in a while."

"Really? I could have sworn I saw her get out of your car the other day at the club."

Bo sipped his drink, bubbles shimmying to the surface.

"She got her license revoked. Third DWI." He pronounced it *dee-wee*. "The owner of the club is a friend of mine. He asked if I could give Brenna a ride, and I did him a solid."

"You hear that she's missing?"

Bo laughed. "Missing? More like her court date is coming up."

"Weird," I said. "Stephen Rhodes said something similar about Dani Burkhardt. That she skipped town after she stole from her boss at the club."

Bo set his drink down on the bar. He tucked one hand under his opposite arm, chin propped on his free hand, studying me.

"What?" I asked.

Bo's lips quivered, as if I'd said something amusing. "You take a personal interest in all junkie whores, or just the ones in Carney?"

"Any idea where Dani is?"

"Probably at some rest stop between here and Cleveland, sucking off a trucker for dope," Bo said.

"Pretty harsh words for someone you used to date."

"Yeah, well, you don't wanna know some of the shit she used to say about you."

"Oh, I can imagine," I said.

Bo removed the stirrer from his drink, set it on the adjacent napkin. "Get me another G&T."

The bartender, a dark-skinned man with a ponytail, set Bo's drink in front of him. He waited until Bo dismissed him with a nod before he moved to the opposite end of the bar.

"So why are you still slumming it in Carney?" Bo twirled the stirrer through his gin and tonic. "Besides to play house with my little brother."

I said nothing, now hyperaware of the size of the bartender.

"You know he's got a kid, right? Ellie. She plays soccer with this kiddie league up by her mom's. Got a mean kick."

Bo's voice cut through the humming in my brain. When I turned to face him, he was smiling, not kindly. Taylor's daughter. He had made it a point to bring up Taylor's daughter.

I reached for my water glass, took a sip only big enough to wet my lips. "I thought you two hadn't spoken since Ellie was born."

Bo shrugged. "We're on different paths. But we're still family."

He held my gaze. I could think of little else but getting the fuck out of that bar and telling Taylor how his half brother had gone out of his way to let me know how much he knew about the niece Taylor hadn't let him meet.

I set my water glass back on the counter, motioned to slide off my stool. "Well, on that note—"

Bo rested a giant paw on my shoulder, pinning me to my seat. "Hold up. What are you doing here, Samantha?"

"What are you talking about?"

"You didn't really come by to accuse me of sending Crazy Ed to rob your uncle's place, did you?"

"I was just curious if you'd heard anything from Dani. That's all."

"I haven't. And I know y'all haven't talked in years, so I'm not sure I understand your concern."

"There's a chance she's dead. You're not concerned?"

Bo drained the rest of his G&T, set it on the counter. "Dani's not dead."

"It's still a little weird to me how you talk about her like you don't give a fuck either way."

A muscle in Bo's jaw pulsed. "You don't know a lot of addicts, do you?"

"Probably not as many as you."

"My mother was an addict," Bo said. "She fucked so many men for drugs they don't even know what disease is the one that killed her."

"And yet you keep creating more. You get your nephew into the family business? Or was it the other way around?"

Bo hopped off his chair, one arm slung around the back, the other finding my shoulders. He pulled me in close so that only I could hear him. "You don't want to go there, Baby Doll. Trust me."

I lifted my eyes to meet his, willing my face muscles to be still. Play dead, wait for him to finish. The look on my face seemed to satisfy him. He smiled to himself as he dropped his arm from my body, let his hand slide down my back.

It took me a beat to remember myself, for the command to travel from my brain to my limbs. Leave. Get out of there. Once in the parking lot, I let loose a violent shudder, my thoughts forming a squall in my brain.

You don't want to go there, Baby Doll.

It couldn't have been a coincidence that he'd used that name. He would have known, because of my father.

Because he was the only person who had ever called me Baby Doll.

I made it to a rest area on 80 with five miles left in the Accord's gas tank. I filled up and called Taylor Edwards, thinking of that picture of his daughter he'd sent me, at the steering wheel of his truck.

"Sam?" Taylor sounded tired, wary.

"Bo killed Luiza Witkowski," I said. "Right?"

I waited for the denial. Instead, Taylor said, "Where did you hear that?"

I swallowed to clear my throat. "How long have you known?"

Did it even matter? Taylor knew that his brother had killed someone, and somehow, he had been able to go about a normal life, carrying this knowledge with him.

"Sam, are you recording this?"

"What the fuck? No. But I am going to the state police about it, so maybe you want to tell me what you know before they come asking."

"Fuck." I pictured Taylor, fingers at his forehead, always searching for the brim of his cap. A beat of silence, then: "Fuck. It was after high school, when I started working at the farm. People were saying a detective was on the farm, asking to talk to my uncle. I guess the girl's mom back in Poland finally got the state police to open a missing person case."

"That's really the first you heard?"

"I mean, there had been rumors for years that Bo hooked up with that girl, and he knew what happened to her, but I thought it was all bullshit. Bo had a really fucked-up life, and people said stuff about us, our mom, that wasn't true."

"But it is true. He killed her and burned her body in the firepit down at the farmhand's cottage."

"I asked him—that detective had people spooked, so I thought Bo should know. He told me it was an accident."

"And you just took his word for it?"

"What was I supposed to do? Everyone said that girl left because her visa expired and she didn't want to go back to Poland," Taylor said. "There was no body or evidence or anything."

"Luiza," I said.

"What?"

"You keep saying that girl. Her name was Luiza." I pressed the heels of my hands to my eyelids. "Did he kill Dani too?"

"I don't know."

Not *Of course he didn't, no way.* Taylor didn't know. Which meant, at some point, he must have considered the possibility that his brother had killed Dani Burkhardt.

Taylor's voice cracked. "I told her, when she said she was back with him—I said she had to leave him or she'd end up dead of an overdose. I never thought—"

"Did Bo kill my family?" I asked.

"Why the hell would he do that?"

"Maybe my dad knew what he'd done. My dad was always there; he would have seen something—" The sentence died on my lips, my overtaxed brain unable to complete the thought.

Chaos. That's how Karl Holcombe had described the murder scene.

Maybe he hadn't meant to kill anyone. He might have gone there to intimidate them, to talk my dad out of telling.

I pictured my mother, at the kitchen sink, turning to face down the barrel of Bo Ealy's gun. My father, trying to plead with him, talk him out of it, just as he'd convinced him to return home after that fight with his uncle.

"When was the last time you heard from Bo?" I asked around the lump building in my throat.

"I told you, it's been years. When Ellie was born, I told him I wanted nothing to do with him if he wasn't gonna clean up his act."

"So he's never met Ellie?"

"No, he hasn't."

"Well, he knows where she plays soccer."

"Hold up—how do you know Bo knows about Ellie's soccer league?"

"He told me himself, at the TC just now."

"Goddamn it, Samantha! This is my life here." Taylor swore under his breath. "Where are you right now?"

"I'm going," I said.

Not back to Gil's, to sit like a duck while Bo Ealy thought of more ways to rattle me via strange men in my basement.

I ended the call, hit "Ignore" when Taylor tried to call me back. And I set my navigation for my apartment.

❧

No traffic at this hour. I arrived home before midnight, crawled straight into bed, and gave in to the pull of sleep.

I woke to my phone rattling by my ear.

"Hi—I'm outside! But there's no key where you said it would be."

The voice was female, belligerently cheery in a way that pissed me off.

I ground my fingers into my eyelids, my blood pulsing. "Who is this?"

"Donna Dolce, from RE/MAX? There was no key in the mailbox. I've been knocking."

The Realtor.

"Shit, I'm so sorry. I forgot."

"Hmm," she said.

I thought of Gil's house key, locked in my car. "Could we reschedule for this afternoon? I can drive the key up."

"How soon can you be here?"

Three hours later. I was uncaffeinated, unshowered, and pulling into Gil's driveway. A petite woman with brassy highlights and big blue Bambi eyes paced the porch. She was about half my height, a clipboard tucked under her massive breasts.

"I'm so sorry again," I told her.

She smiled, said, "Mmm."

I let Donna tour the house while I stood sentry on the porch. When she was finished, she shielded her eyes against the sky. "Should we talk out here?" she asked brightly.

The blinding sun crowded out every thought in my head and Donna's words.

"The market is funny right now," she was saying.

I rubbed my temple. "Funny how?"

Her lips formed a line. She scrawled something on her appraisal sheet, nudged it to me like we were schoolgirls passing notes. "That's the number I was thinking of listing at."

The number was significantly less than my annual salary. "Whatever you think is best."

"It's competitive and will guarantee multiple bidders who are looking to flip."

"Just tell me what I need to sign."

&

Downtown Carney was quiet, the low-lying storm clouds chasing everyone inside, save for an older couple thumbing through menus at a patio table outside Botticelli's, the aging Italian joint at the corner of Main. I admired the relentless optimism, or perhaps the denial.

I paid at the gas pump and grabbed a slimy packaged hard-boiled egg from the convenience store for the road. I would have to explain my swift exit from town when Meacham called again. A shortage of staff at the hospital, requiring me back at work.

A drop of rain, then more, as I turned onto 42. Eyes on the road, but drifting to Ealy's at the last minute. Two marked police cars sat outside the building.

I slowed in time to spot another leaving the lot. I made a hard left, thinking of nothing but Rhiannon.

I threw the car in park and headed for the building. Behind the counter, Hailey was sobbing. A guy in Ealy green had her folded under his arm. In the corner, two more kids in green, huddled, whispering.

I bypassed them and headed down the hall to the office, my heartbeat in my ears. Two uniformed cops stood in the doorway to Rhi's office. A man and a woman. They turned and headed down the hallway, politely avoiding eye contact as they stepped aside to make room for me.

Rhi was at the window, back to me, palming the glass with one hand, the other pressing her phone to her ear.

She lowered her phone, eyes on the screen, and snapped, "Not now."

She turned to me, the expression on her face vacuuming up my insides.

"What happened?" I asked, my hands finding the back of the chair.

"Taylor," Rhi said. "He was stabbed outside the TC last night."

"Okay," I said. "Okay. Is he all right?"

"No, he isn't." Rhi stared at me. "He's dead, Sam."

I shook my head, as if she'd claimed something demonstrably false. The words died on my tongue—*You're wrong*—when Rhi's eyes went glassy, threatening tears. I couldn't recall ever seeing my cousin cry. A flash of her cradling her knee on our back property, blood pouring from the hole an errant stick had made. My own panicked screaming for my mother, at odds with the quiet pinch on Rhi's face.

I gripped the back of the chair, guided myself into the seat. "What—how?"

"They found him this morning, behind the TC." Rhi collapsed into her chair, buried her face in her hands. "A bunch of people saw him get into a fight with Cory Wegner in the bar last night. Cory followed him outside, and neither one of them ever came back."

"Bo did this," I blurted. "Bo killed him."

Rhi moved her hands from her face, her fingers leaving angry splotches on her cheeks. "What the fuck are you talking about?"

"I think Taylor went to the Triple Crown to confront Bo. About Luiza, and Dani."

"Get the fuck out."

It was not rhetorical. She was commanding me: *Leave.* My brain processed this at the exact moment Rhi exploded, her face dappled with red, eyes wild like a cornered animal.

"Are you fucking deaf? Go home, Samantha. Leave."

⁂

I did exactly as I was told. I made it to the Ramapo service area before I broke down. Sobbing, for Taylor, for his daughter. For Luiza Witkowski and Dani and Brenna Corbin. For my parents and Scott. My sister. For myself.

I called Meacham.

"Sam?"

He sounded knocked off guard. I opened my mouth, but nothing came out.

"Sam," Meacham said. "What happened?"

I fucked up. I fucked up.

"Samantha. Listen to my voice."

I shut my eyes, and I did as Meacham commanded. *Listen to my voice. Breathe.*

"He's dead," I said when I finally could. "Taylor Edwards."

"What? When?"

I could not remember. I felt I'd lived a hundred lifetimes since waking this morning. "Can we meet somewhere? Please." I stopped myself from saying it: *I really need to see you.*

"Sam—look, now isn't the best time."

"I'm sorry. I know, I need to stop calling you like this—"

"Sam, it's not that. Hold on."

A determined sort of silence filled the line, prompting me to ask, "What is it? What's happening?"

When Meacham spoke again, he sounded defeated. A professional who'd had to accept that a boundary had been crossed. "I'm texting you my address."

❧

Meacham lived in Middletown, forty-five minutes from the rest stop.

I followed navigation to an apartment complex named simply the Gardens, which boasted luxury one- and two-bedroom units and a café, set to open in the winter. At the security gate, I punched in the code for Meacham's unit. When the intercom connected, I said, "Here."

The line went dead, and the gate arm lifted.

I passed over the doorbell, rapped gently. In the silence that followed, I thought of regret—Meacham's, in particular—and how he'd said he never once regretted becoming an investigator until me.

The door opened. Meacham was in a white tee and basketball shorts, bare feet disappearing into the cushy carpet that had absorbed his footsteps.

The scent of cinnamon was so powerful, I felt as if my nose had been cauterized after thirty seconds in the apartment. I tracked the source to the breakfast nook, where a candle burned atop the marble counter beside an empty bottle of wine.

Meacham ducked into the kitchen, swept the bottle off the counter and into the recycling bin in a fluid motion. I continued into the living room, sat on his couch, a black leather sectional that was so soft it seemed to swallow me whole.

While Meacham puttered around in the kitchen, I took in the living room. Under a flat-screen television was a media cabinet displaying a gaming console of some sort and neatly stacked books. Sports memoirs, *The Road*, *The Omnivore's Dilemma*.

I waited for Meacham to come and tell me he was kidding, that this Yankee Candle–scented apartment was not actually his. I found it impossible that someone with such an ordinary taste in books and HomeGoods wall art spent all day with individuals like Leonard Boggs. I guessed it was probably the whole point.

Meacham dropped into the recliner adjacent to the couch. Another few inches and his bare knee would be touching mine. He pinched the area between his eyes, one elbow propped on the armrest. "I just . . . give me a minute."

"I'm sorry. I know you could probably get in trouble for this, but you're kind of the only person I can trust right now."

"Samantha." Meacham's voice was muffled by his hand. When he lowered it from his face, his eyes were bloodshot. "Today is my daughter's birthday."

There was a heaviness to his voice that twisted my insides like a wet rag. There were no photos in the living room, where one might expect a family portrait, a school photo.

"She would have been two today," Meacham said. "My wife loved to decorate cakes—she had a little business, nothing crazy, but she was real good. Today I woke up and thought she'd be making a cake now."

"What happened to her?"

"Trisomy 18. We found out at twenty weeks."

"I'm so sorry, Travis."

He looked a bit thrown, hearing his first name leave my mouth. "The doctors said she would suffer, even if she was born alive. My wife wanted to terminate. I couldn't live with that."

At my silence, Meacham looked up, thumbs steepled under his chin. "I'm not—I know it should have been her choice. But I needed to meet my baby, only if it was for a few minutes. She lived twelve hours."

I thought of the sister I'd known for only two years, the way I still could not wrap my head around the sheer unfairness of it, even now. All the things Lyndsey never got to do, the person she would never grow up to be. I couldn't help but wonder if my sister was a locum for Meacham's own lost daughter.

"It's funny." Meacham sighed, kneaded his eyelids with his knuckles. "When you called, I was thinking of reaching out to my wife."

"I'm sorry," I said. The words caught in my throat—*I'll leave, I should never have come*—as Meacham said, "No. You did me a favor. I'm the last person she wants to hear from today."

"Not many couples can survive the loss of a child."

"People said we could try again. As if it were like buying a lotto ticket." Meacham looked down at a spot on the carpet. "She tried so hard to forgive me. We did grief counseling, therapy, and all that. Then about a year later, she asked if I would do things differently, if we had the chance. I told her I'd do it all again if it meant I could have those twelve hours with my girl."

I didn't know how to respond. Meacham had offered up so little about himself this past week, and now here he was, giving me everything at once. And what was there to say? CJ was wrong. There was nothing in this world worse than losing a child. I did not understand how a person could go on in the wake of it, to rise each day and continue as if a hole had not been blasted through the center of their universe.

"The other night," I said, horror rising in me. "I made that comment—about your wife. I am such a fucking asshole."

There was a kernel of a smile in Meacham's eyes. "Sam, I choose not to share my daughter with others. No one at the BCI knows why I transferred, and even if they did, it's not everyone else's job to make grieving comfortable for me."

Neither of us spoke for a beat. I took his hand. He squeezed it back, and for a moment something like peace flickered in his eyes. Maybe I was addicted to this part: taking the pain away, no matter how brief the relief lasted.

Meacham closed his eyes, the heat from his hand in mine zipping to my belly. He lifted our joined hands to his face. I palmed his cheek, thumbed the stubble on his jaw, my pulse in my ears as I brushed my lips over his.

His hand went slack on top of mine. "Sam."

The blood crashed from my head. Meacham took his hand back, leaned back in his seat, hands behind his head, eyes closed. "If we'd met any other way—"

"We don't have to talk about it." My voice warbled. "I don't know why I did that, and I obviously know I shouldn't have."

I couldn't pin down the expression on his face. Regret, or pity maybe. It didn't matter. Mercifully, Meacham seemed to agree with me on one point: we didn't have to talk about it.

My heart hammered as he stood and crossed to the living room window, eyed something between the blinds. He said nothing for a long beat before turning to me. Meacham the investigator was back. "Tell me about Taylor Edwards. After you called, I rang Carney PD and got a swift thanks but no thanks for your concern. They've already got a suspect in custody. A Cory Wegner?"

"He's Bo Ealy's nephew."

I wet my lips, thrown by the taste of the wine on Meacham's. Taylor was dead, and that was the entire reason I was here. I rested my elbows on my knees and propped myself up by the chin, the crush of exhaustion threatening to level me. "Last night, Taylor told me that Bo Ealy killed Luiza Witkowski."

Meacham's eyes moved from the window to me. "All I can say is that Bo Ealy is known to law enforcement."

"I think he killed my family too."

"Sam, hold up. Why would Bo Ealy want to kill your family?"

"You said you think the killer was someone who was close to my family. Bo could have done it and had his uncle or someone else go back to set the fire. If Bo let Lyndsey live, his uncle might have taken her. Dropped her somewhere safe."

After a stretch of silence, Meacham said, "Bo Ealy wouldn't have been much older than you in 2001."

"Sixteen," I said.

"Practically a kid."

"He called me Baby Doll!" I was on the verge of sounding hysterical. "That was my dad's name for me. It's like he wanted me to know."

"Hold up, hold up. *When* did this happen?" Meacham's voice was calm, but the look on his face made my pulse tick like I was strapped to a bomb.

"I went to the TC last night," I said.

"Jesus Christ, Samantha."

Meacham retrieved his phone from the coffee table, the glass surface so clean I saw my reflection from where I sat.

"I'm having the state police put a car outside Gil's place tonight."

"The fuck? Why? I'll go back to my apartment."

"I don't have the budget to have NYPD babysit you there. You provoked a very dangerous man, Samantha. How are you still not getting this?"

"I know Bo is dangerous. I'm the one who told you he killed Luiza, and Dani—"

"Samantha." Meacham's eyes flashed. "Bo Ealy did not kill Dani Burkhardt."

The words froze in my throat. *What? How?*

"Dani is alive." Meacham's face looked drawn as he rubbed his jaw. "She used her social security number to apply for unemployment in 2021."

Chapter Fifteen

Dani was alive, and Taylor Edwards was dead. I could not even begin to process this reversal or my role in the events of the past few days.

Brenna Corbin was missing, and Stephen Rhodes was convinced I was involved, thanks to my actions at Cloud 69. And then there was the absolutely asinine move of kissing the investigator on my family's case.

There was no way to quantify the damage I had caused, not just to my family's murder investigation but to people's lives. People I cared about.

I arrived back at Gil's to find a nondescript Honda sedan parked parallel to the edge of the property. I killed the engine and exited my car, returning the driver's wave.

He lifted up his phone, made a big show of dialing. Meacham's guy, I realized. The state trooper. Seconds later, my phone began to buzz in my back pocket.

"Hi there."

"So how does this work?"

"You go about your business and try to forget I'm here. Unless you need me."

"What if you need to take a piss?"

The man chuckled, even though I hadn't been joking. "Enjoy your evening, ma'am. Do me a favor and give me a thumbs-up from the window when you get inside, let me know everything is good."

The bike lock on Gil's cellar door was intact. I entered the house through the back door, into the kitchen. I ended my lap in the living room, flung the lights on, and waved to the state trooper as he'd instructed.

I sank onto my back on the couch. I needed a shower and an Advil or ten, but I was too spent to do anything but exist.

When I closed my eyes, I saw Taylor Edwards at the kitchen table, his lazy smile when he'd admitted he had a crush on me.

Eleven years I'd been doing my job, and it rarely got to me anymore, the things human beings did to each other. But the thought of Taylor Edwards bleeding out in the Triple Crown parking lot threatened to unglue me. I wanted to take it all back, to return to the moment Gil had asked me to come to Carney to help him die.

In my hand, my phone lit up with a text. Camry in your driveway. Do you know them?

I sat up and peered through the bay window. A clunker of a car, sickly beige under the moonlight, was in Gil's driveway. At the edge of the property, the trooper's interior light went on. A figure in black, sweatshirt hood thrown over their head, ascended the driveway.

Nothing but the sound of my breathing, shallow and labored, as I crept to the door. Two angry knocks, punctuating the fear pulsing through me as I trained my gaze through the peephole to find Dani Burkhardt standing on Gil's porch.

The sleeves of her hoodie came above her wrists. There were traces of the face I remembered—plump lips parted and smelling of peach schnapps as she fixed my eyeliner—but I might not have recognized the woman standing in front of me if I hadn't spent the past several days searching for her.

Dani wore no makeup now, and gone was the lurid hair that had earned her the Ariel nickname. Her stubby ponytail was dyed black, her skin clear except for a smattering of freckles.

I stepped back as Dani bristled past me. Beyond her, the trooper stepped out of the Honda, hand at his hip.

I gave him a thumbs-up. He frowned, retreated to his vehicle.

Dani did not look at me as she plowed ahead, clearly with a destination in mind. I texted the trooper: All good here

When I found my voice, I said, "How'd you know—"

"That you're here? Everyone fuckin' knows you're here, Samantha." Dani shut the cabinet door. "What do you have to drink?"

There were three fingers of Captain Morgan left in the bottle Taylor and I had opened the other night. Out of instinct, I moved to the cabinet where Gil kept his glasses before remembering they were sitting in a bin at Goodwill.

"I don't have any glasses," I said.

Undeterred, Dani took the bottle from me and unscrewed the cap. While she sipped, I said, "You're supposed to be missing."

"Lucky for me, no one actually gave a fuck enough to look for me."

"I did," I said, for no particular reason.

Dani eyed me over the rim of the Captain. "Yeah, you're a real fucking hero."

"Either tell me why you're here or get out of my house, Dani."

My voice warbled, but Dani's eyes still widened with alarm, as if she had blinked and I was no longer fifteen years old. I never would have spoken to her this way back then. She wiped her lips with the back of her hand, studying me, as if she couldn't quite work out how we'd gotten here.

"Why did you leave town?" I asked.

"He cheated on me. I mean, he was always cheating on me." Dani raised the rum bottle to her mouth, her too-small sweatshirt riding up. Her stomach was tanned, Barbie-flat.

"I heard from someone at the club," she continued. "The girl was drunk at the TC, and Bo was going to drive her home—they were saying he raped her. I lost my mind. I did a line of blow and I went home and I confronted him. He choked me. I thought I was dead. He told me if I ever talked to him like that again, I'd wind up like that Polish girl.

"I wanted to press charges. I went to the police station and everything." Dani swiped at the area under her eye. "I had the fuckin' bruises and everything. But Steve said it wouldn't matter. Bo would never do time."

"Steve," I said. "You mean Rhodes."

"My wallet and all my shit were at Bo's, and I was too scared to go back there alone. Steve went inside and got my stuff for me and drove me to the bus stop. He gave me forty bucks and looked up a rehab for me."

I thought of Diane Rhodes's story, about the stripper Rhodes had assaulted and left for dead in the cold.

"He's a sociopath," I said. "He could have left you somewhere for dead."

"You ever get choked by a man who said he loved you?" Dani asked quietly. "I didn't care what happened to me, as long as it wasn't getting strangled and burned in a fuckin' firepit."

"Did you know before that night that he killed Luiza?"

"Bo used to say that a group of Mexican farmworkers did it. That they raped her and burned her and took turns clearing what was left of her out of the pit so no one would see them and get suspicious." Dani drained what was left of the Captain, set the bottle down on the carpet. "Maybe if I wasn't so fucked-up all the time, I would've figured it out sooner."

❧

I tamped down the memories of the firepit by the Ealys' guest cottage. The one Bo had steered me past that night, after he had decided to rape me. Had he always planned to kill Luiza? Or had he choked her in a rage after she rejected him?

My mouth went dry, Dani's account looping in my head. *They took turns clearing what was left of her out of the pit.* "Did Bo's uncle help him get rid of the remains?"

"I don't know, but I'd bet my life that they all fucking knew what he did," Dani said. "Every last Ealy."

The couch seemed to swallow me whole, my vision blackening until I saw Clinton Ealy Jr.'s face in my car window, outside Mitch's. *I could use a drink.* I wondered when he'd decided the recon mission was necessary. At the Riverhead Inn, when I started asking too many questions about Stephen Rhodes? Or at the table that night at my aunt's, when I revealed my mother's letter and Gil's falling-out with my family?

I pictured CJ smiling at me over the rim of his beer, the crystal-blue eyes that devastated every straight girl in Carney. I thought of Taylor's assertion that CJ and Rhi had never been together. The way Rhi had blown up at me earlier today, simply for saying Bo Ealy's name.

I swallowed. "Who was the girl Bo raped?"

When Dani looked at me, her eyes were ringed with red. I let myself hope that she would not tell me, or that I was wrong.

"It was Rhiannon." Dani stood, shoved her feet into her flip-flops. "I need a cigarette."

When I heard the click of the latch, I allowed myself to lie down, body stretched across the couch.

I pictured Rhi, in this very room yesterday, Kaylee nestled by her neck. The child's warm brown eyes, taking me in, trying to place me.

I didn't want to keep her.

Rhiannon had green eyes, and CJ had blue eyes. It was not impossible for their daughter to have brown eyes. Unlikely, but not impossible.

I lay very still on the couch until I was the girl in Bo Ealy's truck bed, the cold whipping at my bare legs. Wishing there was no moon so I did not have to see his face. The warning in his dark brown eyes.

Don't fight. Let him finish.

&

Five minutes bled into fifteen. I moved to the window, spotted the empty space in the driveway where Dani's car had been parked earlier.

She had left me again, although this time I'd known it was coming. Dani had barely been able to look at me after she'd told me that Bo had assaulted my cousin.

Even if she now knew what a monster Bo Ealy really was, I suspected a small part of her still blamed Rhiannon. Bo had always wielded a strange power over Dani—even when she was the one to end things, all it took was him looking at another girl to render her a hysterical, jealous mess.

I didn't get it back then. Bo was arrogant and unkind, with a face not even his mother could love. But after Ed Robinette had exposed Bo as King, it made perfect sense to me. It was the drugs, and Bo's access to them, that kept pulling Dani back in. No matter how difficult things got in her life, Bo Ealy was there to help her dull the pain.

I was rinsing the Captain bottle at the sink, adding it to the recycling bin when someone pounded at Gil's front door.

I opened it for Dani. She held a brown paper bag in one hand, her car keys in the other.

"Who's the dickhead casing the place?" She lowered her hood, shook out her black bob.

I decided to go for the simplest answer. "He's there to make sure Bo doesn't kill me."

Dani unsheathed a bottle of Bacardi and uncapped it. "Bo's not gonna do shit to you."

She passed me the bottle of Bacardi. I was transported to that night outside the TC, after I'd caught her snorting coke. *Nothing was going to happen to you.* I realized now that Dani hadn't yelled at me because she felt guilty that she'd left me alone. I think she genuinely believed that girls like me were safe from men like Bo Ealy.

I took a long pull from the bottle, the rum lighting up my esophagus. "Brenna Corbin is missing," I said. "I made her tell me everything she knew about you, and Luiza, and I think Bo got spooked and killed her."

We were sitting side by side on the couch. Dani, butterfly-style; me, my body wedged into the corner. Dani accepted the Bacardi bottle I extended to her. She propped it between her legs. "Brenna's probably fine. She always disappears for a few days when she's back with her druggie loser ex."

She hesitated before lifting the bottle to her mouth, for just long enough I thought it was possible she was lying to make me feel better.

I drew in a shaky breath, allowed myself to say it. "If I hadn't come back here, Taylor would be alive."

Dani blinked rapidly before taking another swig of rum. "He didn't deserve this. He was one of the only good ones."

She passed the Bacardi bottle back to me, my gaze lingering when I noticed we'd drunk nearly half of it already. She caught me staring, zipped her hoodie up to her chin. "I'm off pills and everything else."

When I said nothing, Dani spoke again. "You'll never understand what it's like. When it's quiet . . . I see everything bad that's ever happened to me. Some stuff that wasn't my fault, and lots of stuff that was. After a while, there's no difference. I'll just do anything to make it stop."

"I lost everything." I had never dared say it to another person—I was lucky I was not in the house that night. What did it say about me that I cried not only for my parents and sister and uncle but my things? My favorite Old Navy sweatshirt, love notes from boys whose names I could no longer remember, a Lancôme lip gloss I'd saved up months for.

"I lost my entire childhood, Dani, and I never put a needle in my arm."

Dani had no response for this. I watched her fiddle with the zipper of her hoodie, avoiding my eyes, and I decided to ask the same question I had asked Taylor hours before Bo's nephew had stabbed him to death.

"Did Bo kill my family?"

"There's no way," Dani finally said, reaching to take the bottle of rum from me.

"Why are you so sure?"

Dani drained the rest of the rum and wiped her mouth with the back of her sleeve. "Because if he did it, he wouldn't have been able to keep his stupid fucking mouth shut for twenty-two years."

I woke on the living room floor, my cheek imprinted with stiff carpet fibers. I was alone, an empty Bacardi bottle the only indication that Dani's visit hadn't been a fever dream. I had a glimpse of her passing out on the couch late last night. I thought I'd get her a blanket, go knock out in Gil's bed, but after a quarter bottle of rum on an empty stomach, I'd wound up sliding to the floor like a human puddle.

Outside, a sherbet-colored sky over Gil's empty driveway. I retrieved my sweatshirt from the back seat of the Accord and made my way to the state trooper's vehicle.

The window dropped, Aerosmith leaking out. He cut the volume and said, "All good here?"

"Yeah." I zipped up my sweatshirt, hugged my arms around my middle. "Thanks. I'm heading home now."

He waited until I was in the Accord, backing onto 42, before he reversed and disappeared in the opposite direction, toward the sunrise.

I continued on to the rest area off 80, nursed a Starbucks latte that curdled in my stomach. Visiting hours at the Catskills Rehabilitation Center began at 8:00 a.m.

I had not been entirely forthcoming with the state trooper. I planned to go home, yes. After I visited Clinton Ealy Sr.

My father's boss. The one person who could tell me why my father had gone to the farm on his day off on September 8, 2001. If he even remembered. If CJ had not been lying about the condition of his father's mind.

7:50 a.m., the dregs of my latte cold and sticky-sweet. I dumped my cup and headed for the parking lot, set my navigation.

Just after 8:00 a.m. The automatic doors of the nursing home sent a blast of AC at me, carrying the stench of ammonia and canned peaches.

"Sign in," the woman at the desk commanded me. She looked so old that I suspected she might have a room of her own on the premises. Her hand trembled as she peeled a VISITOR sticker from her booklet and handed it to me. "Who are you here to see?"

"Clinton Ealy." I hesitated, the tip of my pen on the guest ledger. *Nancy Ealy*, I wrote.

The woman directed me to the elevator. I wedged myself in to make room for an orderly pushing a woman in a wheelchair, buried below a mountain of blankets despite the heat.

Clinton Ealy Sr.'s room was on the third floor. I hung back and let my elevator mates funnel out before following the numbers posted outside the doors to a room at the end of the hall. A corner suite, private.

Something stopped me from stepping inside. A flash of magenta scrubs, a small and busty nurse hovering over a bed.

"When is she coming?" A voice, small and gravelly, from under the lump of blankets.

The nurse moved aside, offering me a view of Clinton Ealy. Eyes on the ceiling, sheet pulled up to his chin. The skin at his neck rubbery and white. I had a flash of him at my parents' funerals, handsome.

"She's not coming today, love." The nurse fussed with Mr. Ealy's compression socks, gave him a motherly pat on the shins.

"But she hasn't been to see me in weeks."

"Oh, that's not true, Mr. Ealy." The nurse's voice was kind.

"I miss her. Could you please call her and ask her to come?"

The nurse dropped onto the chair adjacent to Clinton Ealy's bed. Her voice was weary. "Mr. Ealy, I'm so sorry, but your wife has been dead a very long time."

"Liar. Give me the phone. Police ought to know a man is being lied to, kept against his will."

"Why don't you wait for your son to get here, Mr. Ealy? I think he said he was coming this morning. He can explain everything."

A wail, the clatter of a lunch tray hitting the floor, and sobbing. "Why won't he let me go home? I want to go home."

I spun on my heels and made for the elevator, tears hot in my eyes. Shame that I'd witnessed the whole scene, shame that I'd been foolish enough to think I would find answers here.

The elevators opened to the lobby. Clinton Ealy Jr. stared at me.

We locked eyes for a long beat before I brushed past him, eyes on the doors. He fell into step with me easily. "Get what you came for?"

"Leave me alone, CJ."

"I told you, Sam. His mind isn't there."

I stepped through the doors, continued to the parking lot, CJ at my heels. "Samantha—"

"What the fuck do you want?" I spun to face him.

CJ looked tired. He massaged his jaw, said, "We need to talk."

"Then talk."

"Okay." He sighed. "Taylor called me last night. He was saying some pretty crazy shit."

"About?"

"My cousin is dead, Sam. We both spoke to him hours before it happened. Let's not be cute about this."

"Bo threatened his daughter," I said. "I think that's why he went to the TC."

"Bo left before Taylor even showed up. Five different people saw him and Cory going at it in the bar. He's always hated Taylor's guts."

"But enough to kill him?"

"Cory's probably been looking for a reason, ever since Taylor told me he caught him selling while he was on a delivery. He's a fucked-up kid. I bet he'd put a knife in me the second my back was turned too."

CJ jammed his hands in his jeans pockets, his head pitching downward for a moment. He looked up without really seeing me, shook his head. "I just don't get it. He was Bo's brother."

"Someone who mattered this time. Not a migrant worker or a junkie stripper."

"Samantha, do me a favor. Don't get all high and mighty about things you know nothing about."

"You knew about Luiza. Your whole family did."

CJ leaned into my car, palmed the driver's-side door. "Taylor told you that?"

"Does it really matter who told me?"

CJ sighed, massaged his jaw. "By the time Pop and I got home from fishing and heard the rumors, Bo had already emptied the firepit. There was nothing left of her."

"And you never turned him in."

"There was no proof she was dead—Christ, no one was even looking for her," CJ said. "Pop's granddad built the farm from nothing. He would have lost everything if people knew what happened there."

"He deserved to lose everything!" I shouted.

"You saw him, Sam. He's lost all that matters."

A siren split the quiet. An ambulance passed through the parking lot, idled at the loading area by the nursing home entrance.

I swallowed my heartbeat and looked at CJ. "Why are you telling me this? If you knew, you helped conceal a crime too."

CJ shrugged, his hands still in his pockets. "I guess because I know you're not going to tell anyone."

"Because I'll end up like Taylor?"

"I'm not threatening you, Sam," CJ sighed. "I just saw it at Michelle's. The look in your eyes when you saw me with Kaylee. You know I would do anything to protect my daughter."

The glassy look in CJ's eyes brought back the image of my father, in his armchair, watching Lyndsey and me playing on the rug, his eyes wet.

Why are you sad, Daddy? I'd asked.

Because I thought of what my life would be like without you girls.

"You're not going to tell anyone," CJ repeated. "Because you want Kaylee to have a better life than you and Rhi had. You know if I go away or we lose the farm, that won't happen. You know that little girl needs more than Rhi and Mitch. She needs a father."

I lifted my chin to meet CJ's gaze. "Are you even her father?"

"I'm the only father she'll ever know."

"But she's not yours. She's Bo's."

The look on CJ Ealy's face made whatever resolve I had left curl up like ash.

CJ took a step toward me, and I did not see the Golden Boy, the 4-H president, the one person in Carney I never thought might hurt me. With his face inches from mine, he said, "Samantha, my daughter will never know who Bo Ealy is."

But you do, I thought. They all knew, all these years, what Bo was capable of. And what had they done about it?

When I found my voice, I said, "Did my father know what Bo did to Luiza?"

CJ thumbed his eyebrow, shook his head. "I can't answer that, Sam."

"The fuck you can't," I said. "If my dad knew, Bo had a motive to kill him, to keep him quiet. Your whole family did."

Ealy Sr. was in the city with his wife, less than three hours away. How hard would it have been for him to sneak past the hospital staff, head back to Carney to light the house on fire, to cover up what Bo had done?

"Sam," CJ said. "My family had nothing to do with the murders. Just trust me."

"What do you mean, *trust you*? How could you possibly know for sure?" *Unless you know who* did *do it.*

"Please just trust me on this," CJ said softly.

"Fuck off," I said. "You can't just drop something like that and think I'll let it go. I've waited twenty years, you asshole."

My palms met his chest before I realized what I was doing. I'd just shoved CJ Ealy, or made a pathetic attempt to.

CJ glanced over his shoulder. In the fire zone, two paramedics were loading an open-mouthed man on a stretcher into the ambulance. CJ tore his gaze away, found me again, sadness filling his eyes. "The weekend Luiza died, Pop and I were on a fishing trip. Your father got to work the next morning, and he smelled something at the firepit. He saw what was left of her." CJ's voice cracked. "Bo broke down and told him everything."

"No. No," I said. "You're fucking lying."

"Jack got gasoline and helped him burn her down more that night. They dug up what was left and buried it out in the orchard."

I stared at CJ, my jaw pulsating. I wanted to claw my fingers down his face, make him say he was lying, even though I knew he had no reason to lie about what my father had done.

I sank to the ground, barely registering the scorching pavement on my bare thighs. I covered my face with my hands, my insides rapidly sucked up by the vortex until I felt as if I no longer existed.

When I lowered my hands, blinked against the afternoon sun, CJ was watching me, his face impossibly sad.

"When Gil showed up for work, he saw your dad leaving our house real early in the morning," he said. "He confronted Jack about it the day he was fired."

"Did Gil know about Luiza?"

"No, he seemed convinced your dad was using the farmhand cottage to have an affair." CJ shook his head. "All I know for sure is your mom found out the truth and went ballistic. Dad told Jack he could stay at our cottage, that he would talk to Marnie when he got back from the city and they'd figure something out."

"Figure something out?" I shouted. "She never would have kept her mouth shut."

I took a step toward CJ, arms raised, poised to shove him into the side of my car. "Your dad killed them, didn't he? Or Bo did it—"

"Sam." CJ grabbed my wrists. "Pop's car never left the hospital garage, and Bo was in Cortland, with me. Pop wouldn't leave him alone on the farm, not after Luiza."

The plea behind CJ's eyes made the fight leach from my body. My wrists went limp.

CJ released his grip on me, guided my hands gently to my sides. "When we found out what happened, Pop said to me, 'He did it. He killed them all.'"

A flash of my father's face, eyes cloudy in that armchair, watching Lyndsey and me.

Why are you sad, Daddy?

Because I thought of what my life would be like without you girls.

"No," I said. "That's not what happened. It's literally impossible. There was no gun—"

"They didn't *find* a gun. Just like they didn't find Scott's body during the initial search." CJ's eyes glistened. "And the baby—"

"No." I aimed a punch at CJ's chest. He absorbed it, the pain radiating through my knuckles instead.

"Fuck you!" I screamed.

Fuck you and your family for what you asked him to do. My father. A killer. You all turned him into a killer.

She was going to take us away. That's why she'd scrounged up all the money she could and hidden it in her work locker. Mom was going to take Lyndsey and me far from the Ealys, from my father—

"Samantha," CJ began.

"*Fuck* you. And get the fuck away from my car."

CJ stepped away, hands up, as if in surrender. I shut myself in the car and locked the doors, that ambulance sailing past me, the siren eclipsing my own screams echoing in my ears.

Chapter Sixteen

I pulled over on the highway, half a mile from the nursing home, to vomit. Sweating, tongue sour, eyes sprouting hot tears from the violence of the heaves. *Zofran*, I thought. I wouldn't make it back to the city unless I had something to quiet my stomach. Gil had the mother of all nausea drugs in his bathroom, and I'd set them aside for my next hangover.

Gil's was a ten-minute detour from the interstate. I rerouted, unable to think of anything but placing the anti-nausea tablet on my tongue until I peeled into the driveway.

I was unlocking the front door when I remembered, with a swell of panic so fierce I palmed the wall to keep myself upright.

I'd forgotten to dispose of Gil's other medications. I'd meant to flush the pills after double-checking it was safe to do so.

Straight to the bathroom—I passed over the Zofran on the vanity counter and tugged open the drawer, rattling the bottles of Gil's painkillers, the tramadol he hadn't touched. I thought of Dani, her bathroom break before I passed out last night, her wordless exit.

"Fuck, fuck, fuck." I pawed through the bottles until I found the tramadol. Hand trembling, I counted out twenty-nine pills, the exact number I had left the other day after taking one for my headache.

I funneled the pills back into the bottle with a trembling hand. Tramadol didn't carry the stigma that Oxy did, so most doctors I knew didn't really have a problem prescribing it to surgical patients in higher quantities.

Twenty-nine pills. Opening that bottle would have been like Christmas morning to an addict desperate for a fix.

My hand continued to shake as the pills plinked into the container. I was not thinking of Dani and what this bottle might have done to her, to her recovery, had she stumbled on it last night.

Boggs. I could think of nothing else but what he had promised me and what he had begged for in return. The risk to my career, my future, my freedom, to get him these pills. To get my answer.

Did he even see Lyndsey and the killer and his truck at all?

He must have, I decided. Because CJ Ealy was wrong, that my father had killed them all. My father would not have blown off his own hand before setting the place on fire and killing himself. CJ couldn't possibly know that detail, that my father's hand had been shot, as if there was a struggle, because it hadn't been made public. My father died trying to protect his family. CJ was wrong; he would not have killed them all, no matter how ugly things had gotten after my mother learned what he'd done. He never would have harmed my sister, the baby, his entire world.

My father never would have left me here, alone. I pocketed the bottle and I straightened, caught sight of my reflection. The woman in the mirror was a ghoul, hair matted with sweat and saline, lips gray and coated with film.

I rinsed my mouth with water from the tap before sticking a Zofran tablet under my tongue to dissolve. I closed my eyes, pictured the walls around me, the house Gil had wanted so badly for me to keep.

Goodbye, I thought as I left the house for what I promised myself would be the very last time.

The points of the trees in the distance disappeared into mist. I imagined myself driving into it, continuing on north until, eventually, someone stopped me.

I could turn around, in the opposite direction of the Cayuga County jail and the most reckless decision of my life. I could return to my life, my job, and ignore the devastation I'd left in my wake.

The jail parking lot was sparsely populated. No prying eyes for the indignity of the task I had left to perform.

I opened the bottled water I obtained at CVS and shoved the pharmacy bag under my passenger seat, even though I had disposed of my receipt and the box the menstrual cup had come in. A dumpster, behind the gas station I'd filled up at, paying cash.

After I checked that it was still there, inside me, I lowered my mirror and watched myself take baby sips of water. I pinched my cheeks until the color returned to my face.

A breeze lifted the hair from my neck, the sun hot on my skin. The blast of the AC inside the jail, the walls closing in as the guard at the desk greeted me.

"Who you here to see?"

I slid him my license. "Leonard Boggs."

"Boggs? Really?"

I said nothing as I scrawled out my name in the sign-in log.

"You family?" the guard asked when he lifted his eyes from my ID.

"No. He's an old friend of my uncle's."

"Really. Huh." The man studied my license again, forehead scrunching like thick lines in the sand. Finally, he passed it back. "Piece of work, that one. Come on through."

I stepped through the metal detector, stared at a point over the guard's head while he smoothed meaty hands down the sides of my Walmart shorts.

"Enjoy your visit," he said before leaving with a chuckle.

The guard propped by the window offered me a polite nod as I sat. I had not noticed the other day that Disney characters were painted, albeit poorly, on the brick walls. Snow White stared down at me disapprovingly while the inmates filtered in.

Boggs, his skin the color of raw shrimp.

"The detective came back," he said.

"What did you tell him?"

Boggs simply shook his head.

"Good." I reached up the side of my shorts. Boggs sucked in a breath, wet and sticky.

The cup popped out. I shook the baggie into my hand, holding Boggs's gaze.

"Wait until I say to take it."

With my other hand, I slipped the cup into my shorts pocket, eyes on the guard. The guard's gaze flicked over us before returning to the TV overhead, a daytime court show playing on the screen.

"Now," I said.

Boggs slipped a hand below my chair. I put the baggie in his palm, replaced my own hands flat on my lap in time for the guard's next visual sweep.

"It was a pickup truck," Boggs said. "Light colored."

A pickup truck. I called to mind the image burned into my brain. Bo Ealy's Chevy, blue, as dark as the inky sky shot through with stars.

"You're sure it was light?" I asked.

"Yes. The truck cover was black, and it looked funny."

"You don't know what kind of truck?"

"One of those with the little numbers on the side. I think there was a one, and maybe a five."

"You think," I said. "Maybe."

"I wish I remembered more. I wish I could help you find your sister."

"You could have. If you came forward twenty years ago." I found that I was not angry anymore as I said it. I had no hate left in me. I just needed to know for sure.

"She hated coloring, she'd never sit with crayons and paper for long. She loved Minnie Mouse. It was one of the only few words she would say consistently. Mama, Minnie, cow, doggy, and Sammy." My throat was tight. "Twenty-two years. I've gone without her twenty-two years, and it didn't have to be that way. I just need you to know what you stole from me."

When I stood, tears were running down his face. But Leonard Boggs still would not look me in the eye.

❧

I had a missed call from Travis Meacham, no voice mail. Panic, reigniting the adrenaline in my blood that had cooled since leaving the jail.

Had the guard called him? Meacham might have given the jail a heads-up that I would attempt to talk to Boggs. But the guard hadn't stopped me, had wished me a pleasant day when I left. Or maybe Meacham had a more innocuous reason for calling. Perhaps the trooper outside Gil's house had given him a report this morning, perhaps the license plate number of the Camry that had been in the driveway all night.

Meacham might want to know why Dani Burkhardt had paid me a visit hours after I'd left his house, the gears in my head spinning with the information that she was alive after all. Or maybe he had no idea I'd seen Dani, and he was checking in on me after last night, because Travis Meacham was a decent guy.

He was not the type of man to kiss the daughter of his murder investigation's victims, and he certainly wasn't the type to give me a pass on what I'd done to get the information from Boggs.

There was no option but to find the truck on my own. I headed onto 42, drove until a diner came into view. While I nursed a coffee, my phone vibrated in my pocket. This time, a single text, from Rhiannon.

Taylor's wake is this afternoon

I couldn't tell if she expected me to attend or if she was warning me to stay away. I thought of being in the same room as Ellie, Taylor's daughter, and the diner coffee rose up like bile in my throat.

I tamped down the guilt, blinked until the screen of my phone came back into focus. Boggs had said the truck had a string of numbers on the side, possibly with a one and a five in the mix. Within seconds of googling, I had a list of pickup-truck models in front of me.

My heartbeat quickened. There were only two models on the list that fit Boggs's description: the GMC Sierra 1500, and a Ford F-150.

A wire tripped in my brain. The F-150. Why did it sound familiar? I blocked out the chatter of the diner, the blast of the news on the corner TV. The other day, while I was browsing NamUs for missing people in Carney.

"Need more time with the menu?" My waiter, a young guy with a DIY buzz cut, was at the edge of the table, eyeing me impatiently.

"Could I just have a scrambled egg and toast?" I asked.

I did not think I could force even the blandest of food down my gullet, but I needed him to leave me in peace for the next ten minutes.

"What *kind* of toast?"

"Wheat, please. Thank you."

He refilled my coffee with a disaffected nod before disappearing.

I opened NamUs, ran a search for everyone who had gone missing in Carney in 2001. The familiar name rested at the top; the last person to be reported missing that year. Kyle Lawson. Twenty-six years old, white male. No photo.

There were scant details about Lawson's disappearance in his NamUs entry. No information about where he was last seen—only a description of his eye color (brown) and tattoos (the Army medical corps insignia on his left forearm). But at the bottom, there it was, the detail that I had read the other day. The one that had apparently stuck in my mind.

VEHICLE: 1996 FORD F-150.

I waited to feel something. A flicker of recognition at the name. A farmworker, maybe? A friend of Scott's? Kyle Lawson would have been a year behind him in school, if he went to Carney High.

Nothing. I opened a new tab and googled *Kyle Lawson*. There were no news articles about his disappearance, only a lone page on the Charley Project, a volunteer-run website for missing person cases.

My breath caught as the web page loaded two photos of Kyle Lawson. In one, he was fresh-faced, the sides of his head closely shaven, in a flat-topped army hat. In another, his dirty-blond hair was to his ears, his eyes squinting at the camera, laughing, the glow of a bonfire not far behind him.

I waited for the final gear to slide into place. Did I see him at the grocery store, looking at Lyndsey for a beat too long? There was something vaguely familiar about him, but I felt certain I did not know Kyle Lawson, nor did he know my family.

Below the photo was a wall of text.

> Kyle Benjamin Lawson was last seen in the vicinity of Spring Meadow, Pennsylvania, in September of 2001. Reports about the date Kyle was last seen are conflicting.
>
> After graduating in 1996, Kyle joined the army. He spent time as a medic in Kuwait and Afghanistan over

two enlistments before retiring and taking a job at a tractor supply warehouse in his hometown of Spring Meadow.

Kyle did not show up for a scheduled shift on the morning of September 10th, 2001. On 9/11, he called the warehouse to say that he would not be in the rest of the week. However, the employee who took the call could not say for certain whether it was actually Kyle on the phone. Since Kyle lived alone, no one could confirm when he was last at his apartment. Police officially opened a missing person report on September 14th, 2001, at the insistence of Kyle's family.

Kyle's sister Beth believes he may have decided to go to the World Trade Center on 9/11 to assist with the recovery efforts due to his training as a medic. Kyle's friends, however, say he had been depressed since returning home from his second tour of duty and may have been suicidal. Also missing along with Kyle was his gun, a Ruger handgun licensed to Kyle's father, Bill. Kyle has not been spotted since, nor has his truck, a blue 1996 Ford F-150 (see below photo), ever been recovered.

I scrolled to the photo. It was a view of Kyle's F-150 from the back. Over the bed was a black truck cap, just as Boggs had described.

Who are you? I pleaded with his photo. *Why would you take her?*

There was nothing else about Kyle Lawson on the internet. Nothing to indicate why he would have killed my entire family and abducted

Lyndsey. I felt my nerves stretching, fraying with every digital dead end. The answer *had* to be here.

He had a sister, I remembered. A sister who might still be looking for him.

I googled *Beth Lawson NY*, got a hit for a LinkedIn page belonging to a Beth Lawson-Carter. She worked as a mortgage and loan officer at the Chase Bank in Otisville, New York, according to her LinkedIn profile. I matched her headshot to the avatar photo of a Twitter account belonging to Beth Carter.

The last thing Beth Carter had tweeted was an image from the Women's March in DC in 2017, after Trump's election. Prior to that, her tweets were limited to boosting pleas for information about missing persons from *Dateline* and local police departments. On September 11, 2016, she had tweeted a photo of Kyle Lawson, alongside a link to a petition.

> Please help me get my dear brother's name added to the official list of victims of the tragic events of 9/11/2001.

Beth Carter believed her brother had perished at the World Trade Center. No reason to believe that his disappearance was connected to the murder in Carney just a few days prior.

Otisville was two and a half hours away. It was nearing 1:00 p.m. I slapped enough cash on the table to cover my coffee and my as-of-yet-delivered egg and toast before disappearing from the diner.

I was inputting the Chase Bank into my phone navigation when an incoming call interrupted. Meacham again. I sent him to voice mail. It was only a matter of time before he found out about my visit to Leonard Boggs this morning.

I considered the possibility I would be spending Christmas in a jail cell this year. I gripped my wheel with one hand, toggled my phone into "Do Not Disturb" with the other, and hit the gas.

At the Chase Bank, a security guard intercepted me at the door. "What are you here for?"

"I need to apply for a mortgage."

"Sign in, take a seat."

He gestured to the clipboard on the coffee table surrounded by four empty armchairs. I did as I was told, fingers slick around the pen as I wrote a fake last name.

Moments later, a thick-browed guy in a suit emerged from one of the cubicles lining the lobby. He scanned the sign-in sheet, his brow furrowing, despite the fact I was the only person seated in the waiting area.

"Sam?" He looked up at my wave. "What can I do for you today?"

"I'm here to see Beth Carter."

"Do you have an appointment?"

"No. I didn't know I needed one."

He frowned, tapped his pen against the clipboard. "I can see if she's free. I think she was about to go to lunch."

"Can you tell her it's about her brother?" I asked.

The guy's brow knitted, but he headed for the cubicle closest to the front window. I craned my neck, tried to get a glimpse of what was going on inside. After a beat, a woman emerged from the cubicle, her face blocked out by the back of the guy's head.

The woman placed a hand on the employee's shoulder, gently moving him aside. The skin on the back of my neck prickled as Beth Carter summoned me with a finger.

I rose from my seat, the backs of my knees leaving sweat trails on the leather.

"Hi." Beth Lawson did not try to conceal the suspicion in her voice. Her hand moved to her strawberry-blonde bob. "I don't think I know you."

"My name is Samantha Newsom. My family was murdered in Carney in 2001."

Beth's face softened a bit, a question still in the curve of her brow. How was her tragedy connected to mine? "Here, sit. Can I get you a coffee?"

"I'm good, thanks."

"Don't mind me, I'm on my fourth cup." Beth swiveled to face the Keurig machine on the opposite side of her desk. She selected a pod from the Costco-size box on the window ledge. While the coffee dropped, she took me in, her fingers working the rose-gold pendants at her freckled chest. Two of them, each dotted with a birthstone.

"Do you still live in Carney?" she asked.

"God, no. I left after college."

"Good for you." Beth grabbed her mug. It read MARIST. I liked Beth Carter. I didn't think I could come clean about the reason I'd come here, even if it meant leaving with no information about her brother.

Then again, if I told her that a career felon awaiting trial had allegedly seen her brother's truck outside my family's house before fleeing with my baby sister on the night of the murders, she might have security escort me out of here.

"So, what can I do for you?" Beth blew on the surface of her coffee.

"I saw Kyle's entry in NamUs. I just—I really wanted to meet you."

Beth smiled over the rim of her mug. "It's a terrible club to belong to, isn't it? I always told my husband that it was a crime in and of itself, the way the Carney Police handled my brother's case."

"How so?"

"From the moment I reported him missing, they tried to convince me it was suicide. That Kyle couldn't readjust to civilian life, that he had PTSD. A man disappears with his truck and his gun, there's only one explanation, right?"

"I read that Kyle's friends said he was depressed."

"Before he left for Afghanistan the first time, he started seeing this woman. A few months later, she ended things and cut off all contact. It's true, he took it terribly. He was young, and I think he really loved her." Beth sipped her coffee. "But when he came home in 2001, he was over her. Or he seemed to be. I had just had my second son, and Kyle had started a new job—he was happy."

Beth raised her mug to her lips again. "Of course, when the detectives finally opened his case, they tried to tell me that wasn't unusual. That after a person decides to kill himself, he seems happier. At peace. I might have believed it if it weren't for that call to the warehouse."

"The call they're not sure came from Kyle?"

Beth nodded. "A detective advised me not to tell anyone what the caller said, in case it was Kyle's killer on the line. All the man said was that he wouldn't be back that week, that there was an emergency and he was needed elsewhere."

"That's why you thought he might have gone to help at Ground Zero?"

"I was sure of it." Beth offered a wry smile. "That's just who Kyle was. A helper. I wanted to believe he died trying to save people. He was my baby brother, but he was still my hero. But now—I think he was dead before the first plane even struck."

I did not know Beth Lawson, but I did not want her brother to be responsible for what had happened to my family.

"What about the woman he'd been seeing? Did the cops talk to her?"

"I never met her. I knew all of Kyle's girlfriends while he was in high school, but he was very private about this one. I don't think he wanted anyone at work to find out they were seeing each other."

"He had a job between his deployments?"

"Kyle always had to be doing something. He worked part-time, stocking shelves at the Walmart in Spring Meadow."

The blood drained from my lips. "Did Kyle ever tell you his girlfriend's name?"

"No, he was even secretive about that. I didn't push him. I'd just had my younger son. My oldest was a difficult toddler, and I had my hands full. I thought he would introduce us to her when he was ready." Beth worked at the ring on her finger, as if she'd only now noticed it there. "It seems so obvious now that he didn't want us to meet her because she was married."

Beth's hand moved to the photo on her desk. Two children, both with blond shag cuts, hugging, one missing his two front teeth.

"Are those your sons?" I asked.

"Oh no, that's me and Kyle. I was always a tomboy." She handed me the photo. "He's on the right."

I looked at the blond boy in the striped shirt, and my heart stopped.

"My oldest looked just like him at that age," Beth said, taking the frame back. She considered it for a beat. "He was three when Kyle disappeared. They were practically best friends."

Just like him. Lyndsey's face stared back at me from Kyle Lawson's. I ached to reach for it again, to convince myself I was nuts for thinking it. There was no way.

Beth Carter's eyes were still on the photo. "It's silly, considering all the things that Kyle missed out on. But I always thought the biggest shame was that he never got to be a father."

Chapter Seventeen

Who could possibly confirm it, if it were true? If someone knew that Lyndsey was the product of an affair, how could they keep it to themselves all these years? My mother had no friends that I knew of, no social life outside Michelle's occasional drop-ins for coffee.

How could she? I thought. *How could she do that to my father?*

And then: *Of course she could. Of course she did.*

An unhappy woman, suffocated by the demands of her life. Everything she had ever done was for the sake of family: staying in Carney to work a dead-end job to keep the Ginns farmhouse, marrying my father after I was born.

And then, a good-looking boy ten years her junior, probably the first to look her way in years. The affair with Kyle Lawson was probably the first thing my mother had ever done for herself.

I thought of Beth's photo of Kyle as a child, and my stomach turned slippery. I had to find out.

But there was no way to find out, was there? Not without Lyndsey's DNA to confirm. Not unless a strand of hair or some other DNA had survived on that Mickey Mouse blanket over the past two decades.

And to find out if Beth Lawson was Lyndsey's biological aunt, I would have to tell her my suspicions—that her brother had murdered my entire family before kidnapping Lyndsey and starting a new life with her somewhere.

But why? How? Had Kyle Lawson returned home in 2001, only to catch a glimpse of Lyndsey out at the grocery store with my mother? Had he done the math, realized she was probably his child? Beth had said he was devastated over the relationship ending. Maybe learning that my mother had been pregnant, that she'd kept his daughter from him, had made him snap.

Renee Mason, my best friend Caroline's mother, was the closest thing my mother had to a girlfriend. Mrs. Mason was the one my mother called in a panic during minor crises: when she had forgotten that field-trip money was due, when she mixed up her schedule and picked up an extra shift on her afternoon to drive Caroline and me to ballet class.

Mrs. Mason was the one my mother had called that night, begging to let me sleep over.

I knew the Masons were long gone when I pulled to the curb outside their house in North Carney. The lawn was unmowed, and in the driveway was a battered Dodge minivan. Mr. Mason worked at the Birchwood Glenn Chrysler dealership, and Renee would not be caught dead in anything but the newest model LHS.

On the porch, a woman in mesh shorts and a white tank was screaming at a little boy so loudly I could hear her from behind my raised car windows.

I got out of the car and approached the house.

"Hi," the boy said. "You have a hole in your shorts."

"I do," I said.

The woman's expression shifted when she saw me. She lifted her bangs, frizzy and curling, off her forehead. Her voice was bright when she spoke. She nudged her son. "Who's your friend, Eli?"

"I'm sorry to bother you," I said. "My best friend used to live here. I thought I'd drop by and say hi to her parents."

"Renee and Bob?"

"You know the Masons?" I asked.

"We're their tenants." The woman put a hand on her son's shoulder.

"Do you know where they're living now?"

"Fort Lauderdale," the woman said. "They come up a couple times a year to see their daughter."

"Caroline still lives in Carney?"

"Don't know, but she must be close by because Bob sends her over to pick up the rent every month." The woman made a face. "Kind of a stuck-up bitch, that one. You were friends with her?"

At the word *bitch*, I noticed that the little boy shifted his weight to his opposite foot, his knees pressed together.

"Do you have a phone number for Renee?" I asked.

"Yep."

We stood there, on our phones, as the woman read me Mrs. Mason's number. I was aware of the little boy watching me as I retreated to my car. I drove around the block, parked in front of a house marked by a foreclosure sign.

The line rang once before a familiar voice answered.

"Hello?" Mrs. Mason had a way of turning the word into three syllables. *Hell-o-o?*

"Hi, Mrs. Mason. It's Sam Newsom."

"Dear God, Samantha, is it really? Hold on."

A blast of static so loud I had to lower my phone to my chest to escape it. When Mrs. Mason returned to the line, she was breathless. "Sorry, I was by the pool. Oh God, sweetie, it's so good to hear your voice."

"How are you?" I asked.

"Oh, I'm surviving. What about you? What on earth are you doing in Carney? My tenant texted that some woman just came by the house looking for me."

"My uncle Gil died last week."

"What?"

Renee sounded genuinely distraught as I delivered the details. Lung cancer, yes, very sudden. But Gil had always seemed so young, so healthy. Aside from the cigarettes and booze and whoring.

"I should have called you so much sooner," I said. "I'm sorry."

"Oh, Samantha, stop it." A long pause. "I'm just so glad you're okay. I always wondered."

I swallowed the urge to fall apart completely to this woman who had once been like a mother to me. Yet another person I'd left behind when I left Carney. *I'm not okay, actually.* "Mrs. Mason, did you know anyone back in 2001 that drove a Ford F-150?" I asked.

"I don't think so—I'd have to ask Bob to be sure."

"There was one outside our house that night. At least according to a man who says he was there."

"My God. After all this time. How did you find out?"

"An investigator from the state," I said.

"Oh, Travis Meacham?"

My breath stilled. "You know him?"

"He called me, maybe a month or so ago? About the phone call, of course."

The last one my mother ever made. "Did she sound scared?" I asked.

"No, not scared—Marnie sounded distracted. I was on my way out the door to pick you girls up from the movie theater, and I didn't want to be late. I should have asked her if everything was okay, but she said she had to go as well, someone was pulling into the driveway."

"Wait. Someone stopped by that afternoon?"

"Yes, it was in my original statement. The police didn't seem to think it was important back in 2001, because it was just your aunt, but Meacham did."

"My aunt," I said. "Mitch was at our house?"

"Mm-hmm. And for whatever reason, your mother seemed very anxious to get rid of her."

Taylor's wake began at 2:00 p.m. I could not bring myself to go inside Mannino Funeral Home. I knew they would have fixed him up nice, airbrushed away any trace of how violently he died, but I was a coward.

I was early. I knew from the website that there was a viewing for another man running concurrently with Taylor's. A teenage boy, sweating in a suit, pushed an old woman up the wheelchair ramp. She had the resigned look on her face of an elderly widow.

To the left of the building, by a strip of impatiens, I spotted a few guys from Carney High School in ill-fitting button-downs and khakis. Many of them had probably already seen a friend or two buried this year alone, but it was plain from their faces that none of them had expected Taylor to be next.

I popped my glove box open to make sure it was still there. The envelope of cash from my mother's work locker, beside my ancient owner's manual.

Movement outside the funeral home drew my attention. A child, bucking away from the woman who had her by the hand. The girl wore a dress printed with sunflowers; her mother's body disappeared beneath her black sheath dress. Her face was swollen, makeup-free, plump lips whispering an ultimatum to the child. Perhaps the sunflower dress had been a compromise to secure the girl's participation in a ritual she would not understand.

I barely understood the purpose myself, at thirteen. How they could expect me to stand beside the coffins that held what was left of my parents, how any of the well-wishes could possibly ease the weight of knowing I would never see them again.

I looked at Taylor's daughter, and I knew that Taylor confronting Bo had never been about me or my family. Taylor knew what his brother was, and even if he could not protect his daughter from every man in the world like Bo Ealy, maybe he could be the type of man she deserved for a father.

I swiped at my eyes with the heel of my hand. I grabbed the envelope of cash and stepped outside my car, only to come within an inch of colliding with Rhiannon. She wore gray slacks and a black blouse with capped sleeves.

"Surprised you showed."

I shrugged. I had no desire to fight with my cousin anymore. Not after what Dani had told me.

Rhi tucked her hair behind her ear, fingers grazing a small tattoo I had not noticed the past week. *Kaylee Rose.* The sight of it, that fierce need to claim the daughter she had not even wanted, felt too intimate to stare at. "CJ told me you talked," Rhi said. "About Kaylee."

"I won't tell anyone. It's not my business."

Rhi nodded, the closest thing to a thank-you I had ever gotten from her.

"Does Mitch know?" I asked.

Rhi snorted. "So she could tell me I'm an idiot for getting drunk out of my mind at the TC the night it happened?" She shook her head. "It was the first time I'd gone out with friends in years. I'm just always so tired from the farm, you know? I woke up in the apartment upstairs, the one Bo stays at sometimes. He said I didn't want to leave, and my friends ditched me, so he let me stay. The one fuckin' time I tried to have a little fun."

"You didn't want to press charges?"

"I didn't realize what happened until I missed my period. I only told CJ because I wanted time off for an abortion." Rhi swallowed. "I told him I wasn't sure it was what I wanted to do. He told me he'd take care of her, if I kept her. That we could do it together. He's probably the only real friend I've ever had."

I wanted to tell her that I was sorry, that I should have been a better friend and cousin. That I should have done more to protect her from this place. But I doubted that my pity or apologies were what Rhiannon needed from me.

Mercifully, Rhi seemed eager to change the subject.

"They arrested Bo today." When she said Bo's name, my cousin's gaze slipped away from mine and toward the funeral home.

"For what?" I asked.

"Lying to the police about the stabbing and some other stuff. I don't really know."

"Anything about Brenna?"

Rhi looked down at her too-tight flats. "Bo's not talking. But everyone knows he or Cory had something to do with it."

"They're never going to have enough to charge him for any of this," I said, my throat going tight. "The rumors, the confessions. It's not enough."

Rhi tilted her face up to the sky, blinking rapidly. "He's not going anywhere. He didn't get bail, and they're saying the DA is trying to build a drugs-and-weapons case against him and Cory. They get their shit from these guys in Monticello. They're gonna go away for a long time."

I sensed that it was exactly what Rhi wanted and the very same reason she hadn't reported the rape. She needed Bo Ealy out of her life.

Rhi looked over her shoulder at the growing line to enter the funeral home, then back at me without meeting my eyes. "You coming in or what?"

"I don't think that's a good idea."

Rhi nodded. "See you around, then."

"Wait—Rhi."

She turned to face me, a question forming on her lips.

"I spoke to Renee Mason today," I said.

"About what?" Something flickered in Rhi's eyes. Worry, maybe. I swallowed hard against the sinking feeling in my chest.

"She said when my mom called her the evening of the murders, Michelle was pulling up to our house."

Rhi was quiet for a beat. "I mean, she did that, didn't she? Dropped in to see your mom."

"But did Mitch say anything to you? Why she dropped by *that* day?"

"How would I even remember if she did? It was twenty-two years ago, Samantha." Rhiannon's voice held a plea. *Let it go.*

"I think my mom was going to leave my dad," I said. "She had money hidden in her work locker—enough to get us a motel room for a couple weeks."

Rhi swallowed. "Even if it's true, what's any of it got to do with Mom?"

"My mother trusted her." There was no affection between them, but my mom trusted Michelle. That conversation at the table the day I found out my mother was pregnant. She'd told my aunt she did not want to keep the baby. Had she also told her about Kyle Lawson?

Had Michelle told my father? Is that why he skipped out on his delivery that evening and gone home instead? To confront my mother before she could take us away from him?

Chaos, Holcombe had said. But someone had left, alive, with Lyndsey.

"Samantha," Rhi said. "Think of what you're saying."

"I have thought about it, Rhiannon." I thrust the envelope of money at my cousin. "I've got to go. Take this, please."

Rhi's eyes widened at the stack of bills inside. "The fuck for?"

"Taylor's daughter. Start a college fund for her through the farm or something. I don't want it."

Michelle's driveway was empty when I arrived. I did a loop around the block, parked out of sight.

She still kept a key beneath the mat at the back door.

Into her bedroom. Mitch still had her old starchy bedspread. I would come in here sometimes when she was at work, for no particular reason other than that I could. Touching her things, swiping my fingers across her cakey foundation, the only makeup she ever wore.

I had no particular target in mind now. What evidence could possibly be in this house, even if my suspicions were right and Mitch had tipped my father off that day?

Could she have possibly known, all this time, that he wasn't Lyndsey's real father?

Mitch's bureau, the handles brassy with age, held no photos of Rhi or Kaylee. I tugged open the top drawer, found only pilling flannel pajamas and Hanes underwear, folded neatly.

Mitch had said she had no pictures from my childhood when I'd begged, after the fire. Now, the possibility gnawed at me—that she'd been hoarding them for herself, concealing baby pictures of Lyndsey so I would not look too closely at them.

On Mitch's nightstand was a remote to the television mounted over the bureau, the only new addition to the room I could identify. Her reading glasses rested atop a copy of *Soap Opera Digest*. I opened the drawer, exposing a pistol, much smaller than Gil's. A .22 that could fit in my pocket. I swallowed my heartbeat, pawed through my aunt's private belongings.

Melatonin pills, laminated prayer cards from her father's service, from my father's service. Finally, a thin stack of photos: Rhiannon's kindergarten portrait, wallet size. A yellowing photo of Mitch as a girl, her hair in two black braids, perched on her father's hip, her arms around his neck. My father stood beside them, already half my grandfather's height, despite the fact he could not have been older than eight.

At the bottom of the drawer, as if it had been buried there, was a postcard. A painting of a brown-and-white bird, long black beak bent toward its feet, buried in wet sand.

I turned the postcard over a with a trembling hand. Scrawled in black ink was a message: *I love you always, Mitchy. And my girl.*

I read the words again, the slope of the blocky letters sealing my throat shut.

Down the hall, the lock in the front door stirred, and someone called my name.

Rhiannon was waiting for me in the living room. "I had a feeling you weren't going home."

"Where are they?" I asked. I'd meant Mitch and Kaylee, but I thought of the postcard still in my hand. Of the only person I knew of who would ever call Michelle *Mitchy*.

"Mom took her grocery shopping," Rhi said. "They should be back any minute."

My cousin's eyes tracked my movements as I held up the postcard, unable to speak. Rhi's face fell.

"Who sent this?" I asked.

"I don't know."

"But this isn't the first time you've seen it."

"When Mom was hospitalized a few months ago, I wanted to bring her prayer book. She kept saying it wasn't necessary. I already knew about the gun, so I figured it was something else in the drawer she didn't want me to see." Rhi let out a sharp laugh, eyes welling. "I thought I was gonna find a vibrator."

"Did you ask her about it?"

"What was I supposed to say? I pretended to forget about the prayer book. She never asked if I'd been in the drawer."

"It's his handwriting."

"We don't know that. We have nothing to compare it to."

I could tell she didn't believe it. Rhi knew her mother better than I did, and she would not have this postcard in her nightstand unless someone very important had sent it.

"He took her," I said. Not Kyle Lawson, Lyndsey's real father.

Outside, a car door slammed. Rhi moved to the bay window. I followed. We stood there, the two of us, and watched her.

Mitch, hobbling to the back seat.

Rhi fled. I caught the screen door from flying into my face, and by the time I reached the front steps, my cousin was at the door behind the driver's seat. She flung the door open, scooped her child out of the seat, while Michelle, shunted to the side, shouted, "The hell are you doing?"

When my aunt's gaze found me, her jaw set. Rhiannon hoisted her sleeping child up her body so Kaylee's head rested beneath her chin.

I held up the postcard for Mitch. "Who sent this to you?"

My aunt said nothing.

"Answer her." Rhiannon's voice was razor sharp. She nodded toward the postcard in my hand, careful not to disturb her daughter.

The look on my aunt's face turned my guts inside out.

"How could you?" I said. "He killed them all."

"Your mother killed them, with her selfishness." Mitch's gaze moved to Rhi, who held her child closer to her body.

"When did you find out she was leaving?" I asked.

"That afternoon. Marnie had been acting odd for weeks. Something just came over me—told me to drop by the house to check on her. She was packing."

"Did she tell you what my father did? And why she was taking us?"

"I told her she couldn't take you girls from him. He'd never let her. She laughed in my face, told me that Lyndsey wasn't even his. She said her lover was on his way over, and they were going to pick you up from Caroline's, and we would never see any of you ever again."

"So you called him at work and you told him."

Mitch stared back at me. "What kind of person would I be if I didn't?"

"He killed them, Michelle." I did not realize I'd screamed it until the startled cry from beside me. Kaylee. Rhi put a hand to the back of her daughter's head, bounced to soothe her. Torn between wanting to take the child away and wanting to hear it for herself, what her mother had done.

"Did you know he was going to kill them and steal her?" I shouted.

"Of course not," Mitch said. "All he wanted was to keep his family together."

Mitch's voice carried the certainty of someone who had been told this firsthand.

"No one had to get killed," she continued. "Marnie's lover had the gun. He and Jack struggled for it—it went off. Marnie went ballistic. He had no choice." Michelle shut her eyes. "He was trying to clean everything up when he heard Scott in the basement."

"You set the fire, didn't you?" My voice trembled. "They were already gone when you went there and set the place on fire, right?"

"He came by the house. He wanted to get you from the Masons'. I told him he couldn't. You couldn't be trusted to go along—he had to leave you with me, and he and Lyndsey had to leave, right away, and get rid of Marnie's lover's gun and truck."

"He'd just killed three people!"

Kaylee began to wail, and the dogs next door began to howl. The groan of a gate and a woman stepped out. "You lower your voices or I'm calling 9-1-1."

Rhi swiveled to the woman. "Fuck off and mind your own goddamn fucking business, Dottie."

At the look on Rhi's face, Dottie took two steps back and disappeared behind her gate.

During the transaction, Mitch had seemed to come to terms with the gravity of the situation. There was panic on her face. "Rhiannon, you get that baby inside."

"Don't." Rhi's voice held a dozen different threats. *Don't talk. Don't tell me what to do ever again.*

"Where did they go?" I asked.

"Jack never told me," Mitch said.

"Bullshit. He sent you this."

"Samantha." There was a plea in my aunt's voice. She reached for me, and it dawned on me how weak of a woman she was. I could knock her over with one arm, watch her lie bleeding on the pavement, and I would enjoy every moment of it.

"Give that to me," she said. There was fear in her eyes, the prospect of losing it forever. All that remained of her Jack.

"Samantha! Give that here right now!"

I set off toward my car, the sun hot on my back, the dogs and the child continuing to howl.

Chapter Eighteen

I made it back to my apartment in time to hear the couple next door screaming over the *Jeopardy!* theme.

I scrounged an Ambien from my medicine chest and crawled into bed. The space felt foreign to me after those nights on Gil's couch, but I slept. I slept an entire night, for the first time since my family was murdered. Since my father murdered my mother, my uncle, and Kyle Lawson.

I woke to banging at my door, rattling the latch. Sunlight through the window over the kitchen, shouting and jackhammers out on the street.

Through the peephole in my door, I saw Travis Meacham, arms folded over his chest, standing next to a very pissed-off-looking woman in an ill-fitting gray suit.

I opened the door and folded my arms over my flimsy T-shirt. The woman spoke first.

"Detective Tanya Reeder," she said. "I'm with the New York State Police."

"May we come in?" Meacham asked.

"How can I help you?" I asked as Tanya Reeder invited herself into my apartment. I put the detective anywhere between forty and fifty. Her lipstick bled into the corners of her mouth, and her hair, coarse and graying, was twisted up and held by an alligator clip.

She looked at me. "I expect you know why I'm here."

No, actually. Was it the smuggling narcotics to an inmate? I said nothing, thinking of TV scenes of two-way mirrored rooms and demands for lawyers.

When I said nothing, Reeder reached inside her jacket pocket, retrieved her phone. "I understand you made statements to my colleague about the murder of Luiza Witkowski."

I looked at Meacham, who stared at a point on the wall over my shoulder. "It's in your interest to cooperate, Sam."

I had only two chairs at my kitchen table. Reeder and I sat opposite each other, while Meacham hung by the fridge.

Reeder scrawled notes on a legal pad as I answered her questions. No, Taylor didn't tell me he was planning on confronting his half brother the evening he was killed. No, I had not had any interaction with Cory Wegner prior to that night at the orchard, nor did Taylor ever mention Bo's other brother to me.

Reeder paused her scrawling, asked, "And why did you accompany Taylor Edwards to Ealy Farms that evening?"

"I was helping him break up a party."

Reeder didn't look up from her notepad, where she had written, simply, *Party?* "What, exactly, was the nature of your relationship with Taylor again? I'm still unclear on that point."

I was aware of Meacham, by my fridge, peppered with save-the-dates and baby shower invitations for other people. For the first time, I felt ashamed at admitting how alone I was.

I stared at Detective Reeder. "We had casual sex. Is that clear enough?"

Meacham said nothing while Reeder sipped from her bottle of Dasani. She recapped her water, said, "Did Taylor or anyone else implicate other individuals in Luiza Witkowski's death?"

I thought of how I'd screamed at CJ Ealy in the parking lot of his father's nursing home when he'd told me my father helped Bo dispose of Luiza's charred remains.

"Samantha?" Reeder set her water bottle down on my table. "Do you need a break?"

I shook my head. I guided Reeder through the maze of lies Bo Ealy had constructed around Luiza's disappearance. When I told her that Ed Robinette claimed Stephen Rhodes had killed my family because Scott saw Luiza's passport in his back seat, Reeder stopped scrawling and looked up at me. "That couldn't have happened. Luiza Witkowski's passport was found in the room she was renting."

"Obviously it didn't happen," I said. "Bo started the rumor because *he* killed Luiza, and you're sitting here bullshitting with me about it instead of getting him to tell you where Brenna Corbin's body is."

Reeder set her phone on my table, swiped a finger across the screen to check the time. "Brenna Corbin has used her credit card multiple times since Bo Ealy was arrested, as well as her cell phone."

Brenna was alive. I looked to Meacham for an explanation, but his face was neutral.

"I don't understand," I said, holding his gaze. "Rhodes tried to question me after she went missing. You were *there*, at Gil's house."

"Brenna Corbin was never reported missing," Reeder finally said. "Stephen Rhodes was attempting to question you under false pretenses, and he's been suspended pending a full investigation."

"What the fuck?"

"Brenna Corbin's ex-boyfriend was an informant in a drug case of Detective Rhodes's," Detective Reeder said. "The informant skipped town before he was supposed to testify, and Rhodes's case fell apart. There have been complaints that he's been intimidating individuals that he believes know where the informant is."

Brenna was alive. Any relief I might have felt was eclipsed by the fact that Taylor Edwards was still dead, and so was Luiza. The thought of Bo Ealy never having to answer for either of these things filled me with an anger so intense that I stood, my legs trembling.

By the fridge, Meacham shifted his weight, watching me, as if I were an uncaged animal. I crossed my arms over my chest, heart thumping wildly, and glared down at Detective Reeder.

"So what now? Rhodes gets to retire with his full pension, Bo gets a couple years in prison for the drug charges, and the fucking Ealys get away with covering up a murder for twenty-two years?"

"Samantha," Meacham said. It was the first thing he'd said in nearly an hour. Tanya Reeder offered a tight smile as she rose from the table.

"You have my card," she said. "If you can think of anything else."

Detective Reeder paused in my kitchen doorway, her face forming a question when she noticed Meacham hadn't moved to follow her.

"I'll be out in a minute," he said, his eyes on me.

The front door clicked shut behind Detective Reeder, and we were alone.

"You saw Boggs," he finally said. "Twice."

I sat back down at the kitchen table. When I did not respond, Meacham moved his hands to his belt loops, pushing his jacket back. "Jails have these funny things, Samantha, called visitor logs."

"He didn't tell me anything," I said.

Meacham smiled, shook his head. "Does the name Kyle Lawson mean anything to you?"

"No."

"Funny, because I spoke to his sister. She says a woman who identified herself as Samantha Newsom came by her bank yesterday asking about Kyle."

I met his eyes. "What do you want me to say?"

"That you give a shit whether or not this woman, who has been waiting twenty-two years for news about her brother, gets to know how he died."

"How long have you suspected it wasn't my father in the house?"

"Since I got the case. I reread all of the tips that had been called in over the years—there was one that was never followed up on. A year after the murders, a man saw your mother's picture on the news. He claims he met with her in September '01 about renting a two-bedroom property he owned. He was sure it was Marnie Ginns he spoke to, because he saw a little girl in the truck at the curb."

"Why didn't Holcombe follow up?"

"He did. The landlord couldn't describe the truck, or the guy driving it. Holcombe wrote it off as a false sighting."

"But you didn't." *And you didn't tell me. You son of a bitch.*

"I requested all the remains be exhumed and retested," Meacham said.

When the spasming in my throat quieted, I said, "When will we know for sure?"

"Even if there's usable DNA, it'll take a long time. But at least now we have yours for comparison."

Anger rose in me. "You lied about why you wanted my DNA."

Meacham hesitated for a fraction of a second before he shook his head. "I didn't. Finding Lyndsey is still crucial to building a case."

"You had another purpose, and you kept it from me."

"I was only doing my job."

His voice had cooled, and I thought of how he'd opened up to me about his change in career, about his divorce. How he'd treated me like a friend and earned my trust in order to prove my father was a murderer.

"What about Luiza?" I asked.

Meacham's gaze flicked to the door. "Detective Reeder is working on getting a warrant to search the farm, based on a tip."

My body went cold as I thought of my father, under the moon, alongside Bo Ealy, burying that poor girl's bone fragments.

"Sam." Meacham's eyes found mine. "Is there anything you didn't tell Reeder about Luiza that you'd like to share with me?"

Fuck you, I thought. *You knew, all this time, what my father really was.*

"I need to sleep before my shift," I said.

Meacham's jaw set. "There's no point protecting him, Samantha. I can't even pretend to understand why you would want to."

"If that's what you think this is about, okay."

He laughed, shook his head. "That's it? *Okay?*"

When I said nothing more, Meacham slammed a hand on my counter. "Goddamn it, Samantha! You're not the only one who's hurting."

His voice warbled. I felt the impulse to look away, as if I'd walked in on him stark naked, but I couldn't. He broke my gaze. "Beth Lawson—how could you be so selfish?"

If he'd hesitated half a second less before issuing the amendment, I might have believed his anger was solely on behalf of Kyle Lawson's sister. I thought of Meacham on his couch, the malbec-stained wine glass, the lonely way he'd marked his daughter's birthday. My own anger at how he'd played me.

"Finding Lyndsey is not going to bring your daughter back," I said.

Meacham stared at me. He stopped, palmed my door, before turning his body halfway to meet my gaze. "I hope you can live with yourself."

I shut my eyes against the click of the door.

I was at the bodega a block from the hospital, my usual place, an hour before my shift. I nursed a tepid cup of coffee while I waited for Jim Ryan. I did not know if Ryan was his surname or if he went by his middle name, to maintain the illusion of anonymity, to give clients the impression he was a man who blended in.

All I knew of Jim Ryan was that he was former NYPD, like the majority of private investigators in Queens. Unlike the others, he had agreed to take a full cash payment, up front, in exchange for agreeing to keep no formal record of me as a client, save for a signed piece of paper that I agreed to pay his expenses in cash on return from his trip to South Carolina.

He sank into the seat opposite me. The postcard from Mitch's drawer was clipped to the front of a manila folder.

"I know it wasn't much to go on," I said.

Ryan lifted his eyebrows. "Do you want to hear what I found or not?"

He had tracked down the artist who designed the postcard. At the time it was mailed five years ago, he only sold to three shops within ten miles of the town the postcard had been mailed from—Sullivan's Island, South Carolina.

"One of them kept meticulous records," Ryan said. "A mom-and-pop shop—the woman has marble notebooks with the dates of every sale of merchandise going back to the nineties."

He had flown down to South Carolina to meet with the owner in person. He'd shown her the postcard, and she hadn't even needed to consult her sale log.

She remembered the man who bought the postcard, because he and his family had rented a beach house every summer for the past few years. The kids came into the store often, three of them, and the mother was kind, chatty. The owner thought the woman's name was Ellen.

Her husband visited only once, though, to buy the postcard. He paid cash—the wife always did too—and the owner never got his name.

My heart sank. I had paid thousands to track the postcard to a dead end.

"I'm not done," Ryan said.

The shop owner consulted her notebook. She remembered that the man's son came in toward the end of the trip. He needed condoms. He was sheepish about it, because the owner kept them behind the counter. Too many teenagers stealing them.

The guy paid for a pack of Trojans, a case of Bud Light, and some snacks. With a credit card.

"His name is Chase Bolling," Ryan said. "I found someone by that name that fits the age and description of the man's son."

Son. My father didn't have a son. The thought looped in my brain as Ryan passed a folder.

Inside were printouts, screenshots of a Facebook page for a man named Chase Bolling. He was an English teacher in Nashville, and he was tanned and good-looking. In his profile picture, he was dipping a dark-haired woman in a wedding gown.

Ryan tapped a fingernail, yellowed by tobacco, on the couple standing to the side of Chase and his bride. Chase's wedding to the dark-haired woman. A woman with copper hair twisted in a chignon, in an ugly eggplant evening gown, a clean-shaven man in a tux at her arm.

The sight of him in formal attire was almost as jarring as the sight of him, very much alive. The twenty-two years that had passed since I'd last seen him were obvious in the lines marring his face, the slump in the once-solid shoulders that had carried Lyndsey and me around the house.

I closed my eyes, fighting off the image of myself, running into his arms after he'd come home from a long route. *I missed you, Baby Doll.*

You can bury the past, starve it of light and oxygen, but it will still find a way to survive.

All thoughts of my father, and where he might be, dissolved when I remembered what Ryan had said about the shop owner on Sullivan's Island. *The kids came in often. Three of them.*

I swallowed to clear my throat. "What about Chase's siblings?"

"One is older, one is younger. Mia is thirty-one, and Elizabeth is twenty-two."

Lyndsey would be just shy of her twenty-third birthday, if Chase's younger sister was actually his stepsister via my father.

She had been small for her age, though. Quiet, slow to talk. It would have been easy for my father to lie about how old she was when he met Ellen Bolling and her two children, pass his own daughter off as a year younger than she actually was.

If I was right, and it was her—how could he?

"The man," I said. "What did he go by?"

"John Bolling," Ryan said. "He took his wife's last name when they married in '03. Couldn't dredge up anything on him prior to that."

"Do you know where he is now?"

The look on Ryan's face made my heart sink. "I called the wife. She said she hasn't heard from John in four years."

"They divorced?"

"He walked out on them."

That postcard to Mitch. *I love you always, Mitchy. And my girl.* Had it been a final goodbye? My father had brought his new family to Sullivan's Island, he had stuck around for Chase's wedding, and he'd left them, just like he'd left me.

"The last address for him was a house in his wife's name that sold four years ago," Ryan said, off my expression. "Social security doesn't have a death record for him, and Google is no help. John Bolling shares a name with the mayor of the Virginia Colony."

"Thank you," I said. "I appreciate everything."

"That's it?" Ryan cocked his head. "I've got an address for the kid, Chase. He lives outside of Nashville."

I shook my head. Jim Ryan had done what I had hired him to do. He had found the man who had sent Mitch that postcard.

"You take care." He stood, hesitating for a bit, as if contemplating whether to give me a fatherly squeeze on the shoulder. He nodded to me, and then he was gone.

I opened the folder he had left on the table. Inside were his itemized expenses. A round-trip flight to Charleston Airport and one night at a nearby motel, both booked through Expedia. I slipped it in my backpack, and I headed to work.

❧

It had been a drama-free evening in the ICU for the most part, considering Farkas was the attending doctor on call. The hour hand had been hovering over three for an eternity. Every patient on the unit was either asleep or slack-jawed in front of muted *Forensic Files* reruns when I sank into a chair at the nurse's station to submit a patient's request for an antacid.

I caught myself kneading my eyelids, trying to fend off a bone-deep tiredness.

The dark hour, Nancy called this. That last stretch before the end of the shift where minutes felt like days, where a hard-earned moment of peace could be stolen in an eye blink by a stray bullet or a cabbie blowing a red light.

I got up to start my rounds, paused at the door to 11A. A nursing home transfer, old man with pneumonia. Over his intubated body, Dr. Farkas was shouting at an intern.

The girl was half his height, honey haired. I knew her name was Grace. She was one of the better interns, but prone to tears, and excuses. An easy target for Farkas.

I watched, heart moving into my throat, as she shook her head. I did not catch what Farkas was laying into her for, only the way his arm shot out and grabbed her wrist when she tried to leave.

I stepped into the room. "Don't fucking touch her."

Farkas stared at me. "*Excuse* me?"

Dr. Grace Whatever kneaded her wrist where Farkas had grabbed her, eyes wide.

"The patient is in a coma, so I'm not sure who you're swinging your dick around for," I said, my voice warbled with adrenaline.

I did not hear the stream of words that left Farkas's mouth. I was aware of him storming out, Nancy running into the room. The medical intern staring at me, Bambi-shocked eyes, before I fled for the break room, trembling and sick.

I collapsed onto the couch, buried my face in my hands. The click of the door, and then Nancy's voice.

"Samantha. The hell was that about?"

"He grabbed her, Nance."

"She says he didn't."

"Because she wants to keep her job!"

"Yeah, and our job is to take care of patients, not play Mommy to the interns."

"I can't be here," I said. "I can't fucking be here."

"I'm glad you suggested it." Nancy's voice was cool. "You're obviously not ready to be back."

I felt as if a wound had been lanced, and now it was all pouring out. I would do anything to escape the pain. I thought of Luiza Witkowski, who would never get justice unless some trace of her was found someday. I thought of Taylor Edwards's body being lowered into the ground and that little girl in the sunflower dress. Kyle Lawson, his hand blasted away by his own gun, trying to protect my mother before my father killed her too.

"I fucked up, Nancy," I whispered.

I was aware of her shape sinking into the couch next to me. The shushing sounds leaving her mouth as Nancy pulled my head to her massive chest while I wept.

❧

It's very easy to get a doctor's note for extended medical leave when you work in a hospital. Some more crying, my tears blotting Nancy's scrub top, and then a trip downstairs to the psychiatrist on call for an evaluation.

He determined I was not fucked-up enough to turn in my cell phone and any sharp objects and go upstairs. He recommended an outpatient program and some time off work.

Nancy was the one to bring up the Healing Spring, a facility in the Everglades. Her bipolar daughter had spent a week there, gotten *her head on straight*. According to their website, the facility prided itself on the beautiful scenery and a holistic approach to substance abuse, eating disorders, and in my case, post-traumatic stress disorder.

When I landed, I texted Rhiannon. The last I'd heard from her had been two days ago, after she'd formally accepted my proposition: she and Kaylee would move into Gil's house, and in exchange for reduced rent, Rhi would slowly fix the place up.

Donna Dolce was not pleased I decided against selling. But Rhi and Kaylee needed a place to stay, fast. Selfishly, I hoped Rhi would make the house her own, ask me to sell it to her, because I knew how happy it would make Gil to have a child grow up in his house.

I'd asked my cousin if she'd spoken to her mother since the scene in Mitch's driveway. Rhi had replied with a perfunctory no that did not invite further inquiry. Meacham had spoken to Mrs. Mason; he already knew that Mitch had been at my house that afternoon.

I could only assume he hadn't told me because he thought I might tip off Rhi, or Mitch herself. Mitch hadn't admitted to being the one to set the fire, even when confronted with the postcard. I doubted anything *could* make my aunt fully confess to her role in what happened—she barely seemed to believe it herself the other day outside her house, when she confirmed she'd known all along that my father and Lyndsey had survived.

Rhi hadn't asked me what I'd done with the postcard I found in Mitch's nightstand. She probably assumed I'd turned it over to Meacham, because that is what any levelheaded person might have done.

I thought of the missive on the Healing Spring's website: *Cell phone privileges are limited to 7–8 PM to maximize healing time.*

I might be unreachable for the next couple weeks, I texted Rhiannon, along with the phone number for the Healing Spring, even though I was not due to check in for another two days.

"Welcome to Charleston," my pilot drawled, followed by a chorus of seat belts unclicking. I retrieved my carry-on suitcase from the overhead bin and disembarked, following the signs pointing to the car rental area of the airport.

My phone buzzed in my pocket. Not a response from Rhi but a voice mail, no doubt from a call that had come in while I was in the air.

The sight of Meacham's number sent me into a seat at the nearest gate, my knees trembling.

Samantha. Call me back as soon as possible.

It had only been a week since he'd left my apartment with Detective Reeder. I hated how badly I wanted to hear his voice.

"Sam." The sound of a blinker. Meacham was driving.

"What's going on?"

"Your DNA—there was a match in NamUs."

She couldn't be dead. Not when I came all the way here to find her. I closed my eyes, willing the din of the airport to quiet. "Lyndsey?"

"No. The remains belong to an unidentified man who died in Georgia."

My heartbeat picked up. Meacham's voice was gentle when he spoke again. "There's a one in a billion chance the man is not your biological father."

My father was dead. I had known this for twenty years. And still, Meacham's words leveled me. I was thirteen again, Mitch delivering the news as I shivered in the front seat of her truck. *They're all gone. None of them made it out.*

"I don't . . . How did he die?" I asked. "When?"

"Two and a half years ago. He didn't have any ID on him. He was found on a park bench not far from a homeless camp. Official cause of death was hypothermia, but he had pretty advanced cirrhosis."

He'd known he was dying when he brought them to the beach. He'd sent his sister that postcard, and his last cowardly act was to abandon his family.

"And my sister?" I asked.

"No hits in CODIS or NamUs. It's going to take a while to go through the others. There's a backlog, and her DNA might not even be in any sort of system."

I said nothing, thinking only of that shop owner's memory. My father had had three kids with him.

"Anything you could tell me about what happened with your aunt last week," Meacham said. "Anything at all that could help me find your sister."

I thought of the postcard, in an envelope on my kitchen counter, addressed to Travis Meacham at the New York State Bureau of Criminal Investigation in Port Jervis. I'd left a note for Nancy to drop it in the postbox when she fetched my mail over the weekend.

Meacham would have what he needed soon enough. I hadn't put a return address on the envelope, but he'd see Mitch's address scrawled on the postcard inside.

He would know that I'd sent it. He might think I'd resisted turning over the postcard because it would implicate my aunt, the woman who took me in after the murders. The little family I had left.

Truthfully, I wanted nothing more than for Mitch to spend the rest of her pathetic life in a cell for what she had done. But if Lyndsey really was alive—if she had lived out the past twenty-two years as Elizabeth Bolling—I could not let Meacham get to her first. And it wasn't because he had betrayed me by lying to me about why he wanted my DNA, or because he hadn't shared his suspicions about the body in the house not being my father.

My sister, if she was alive, would be a grown woman. It would be her choice whether she wanted to be reunited with the family she was taken from. Her loyalty to the only family she had ever known—my father, the Bollings—might lead her to reject the truth. To reject me.

When my silence had stretched on long enough, Meacham let out a sigh that was quickly blotted out by an announcement at the gate behind me.

"Where are you right now, Samantha?" he asked, his voice hitching with interest.

"Fort Lauderdale Airport," I lied. "I've been having trouble dealing with everything. There's this place—I'm getting help."

Meacham was quiet for a solid minute. "Good for you."

Eleven forty-five a.m. I was showered, smelling of hotel bar soap, staring down a hostess at the Beaumont Hotel restaurant outside Charleston.

"Do you have a reservation?" she asked.

According to a LinkedIn profile I found, Elizabeth Bolling had just graduated from the University of South Carolina. She had attended Fort Mill High School, just like Chase Bolling, according to his Facebook page.

There was no photo on Elizabeth's profile, and her information was sparse. She had majored in psychology, and she currently worked as a server at the Beaumont Hotel restaurant.

"I don't mind sitting at the bar," I said.

I'd called the restaurant last night, after I booked my 8:00 a.m. flight to Charleston. I'd asked if Elizabeth would be working today. Brunch shift, the hostess had informed me.

I scanned the room, the chatter in the restaurant dissolving in my ears when I saw her.

I did not breathe until she was in front of me, filling my coffee cup. Hair the color of honey, held back in a jaw clip. She was tanned, toned. A sorority girl, certainly.

"How are you today?" her smile was bright. "My name is Lizzie."

Lizzie. Lyndsey. When had my father made the shift? How long had it taken my sister to respond to the name?

My throat sealed. A beat of silence too long. Lizzie's head tilted, mistrust filling her eyes. Maybe thinking of the mystery caller from last night, who had inquired whether she would be working.

"You look familiar," she said. "Have we met?"

"No. I'm not from around here." I sipped the coffee. "My name is Samantha."

Lizzie smiled. "That's my favorite girl's name."

"Really?"

"My parents got me the American Girl doll for one of my birthdays." Lizzie looked sheepish. "I always said if I had a daughter, I'd name her Samantha."

My parents. My heart dipped behind my ribs. I'd done this to myself. I knew the answer before I came here. There was no way a child her age could remember the family that had been stolen from her.

"Do you need a few more minutes with the menu?" Lizzie asked.

"Can I have the Belgian waffle?" I asked.

She took out her order pad. "Do you want ice cream with it?"

I forced a smile. "Gotta have ice cream."

Lizzie smiled. By the time she returned to check on me with my food, I was crying.

She set my plate down. "Oh my gosh, are you okay?"

"Yeah. I'm so sorry." I dabbed my eyes with my napkin, debating fleeing before I could say anything else. "Sorry. I'm really sorry."

Lizzie's eyes widened. This was above her pay grade. "Do you . . . do you need help? Is there someone I could call?"

"No, it's not like that." I swallowed to clear my throat. "My father died. It was a long time ago, but I only just found out this morning."

"Oh my God. I'm so sorry." Lizzie pushed some napkins toward me. "I wish there was something I could do."

"Don't worry about it. You being so nice to me is helping."

I couldn't take my eyes off her, as rude as it was to stare. She was beautiful, all of my mother's radiance and none of the signs of wear on her face—exhaustion, worry. But the heart-shaped mouth, the dirty-blonde hair, and the golden smattering of freckles on her nose all belonged to Kyle Lawson.

I suddenly felt a deep sense of shame that I had come here. Even if I told her who I was, who *she* was, she would not believe me. Who would?

Even worse, what if she did believe me, and it changed nothing? My father's new wife, Chase, the older sister, Mia—they were Lyndsey's family. They'd had her for twenty years, and I'd had her less than two.

What if she accepted the truth about what my father had done and decided to reject me anyway?

Lizzie's fingers found the pile of napkins I hadn't touched yet. She smoothed down the one on top, her eyes finding mine. "I didn't get to say goodbye to my dad either."

"What happened to him? I'm sorry. That's probably not something you want to talk about with a stranger."

"No, it's fine. He left when I was in high school. He called a couple times, and then he stopped." Lizzie shrugged before beginning to blink rapidly. She grabbed the coffeepot behind her so she had something to do with her hands, even though my cup was practically full.

"My dad left me too," I said. "I'm so sorry."

"He had a lot of demons. But he was a good dad, and I miss him." Lizzie smiled. "You would have liked him. He always had a scoop of ice cream on his waffle."

She tapped her fingernails, painted a jaunty tangerine, against the countertop. "Let me know if you need anything else, okay?"

The remaining tables in the bar area had filled, pulling Lizzie's attention. I cut a quarter of the waffle into tiny pieces, managed to get them down before I flagged another server. By the time I was ready for the check, I'd lost sight of her completely.

"Did Lizzie leave?" I asked her.

"She's on her fifteen. Can I get you anything?"

"Just the check, thanks."

My heart hammered as the waitress returned with a check holder.

I signed my name. And then I left.

I paused with one hand on my rental, tilted my head to the sun, eyelids shut.

She looked happy.

It's her job to look happy. There's no way the glimpse I'd gotten of her life could capture the real Lizzie Bolling. Her heartbreaks, the pain of her father leaving, the sliver of memory she couldn't explain. Maybe a woman, her hands smelling of Jergens.

Someone was calling my name. I looked up in time to see Lizzie, flying down the wheelchair ramp, the bottom pieces of her hair escaping her bun. The sight of her, that smiling girl, took my breath away, because I knew.

This girl was happy. She'd had a beautiful life. Even with all my father had stolen from her, she'd had a family and friends and dreams for the future. And none of it would ever mean anything again, once she learned the truth.

"You forgot your credit card!" Lizzie said when she reached me.

"Thank you." I wrapped my hand around my card, still warm from her touch.

She smiled, her body pitching forward slightly, as if I were an old friend to be hugged goodbye. Lizzie caught herself, waved from a respectable three feet away before saying, "I hope you enjoy Charleston!"

And as fast as she'd gotten to my car, she was gone again.

I thought of following. I stayed in my rental car until the sky turned the color of ash, and then I drove back to my hotel and set my alarm to leave early in the morning for Fort Lauderdale.

Travis Meacham would find her, once he opened the postcard. He had found my father, after all, and I knew he would not give up until he found Lyndsey too.

He would tell her the truth about who she was, how her real parents had been killed. Maybe she would want to meet me and Beth Lawson. Likely, she would take one look at me and hate me, remembering what happened here today. How I didn't have the courage to be the one to break my sister's heart.

There was no sense dwelling on the decision. I'd already made it. There would be no absolution for me either way. I would get in my rental car, and I would drive to the Everglades. I would try, in earnest, to heal, while Meacham found my sister and closed his case.

And he would find her. I only hoped that by the time he did, I would be the sister she deserved.

ACKNOWLEDGMENTS

Writing careers are long, and there are so many people who have helped me arrive at this exciting new juncture, but I'll nonetheless try to keep it short. Endless thanks to the following people:

Sarah Landis, one of the first to believe in this book—thank you for being my bulldog and always being there with a brilliant solution. Will Watkins, my film agent, who is probably the smartest and kindest person I've encountered in Hollywood (and for better or worse, I have dealt with a lot of people in Hollywood). Thanks to the entire team at Sterling Lord Literistic, and to Rebecca Vail and Alex Maggioni, the OG fans of this book. Your excitement and belief in Sam means the world to me.

Megha Parekh, the fiercest champion for this book I could have hoped for, who understood what I was trying to do and helped me get there. Emily Murdock Baker, for your sharp editorial insight. Sarah Shaw, Grace Doyle, Rachael Herbert, Jon Ford, Caroline Teagle Johnson, Adrienne Krogh, and the rest of the team at Amazon Publishing.

All the friends who read bits and pieces of this book over the years and provided feedback and encouragement, especially Courtney Summers, Veronica Roth, Kaitlin Ward, Erin Craig, Elle Cosimano, Maurene Goo, Kit Frick, and Laurie Elizabeth Flynn.

And most of all my husband and son, who have had to endure quite a few "Mommy is BUSY!" writer fits over the years. Thank you for always being there after I type *The end.*

ABOUT THE AUTHOR

Photo © 2022 Charles Santangelo

Kara Thomas is a part-time librarian and an unsolved-mystery enthusiast who dreams of one day solving a cold case. She lives on Long Island with her husband, son, and rescue cat. She is the author of *That Weekend*, *The Cheerleaders*, *Little Monsters*, and *The Darkest Corners*. For more information, visit www.kara-thomas.com.